thrall

thrall

Steven Shrewsbury

SEVENTH STAR PRESS

Cover art and illustrations: Matthew Perry
Cover art and illustrations in this book Copyright © 2010 Matthew
Perry & Seventh Star Press, LLC.

Editor: Louise Bohmer

Published by Seventh Star Press, LLC.

ISBN Number 9780983108634

Library of Congress Control Number: 2010939791

Seventh Star Press
www.seventhstarpress.com
info@seventhstarpress.com

Publisher's Note:
Thrall is a work of fiction. All names, characters, and places are the
product of the author's imagination, used in fictitious manner. Any
resemblances to actual persons, places, locales, events, etc. is purely
coincidental.

Printed in the United States of America

First Edition

FOREWORD

After the genesis of man, and before the destruction of the Earth by water, there existed a misty realm shrouded from times past. I believe we have forgotten more about history than we have recorded. Journey now to a foreboding place of adventure, evil, and excitement where even gods walked the earth and fables were real.

DEDICATION

This one is for my family
John August Shrewsbury
Aaron Kenneth Shrewsbury
Stacey Lynne Shrewsbury

Deliverance Will Come

ACKNOWLEDGEMENTS

Thank you to Shana Sidfrids for her various comments that pushed me on to write this. If not for her, I would have finished other books first. Thank you forever.

Thanks to Louise Bohmer, Mark Boatman, Kent Gowran, Mark Hickerson, Peter Welmerink, Bob Freeman, Angie Hawkes & Christopher Fulbright, Joe & Kay Howe, Amanda DeBord, Stephen Zimmer, Matt Perry, Brady Allen, Mark Shrewsbury Sr, Mark Shrewsbury Jr (the Godson), Amy Shrewsbury, Jim MCleod, Tod Clark, R. Thomas Riley, Bill Gagliani, Cody Goodfellow, Cheryl Lynne Staley, Randy Chandler, Gina Ranalli, Charles Gamlich, Jodi Lee, David Wilbanks, Martel Sardina, Weston Ocshe, Mari Adkins, John & Becca Hay, John Little, Nikki Threat, Scott Colbert, Ginger May, Fred Grimm, Rhonda Wilson, Mark & Jeannie Worthen, Donnis Lovell, Ty Schwamberger, Evyl Ed, Jen O, Alien Motives Bill, Tracy West, DezM, Deb Patterson, Shawn Reeder, Debi Hulbert, Mark Johnson, Nate Kenyon, Kelli Miller, Alex McVey, Kimmi Jo Greenwell, Gregory Hall, Elizabeth Donald, Scott Nicholson, Andrew Wolter, Hank Schwaeble, Sara Harvey, John Hornor, Rex, Kurt (Dathar), Dean Harrison, Alkilyu, Seth, Cat McCinn, Mr. Solow, Gail, Minh, Angel Lesa, Noigeoverlord, Keevah, and Brian Knight (thanks for the coffee).

Thanks to Brian Keene for the use of his demon book and bad angel names.

Also, for their advice and encouragement: Norm Partridge, Bryan Smith, Ron Kelly, Steven Saville, Harlan Ellison, James A. Moore and John Skipp.

Thank you always to my family, Stacey, John, and Aaron.

Steven
Rural Central Illinois

CONTENTS

"Providence often preserves a fated warrior when his audacity is superior."

-Anonymous

Chapter I

TAVERN UPRISING

"By the gods, pull the damn sword out," the man on the floor howled out into the tavern. Although down the bar, Gorias' ears heard him clear enough. The aged warrior looked over at the figure laying face down on the dirty boards. A man screamed in agony while a halo of patrons surrounded him.

Gorias took a drink from his tall flagon, pulled his cloak closer, and said to the slender bartender, "The sword isn't in him, Michael."

The barkeep checked the floundering man then pointed to the swinging door. "Close that. Though winter's gone, but it's still cold as teats on a celibate outside. Besides, his assailant is long gone."

While a plump drunkard shambled over to shut the wooden door, Gorias' leaned out from the far end of the bar. He made sure his cowl covered his long face before saying, "And yet, he bleeds."

To the all assembled in the smoky saloon, it appeared as if a sword lay across the whimpering man's back. When a rather jaunty, short-haired woman in dark leathers grabbed the sword hilt and winked at the bartender, Michael muttered, "Leave him be, Shavon," but she never listened. Shavon planted her boot on the long metallic mesh on the floor, meant to provide sturdy footing near the bar, and with a savage jerk, removed the sword away from the man's tunic.

Two things became apparent. One, no blacksmith crafted the sword in steel. Two, the drawing away ripped the clothes and flesh from the man. Shavon giggled at this revelation as a few men armed up their fallen comrade.

Michael remarked to the patrons, "The constables have been summoned." Though clear to Gorias the barkeep did this to instill calmness in the masses, many still nervously gaped at the bloody man.

While a few men carried the wounded patron outside, Shavon studied the weapon and said, "It's made of wood, but with

1

hooks, nails, and glass shards on the underside. Devious." She took a couple steps and slapped the fake blade onto the wall. The object stuck to a support beam. Shavon walked through the bits of straw matted over the metal mesh before returning to the main hardwood floor of the tavern. Hands to her slender hips, she looked back and admired her work. "A fine decoration, no?"

Michael sighed, and Gorias peered into his drink as a sense of normalcy returned to the crowded tavern. The bartender muttered, "Who ever heard of a big man wielding a fake weapon?"

The aged man brooded over his drink and said, "It's a proto-sword."

"A what?"

"You're mistaken," said Gorias, the hood of his over-cloak receding a bit to show his coarse, matured features. "The weapon proved very useful indeed. The small objects inserted in the counterfeit sword did just what the aggressor planned. It caused shock, pain, and ultimately rent the skin off Silas's back. Then again, he had some help from that sweetheart in leather over there."

"Who makes such a thing? It's a savage weapon..." Michael's voice trailed off as he ceased to wipe the bar down. "Barbarians? Here in Shynar?" His voice lowered and he scowled. "I know there're many mercenaries in Khabnur City due to the rumors of war surrounding us, but hell, barbarians? They're over a thousand miles away."

Gorias shrugged and a muffled grinding sound emerged from his cloak. "Zenghaus Mountain is two thousand miles away, to be exact, but yes. That big fellow who ran out came in ill dressed, in his breeches and garnache, which makes me think he stole them. They way I saw him fidget, he probably prefers being naked."

The bartender laughed, still speaking so only Gorias could hear him. "Perceptive of you."

"My eyes aren't as good as they used to be, kid."

Fingers drumming on the bar, Michael said, "I never saw a barbarian run from a fight that easily." His eyes narrowed at Gorias, taking in his great size. "Certainly a large man for these parts. Didn't you see him?"

After a nod, Gorias responded, "Maybe he wasn't here to fight but to pay attention."

"A barbarian spy? That's a swell jest. I haven't heard much of the barbarians on the move since the army of Nosmada tangled with them a few years back. Before that it was the old fable of La Gaul slaying the Nephilum in the Zenghaus Mountains." Michael pointed to Gorias' flagon. "You need another one, old timer?"

"Sure, youngster," the slouching man agreed, and pushed gold toward the server. While Michael definitely wasn't a young man, his withered face smiled at the name the ancient brute called him.

Voices bombarded Gorias as he drank from the full flagon. The drunks paid him little mind as he slumped over his drink, but their conversations rang in his sharp ears.

"Blood! I'm sick to freakin' death of hearin' 'bout blood all the time. 'Cause no matter how much damned blood the priests, holy or not, surrender up, it's never enough to appease the gods or devils."

Another voice said, "I heard tell no 'mount of sacrifices can stop these uprisings of the dead ones. Bugger me, all this necromancy afoot with a bloody war brewing as well makes my ass chew crackers."

Shavon shot back, "You besotted idler! They dead arise and drink the blood of any and all takers, then walk like fools to the south." Her boots clicked on the floor as she spoke. "Even the guards around the Foundry of Syn never have to draw steel to kill a leech. They walk on past. No loss."

Michael wrung the bar rag and murmured, "Aside from the idea of barbarians nearing the curtain wall of Khabnur, that leech circumstance is the craziest thing I ever saw, or my name ain't Michael Galenson, and it is."

Gorias shot back, "You want an award, rawboned man? Buy yourself some steak to feed that body of yours, and you might not be deemed food for the risen dead."

Michael chuckled in good humor as he pointed at a man in the far corner of the bar. "We get all kinds. You see that one there?

The tall man with dark hair, who looks too clean to ever have been dirty? He just comes in here to read parchment every so often. He never drinks."

Gorias glanced at the person indicated, and then looked back at his slurry brew. "That's Ezran Gavreel. He wouldn't be drinking."

"You must know everyone, or have a ready answer for anything, old timer. Is he a spy of some kind as well?"

Gorias shook his head. "No, not really. Ezran watches a lot though. The bastard never gets any older, either."

The talks around them went on.

"They say there's a blue dragon afoot in the North-east, screamin' his lungs out beside the great rivers of Gemini. They say it flounders in the cursed desert of Dundayin by the ruins of Larak."

Shavon cursed the speaker. "Javed, you are drunk and dense. A lethal combination, however, not an uncommon vintage."

Javed continued, "It's said the Cult of the Dragon used a fragment of the Daemonolateria in the resurrection of that dreaded creature. I heard tell they are around here, too."

Many guffaws echoed and more people told him he was loaded, yet a few agreed with Javed's words.

One man across from him slobbered as he spoke. "They say not all the swords in the Foundry of Syn could penetrate the dragon's flesh."

In the far left corner of the saloon sat an enormous persona, twice the size of any man, drinking from an enormous pitcher. At the mention of the Foundry of Syn, the ogre lifted one deformed eyebrow, but kept drinking. Every so often, he inhaled from a hose attached to a tall ceramic tube smoldering at a spot low in its construction.

A different male voice thundered in the ears of Gorias. "Bah! That's a damnable fairy tale. Daemonolateria, fah, my sore ass in a sling. Besides, the last of the blue dragons was slain by Gorias La Gaul, damn, must be thirty or forty years ago. I heard he gutted and fed the thing to the folks in the village of Oliverian."

Many grumbling voices agreed on this point and the ogre added in a bottomless voice, "That was about when the first of these accursed leeches were spotted, no?"

Shavon chattered with mirth. "Gorias La Gaul? He's but a fairy tale, like dragons, as well. It's tough to accept one man could slaughter a dragon, be he a keen fighter like Gorias La Gaul was supposed to be or not. Think of how silly that is." She spoke on in strident tones. "Could all the axes they craft in the Foundry of Syn be enough to butcher a giant beast like a dragon? That's lunacy, seeing the platelet flesh dragons bore, right?" She waved her thin hands in the heavy smoke and pointed at the corner. "You, ogre! Are you not, Mitre, the foreman of the foundry?"

The massive individual only grumbled, blowing smoke from its nostrils, thus giving a command in the affirmative. Mitre swirled the settlings of his pitcher and demanded more drink.

Michael motioned for a serving woman to attend the ogre and whispered, "That gal will get the business end of ol' Mitre Stillwell's wrath if she prods him enough. Dragons, heh."

Gorias closed his eyes, dreamt of the way the ice of the northern lands used to stiffen his beard. His back ached, and he recalled how the cold treated his bones then. He also remembered the sounds of a dragon's scream, filtering down his ears and into his spine. Motioning for another round from Michael, he noted the short-haired girl in leathers left the ogre alone.

As he set down another drink, Michael gazed toward the table in the corner opposite Mitre in the crowded mead hall. "Cursed kids these days. They know naught of which they speak."

The grizzled drinker gave a fatigued shrug and put the mug to his lips. Before ingestion, Gorias said, "They walked in here wearing blades. I never saw a kid carry a curved sword like that mouthy assassin does."

Michael blinked, confused. "Shavon? An assassin? How did you spot such a thing in the dim firelight? Didn't know you would care for such a matter, old one. Seldom do folk come into the Aragon barroom with such keen senses. Hell, they sure don't leave with them."

"Why do you think I keep my back to the wall here and not to the saloon main floor? That's why that screaming fool was hauled out of here. He turned his back on the big barbarian he started a fight with."

"I thought maybe it was the brace you wear. I see you never take off your backpack and scratch at it under your leather jerkin. I figured you propped yourself up there to rest."

Gorias felt the stiff portions of the long bundle and inner brace on his sore back. "Astute of you. Do you want a medal?" He shot a glance at Ezran, who still read. "How in the Hell did you come by the name of Michael?"

The man rubbed his thin black beard and giggled. "My mama said it was after the Arch-angel."

"Huh. I doubt you're his son. You would be taller." Gorias gazed back across the smoky tavern and Ezran Gavreel met his stare. The man at the bar returned to his drink.

Shavon pranced in her tan leather boots and shouted, "You all carry on about La Gaul as if the children of demons didn't invent him. They do that to bestow false hope on this besotted realm." She slammed her fist down on the table to gain the complete attention desired. "If Gorias lived, wouldn't he be fighting the resurrected dead men of Nosmada, or offering his services to the local tribal kings? They're out there gathering up every mercenary they can in fear of Nosmada's army trekking past Khabnur. These chieftains, they have secret plans, and lives they need silenced in their schemes. They never sent out word for an old legend, they sent for me."

Gorias eyed Michael, half smiling, and his server whispered, "That's Shavon from Politi. She has been through here before, but you said she was an assassin?"

"Yeah."

"How do you know that?"

"Silence is not her strong suit," Gorias said. "But I can see by the embroidery of her boot tops that she attained them afar off, not on this continent. Aside from that and the way she moves, Shavon smells of amber hash. I noticed it when I walked past her. All the opiates that ogre is inhaling cannot hide the scent of the amber lilies of the Caliph of Damavand. He's the father of an assassin's cult. That mouthy gal reeks of it. That's how they pay their trainees--

keep them plied at first."

Stunned at this revelation, Michael said, "Damavand isn't that far off, but Hell, that's wild. Do you think she got that curved blade in the East?"

Gorias frowned. "I hear in the underground factory at Syn they can make a mock up of any weapon. She doesn't look road rough enough to have traveled that far. Her gait, her complexion, all too fresh."

Mitre Stillwell again grumbled, but only to motion for more drink. From under his table scurried a tiny man, smaller than a dwarf, but dressed in the same fashion as Stillwell. The small man adjusted his loose brais pants, re-lit the bowl of the long tube, and ran to the bar.

Michael drafted Stillwell a drink. "From what Shavon declares openly, she's here at the request of the local magistrate, Lira Rhan. There's some devilry afoot with a group of young cultists. Rumor is the local youths pray to the images of Nosmada, dark Son of Man from —"

"I know who Nosmada is," Gorias snapped, his gaze on the ogre, then to Ezran, and then back to the bar. The scurrying servant returned to Stillwell with the pitcher. After adjusting the rather feminine barbette on his tiny head, the lackey vanished under Mitre's table.

Shavon threw up her arms and clucked. "I heard the tales of Gorias La Gaul from my youth. His two swords and such moves." She mocked a man fighting with two blades, "I knew them from my cradle on. They are stories, nonetheless, from a forgotten age, like lies told of *one* God when we know there are thousands."

The man across the table from her shot back, "You should mind your tongue, girl. Show more respect. Gorias La Gaul came from North of here —"

Shavon drew out a dirk and stabbed it in the table near the hand of the man who shouted at her. "I accept no quarter from a man who insults me, Arius." She gripped the edges of the table with both hands. "If you can grab it before me, you can have my self for the night."

The entire tavern quieted and turned to face her. Gorias winced as he straightened up. Even Ezran took time from his reading to look over at Arius facing Shavon. Michael glanced at Gorias when he stood up straight and towered over the room.

Across from Shavon, the patron Arius shook off the cling of his grimy clothes and grinned. He removed his woolen cap and grabbed the sides of the table. Arius licked his lips, and Shavon's eyes glowed by the flames of the hearth.

"She'll murder him," Gorias said casually and put down his drink. "He'll rise from the dead tomorrow to join the unholy horde of Nosmada, unless they burn his filthy ass. I'd bet another round on it."

No sooner had Gorias spoke than Arius made a play for the dirk. The woman moved, but not toward the table. Shavon reached toward her left forearm and came out with a tiny, curved blade. As Arius raised the dirk triumphantly in the air, Shavon sliced his neck clean across. Arius' smile remained stuck in place as his throat gaped open, vomiting out blood on the gaming table.

"So much for those cards," Gorias quipped.

Mitre Stillwell smiled and drank, coughing on some of it. His minuscule servant peered out from his cover then returned to his spot under the table.

"I'll take that," Shavon said with a grin, snatching the dirk from the dying man's grasp. Arius fell over the table, sending bloody cards to flight, and the room gasped for the most part. She bent close to his ear, whispering, "Was it as fine as you thought?"

As Shavon cackled loud, Gorias faced the door to the mead hall. It lay twenty feet away. He stepped forward, never picking up his walking staff. Wiping his boots on the mesh on the floor, he moved from the bar with some speed.

Shavon stepped into his path. Her trim frame lolled back on her right hip, arms folded. She stood about half way to the door and giggled. "What're you trying to do, old wretch? Run home to your fat woman now? Are you that faint at the sight of blood?"

"I'm just trying to get to the door, sister." Gorias planted his feet square to his shoulders. His hood fell back and a great mound of graying locks spilled out around his craggy, long face. He loomed over her, cutting an imposing figure.

Mitre Stillwell put down his pitcher. The tube fell from his lips.

"Goodness," Shavon cooed, unafraid, her left boot heel tapping. "You must've been quite a man…once."

"Yeah, well, it still works, even if my back doesn't, much," Gorias said as he put coins on the bar, wearing no expression of concern for the killer in front of him.

Shavon didn't move as she pouted. "You're either courageous or too stupid to realize your danger, elderly fool. Do you know who I am?"

"Does it matter? The whorehouse is down the street."

"You're drunk." She laughed.

"And you are really ignorant, sister. Funny thing is, though, I'll be sober come daylight."

Her eyes flared and the tavern drew a collective breath. "Why you insane duffer, do you know who is going to slay you?"

"Doesn't matter." Gorias glanced at Ezran Gavreel. "Deliverance will come."

A few in the bar spit their drinks at his words, and Mitre coughed loud, almost laughing, but she ignored all of this and went on to say, "I have traveled far and wide. I have killed everything that walks or crawls! I have…"

In the middle of her great boast, Gorias hunched over. While he braced himself on his knees, no one paid this much mind, not even Shavon. So weak went his movements, surprise took her completely when he dropped to the floor like a cat, seized the long straw covered mesh under her boots, and yanked back. The crude rug ripped from under her pointed heels and she flipped backwards. After her rump rolled over her head, she hit the floor on all fours, stunned, braced, and laughing at what happened.

But as she fell, he reached his hands just under his waist to the bottom of the stiff backpack. From out of slots came two blades, each near to three feet in length. Since he stood quite tall, and his pack so long, he easily concealed the two sword scabbards. When he stepped forward he swished the swords, lancing the smoke in the air then driving them down on either side of Shavon's braced form. The blades sliced clean through her arms at the elbow joints.

She slammed these bloody stumps into the floor, gasping in shock. The rest of the bar hissed a name that made her look up at her slayer.

"*La Gaul!*"

Over her towered the ancient warrior, the fable himself, Gorias La Gaul. His eyes stared at her more in pity than anger. Her crimson blood dripped from legendary blades that gleamed brighter than steel should. She watched him turn the blades down and hold the two swords like daggers, knuckles side by side.

"You're...not real. I thought...you were dead..." she choked, tears streaming from her brown eyes.

"Not quite yet, sister. Do you think I've lived so long on strength alone? If you would've gotten old, you would've known to save the talking for after the fight."

With that he planted his blades in her back, pinning Shavon's heart and lungs to the wooden floor. This action made the crowd grunt then fear to breathe again. The thud rang with finality.

While he snuffed, he broke the silence with the scuff of his boots. After he stepped on her neck and pulled his swords out, he wiped the blood on her short hair and said, "Which way is that whorehouse, Michael? It has been quite a spell since I was last visited the one in Khabnur."

The door to the mead hall opened and two men stepped in with drawn swords. By the insignia on their black leather coats, Gorias figured them members of the constables' guard. At last, they answered the summons for the man injured by the barbarian emissary.

La Gaul looked at the amazed patrons, then to the giant ogre who arose from his bench. Beyond the men from outside Gorias spied Ezran Gavreel, smiling. He never recalled seeing Ezran leave the bar.

"Looks like I will have to go later."

CHAPTER II

MAGISTRATE

The constables allowed Gorias to mount up on his white horse and ride to the Magistrate's office located in the castle keep. Since this Aragon barroom sat near the outer reaches of the curtain wall, a long ride lay ahead of them. Security ran very high. The sprawling city of Khabnur bustled with activity, full of folk from afar. Many were mercenaries, he concluded, by their weapons and light armor, in town for the brewing war. *There is money to be had and not much work to be done,* he thought, *so the rabble who thought they could fight came.* He felt certain the nominal show up fee gathered quite a few of them.

Diverse races and warriors of varying degrees stumbled out of saloons. Gorias looked down from his mount on the gaggle of humanity and made note of their number, if not their ability. Many carried a khopesh, a short bronze blade manufactured en masse just about anywhere. A crude weapon, it certainly could kill, but in the long run the sword couldn't stand against steel or iron. Since the mercenaries hailed from diverse lands, their weapons varied. A few even sported well-dressed rapiers and broadswords so heavy they required two hands to use.

Word that the legendary warrior arrived in the city of Khabnur spread like a plague, and since the winter lessened, many who weren't fighters crowded the cool streets to see the fable pass by. Though hemmed in by four constables, Gorias rode his great steed with a placid face. He never commented on the muddy city, well built as it was, or the legions of urchins in the streets at such a late hour.

Soldiers and men on the high walls or in the embrasures pointed at Gorias, a few used long scopes to get a better view. Soon every eye in the crenellated ramparts focused on him. Men staggering drunk near the pilaster reinforcement beams paused to

11

hear the tale and look at him as he passed.

A baritone bark of the name, "La Gaul!" broke the peculiar silence.

The guards hesitated when they saw the gigantic form of Mitre Stillwell lumbering up the avenue. At his heels skipped the dwarfish lackey.

Gorias assumed these guards were acquainted with the foreman of the Foundry of Syn or they wouldn't have allowed Mitre to walk beside him.

"Mitre Stillwell?" said Gorias with a half smile, as he waved back at a few men greeting him with bows on the nearest merlon. "It's been decades, you red headed jackass. I didn't recognize you out of your usual digs in the desert, swindling the stupid out of religious relics."

The ogre trudged on, running thick fingers through his thinning bowl of reddish gray locks. "So the dead walk for real, apparently not all as vampiric leeches, you wormy dog."

"So it seems." He chuckled, hand resting on the pommel of the broadsword sheathed on his saddle. "You're supervising the Foundry of weapons? That's like bears in charge of feeding fish."

Mitre's immense shoulders receded and he sneezed. "An ogre must eat, old fool. I could only defraud the religious masses in the desert for so long. My days of high or even low timed adventure are over."

Gorias' focus kept to the cobblestone road ahead that led to the keep. He never looked at the giant who strode near to eye level with him as he said, "Who is the fool?" He leered at the small one at Mitre's heels, and the dwarf registered terror then ran into an alleyway. "I wager keeping working slaves in line must be boring for you after your career of fighting and whoring."

With a poke of his hand to La Gaul's spine, the ogre said, "My back has seen better times, as has yours, jackanape. Keeping tabs on chattel is easy work, and the rest of the world beats a path to my stone doorway."

"No matter who the customer?"

"Wealth is wealth, hoary dog. You know my credo. That's to

never hold a belief that cannot be erased easily enough in favor of a more profitable one."

As he thumbed the ferrule band on his broadsword's grip, Gorias said, "War is coming, I hear."

"Bah, war is life. War is like breathing and there's no use trying to suppress it. After a while, it feels natural."

"I see."

Stillwell coughed, belched. "What're you doing here, anyhow? When I saw that saintly bastard Ezran back in the tavern, I thought you two rode in together."

Gorias adjusted his back brace and said, "Unlikely."

"Whenever I see him, I get nervous. I don't care for feeling nervous, La Gaul."

"I'm just passing through."

"Hah! Passing through my ass, you are."

"Now that would be a mean feat."

Even the guards laughed at this and Mitre smirked. "Really, though, you still out trying to scare up money, still relying on the good graces of the Angels to save your sorry ass at the moment of your death?"

"Still leaning on midget lovers? They have to try less to kiss your ass that way?"

"Fah, you're a filthy old prick." Mitre waved a massive hand, dismissing him. "Careful you don't use it in the incorrect way around here. Even a legend can end up wishing he were born a woman."

The ogre trudged off in the direction of the billowing smoke-stacks of the Foundry. Those in the streets provided the massive figure a wide berth.

One of the guards spoke to Gorias. "Sir, were you friends with the ogre?"

Eyes narrowing at the guard he shrugged. "Ogre?" He said the term as if the word told a joke to him. "We got drunk at the games centuries back. Mitre wasn't all bad then. He's a selfish bastard. A lot of folks are. He's a damned ogre, correct? Did you expect great manners?"

Once the group reached the outer wall of the castle they

dismounted. They gained access to the inner ward, and one of the constables whispered to his partner, "Shouldn't we disarm him before he meets with Lira Rhan?"

The older of the two constables eyed Gorias and said to the other man, "You're a young pup. Go ahead and disarm him if you think you can. He isn't under arrest."

Gorias raised an eyebrow, studying the tall fore building and the turrets of the castle, muttering, "Well, that's good news. Hey, can I pass some water before we go inside? I'm not as young as I used to be and I've been drinking." Not waiting for approval, he leaned his left hand on the brick wall outside the Magistrate's office and fumbled with his trousers.

While he relieved himself, a small man emerged from the wooden door just outside the castle's first wall. A soft featured man, very young, he arrived dressed in a long velvet robe with an open front. His embroidered doublet under the robe showed his class if anyone missed his manners. The man did a double take as he glanced toward the spectacle of the giant warrior leaning on the wall, flanked by constables.

"Gimme a minute, all right?" Gorias said to the constables who watched him. "I never do well with an audience."

"This is the renowned warrior?" the small man said to the snickering constables.

"Step a little closer, kid, and you'll be impressed."

The constables all laughed louder, but quickly straightened their expressions as the well-mannered youth shot them daggers with his gaze. He turned and went back through the wooden door.

"Who's the pretty punk?" Gorias straightened his trousers.

The older constable informed him, "He's Lemach, son of Nazor, administrator to Magistrate Lira Rhan."

"That's a mouthful. Nazor? It seems like I met him years back." He thought, *One forgets after a few hundred years.*

From foot to foot, the constable shifted then nodded. "Nazor was a general and became a politician later in life."

Gorias rewarded him with a rich laugh. While his head lay back, he eyed the apex of the castle high above them. "Helluva fate that one, huh?"

The constable grunted his agreement and took a nip from a small leathery flask. "I won't argue there, sir. Lemach is a very intelligent boy, just not cut from a warrior's cloth."

Gorias adjusted his manhood, winked at the constable. "Bad seeds tend to grow fast, eh? Well, if I'm not under arrest, why in the world am I here?"

The constable motioned for him to enter. "You'll find out soon. Incredible to meet you, sir." The man offered Gorias his hand.

La Gaul clasped the smaller man's gloved hand with firmness and shook it. He then turned to the doorway.

"I don't mean to embarrass you, sir, but I have read about you my entire life and heard so many ballads about you." The constable spoke with reverential respect. "I never knew you were real. I thought you a fable."

"Just because I never got myself killed doesn't make me a legend. I appreciate the friendly talk, though. Yeah, usually the folks that meet me want to kill me."

Confusion spread on the law man's face. "Why is that?"

"Think about it, son. All of those bard's tales you hear in a tavern. The fella that kills the old legend is remembered, too. Even if he's barely able to let go of his mother's tit, his name lives on."

"They say you talk to angels."

His hand on the hilt of a dagger in his belt, he smirked. "Doesn't everyone?"

Gorias walked in as the constable called out, "I curse the man who slays you!"

He mumbled, "I'm still looking for him."

The passageway through the connecting stone hall felt close and dreary to him, but the way soon opened up into a longer chamber. The wooden features on the walls and long tables denoted a place where someone meted out justice. He recalled the scaffold he'd ridden under on the way in, so he understood evenhandedness still traveled swift in the land of Shynar.

Lemach approached him as he stopped to rest in the flickering torchlight. "Lira Rhan will be here momentarily."

"Fine, son of Nazor."

The youth's brows lowered as he took in Gorias' hearty smile then folded his arms, fine tippet strains hanging from his elbows. "You knew my father?"

"I knew a lot of folks, kid."

"I'm the administrator here, or castellan if you prefer."

"Well, good for you. It suits you well."

"I am the youngest of Nazor's sixty-seven children."

Gorias moved one of the wooden chairs out from the nearest table and sat. With a wince he said, "I'm happy for you. Why did he stop having kids?"

"My mother died," Lemach replied curtly, his expression mask-like.

"I figured maybe she grew tired of being a mother."

Lemach raised an eyebrow. "More like Nazor was weary of being a father. He killed her in a rage."

Hands on his knees, Gorias sighed. "You'll have that, I guess."

"The world is getting over populated," Lemach said, still emotionless, his nose raising as if smelled those of which he spoke. "These tramps in the street produce like brood sows, one a year. The more rabble that breath, the stupider they become. That is why you get followers of an evil man like Nosmada."

"I thought the followers of Nosmada were just resurrected dead folks." The constables in the chamber grinned at his jest. Gorias appreciated the fact that these arisen dead, or leeches as many called them, never seemed to appear again once they gorged themselves on blood and disappeared to the south into Nosmada's citadel.

Undeterred by the taunt, Lemach said, "Either that or brain dead youths theorizing death and darkness are the answer. They submit to Nosmada's forbidding will."

Gorias reflected that he could understand why many youths joined Nosmada's army. The pay was good and the discipline was something they never received from a parent. They were the trained troops that enforced whatever agenda Nosmada had, leeches present to not.

Lemach smiled. "Did you know, though, that some of them willingly take on the blood sickness to become one of his inner circle darklings?"

Gorias nodded, brooding over the blood disease Lemach referred to, running rampant in the world. No one had a cure. "There're a lot of stupid folks, Lemach. They need an identity. They think being a member of the living dead is great, or a means of being powerful, or different. Hell, they're Nosmada's kin one way or another." He then fell silent, wondering why Nosmada's army currently marched north. What was it that they desired thereabouts in Shynar?

Lemach ignored his words, walking in a small circle with the delicacy of a dancer. "Do you have children?"

Hands falling to his sides, near the pommels of the twin swords, Gorias chuckled. "I'm sure I do."

His steps halting, Lemach's nostrils flared. "From a wife?"

"Yeah, at least one that way--a son."

"Is he dead?"

"I should be so lucky. Look, where's this woman I'm supposed to see? I have business in this town even if you don't want to kill me."

"Lira is on her way, and the legion of mercenaries can live without one more for a bit."

Gorias didn't arrive with the glut of mercenaries, but didn't related this fact. "Quite a bunch they are."

Lemach showed wry humor in his rigid face. "You are not impressed by these fighting men?"

"Not specially," Gorias said, his middle fingers tapping on the grips of his blades. This action made the guards stare at him with keener eyes. "Those mercs are high on intimidation and low on delivery. That's the way with most mercenaries from afar." He smiled at that thought, for many folks thought people from distant lands possessed a sort of clandestine method of fighting or killing. They really didn't, by and large, he reflected, but their alien nature could be used to an advantage.

Lemach nodded and thought for a while. "Back to your son,

Lord La Gaul. I would guess being your offspring would carry great baggage, no? I mean, walking in the shadow of a parable…"

"Lord?" Gorias shrugged. "Life is what you make it, youngster." Looking at the supple featured man, he thought it was never a pleasant thing to realize your own blood had become something this planet could do without. After a while, though, you got comfortable with it, he reckoned. Life went on and on.

Lemach licked dry lips, looked about with a sudden discomfort. "Do you have grandchildren?"

Gorias leered at him. "Funny you mention that. Maybe I'm in Shynar visiting one, eh?"

At the head of the room, a long line of castle guards emerged from the single doorway. All of their clothes, from breeches to tunics, were woven in a heavy brown leather cover. These men in spiked helmets stepped with purpose, lean and fit, carrying tiny cross bows. Their manner and eyes told Gorias they stood much more apt for war than the relaxed constables.

Lira Rhan, Gorias assumed, was the amazingly tall woman who emerged from behind them. A small dwarf followed her dressed in black, but Lira demanded Gorias' attention. Very pale with green eyes and arching cheekbones, Lira wore a floor length houppelande gown made from woolen Kersey cloth. While not the velvety Fustian material Lemach seemed to favor, her Murrey tinted garment showed her aloofness from the dark warrior class. Her long, spider-like arms were encased in samite gloves to the elbow. Her collar, high and tight, hemmed her neck like ravens on each side.

The guards lined the wall opposite Gorias and Lemach. The dwarf pulled back his slate colored cowl, stroked a jewel hanging from his neck, and gaped at Gorias. Lira stood behind the table, but when it became apparent he had no plans to rise and turn to face her, she stepped around the edge of the counter.

"Evening," Gorias said. "Excuse me if I don't jump up and salute. I've had a helluva day."

"I would have had you thrown in chains, La Gaul," she said, her voice husky but tight.

"What stopped you?"

She folded her arms, and Castellan Lemach dropped hands to his sides.

"We could not justify the causalities it might result in. On to other matters, Shavon was on retainer from our chieftain."

"I guess you dropped that money in the waste hole, huh?"

Unamused, Lira said, "She is a fine warrior."

"She *was*, anyway. The gal had a big mouth for a killer. I guess they don't have to worry about paying her in hash or whatever now."

The dwarf spoke up in a stinging tone, "She was the best stock for the duty at hand, La Gaul. They are a rare breed."

Gorias never faced the dwarf. "She was young, I guess. Hell, she'll be young forever. If she was that good of a killer, better decapitate her and burn fast so Shavon can't rise from the dead and join Nosmada's horde in the south. For now, they feed and move on, probably to Kanoch. I'd hate to see her fight like that as an undead."

Lira's roared. "We know how to stop that." Her manner calmed as many guards stiffened. She unclenched slender fists. "This is our chieftain's mage, Robyn De Balm."

Again, Gorias never looked in the dwarf's direction. His hand smoothed over a dirk in his belt and the small jewel on the handle.

"Don't think about trying to fight your way out of here," Robyn said, the small metal helm on his head slightly askew. With quickness, he righted the strap on his chin. "Perhaps in your youth you would have challenged these guards, but..."

Gorias sighed loud. "Is that all you folks think about is killing people? Did you bring me down here to execute me? How? By boring the piss out of me?"

A few of the guards raised their crossbows. Gorias dropped his arms, palms on the grips of his two short swords. He was certain each young guard thought the arrow they had set carried death for Gorias La Gaul. He gave them a cold glare, challenging them with the unspoken question: *Who will die first?*

Lira remained steady. "You question our methods?"

"I wasn't expecting an answer, sister."

"Gorias La Gaul," she said. "You have no idea why Shavon was in Shynar?"

"I never caught why she was here, no. Every dog screwing fool who fancies themselves apt at killing for hire is here. What was one more tramp with a sword and a bad attitude?"

"Shavon came on retainer to us for a service, not to serve amongst the protectorate against the legions of Nosmada. It's a very important duty she was trusted with, and one not just any soldier could perform. One would have to be a fierce killer with little soul to do this job."

Gorias exhaled noisily, guessing her intent. "Oh great. You have me to take over her job since I killed her arrogant ass? I'm only in town for the booze, whores, and to see my grandson. Why not go find a younger swinging dick amongst the mercs? Go ask that freakin' assfaced ogre at the foundry for his hand. I know he can be bought."

"You slew our hired woman," Robyn said matter-of-factly mid rapid blinks. Gorias stared at the guards. "And you will kill my sorry carcass if I don't comply, huh? Just splendid."

"A group of youths obsessed with gaining the favor of Nosmada are planning to go to the marshes and resurrect Carlato Wyss," Lira said while folding her hands. "They have been in league with the Cult of the Dragon."

"Wyss."

"I imagine, at your advanced age, you recall his incidents."

"Haven't heard that name in quite a spell. Incidents? That sounds mighty clean." He recalled tales of Carlato Wyss, the evil bard or performer, who slaughtered and raped so many people the exact count eluded authorities. "They tied rocks on his legs and sank him in a bog north of here." Gorias laughed and unnerved the room. "Yeah, a cult leader if my memory serves, at least by today's reckoning. These punks are out to resurrect him? Why?"

"That is a matter of some debate." Lira sighed, fingers drumming on her forearms. "Some say to curry favor with dark Nosmada and further his evil claims for blood. Others say it is out of a bizarre hero worship of the late bard. At any rate, they've slain many for their blood rites and thus, need to be stopped."

De Balm said, "Many believe they want the location of an ancient book that will unset the world--the Daemonolateria. Wyss knows where it is."

"Is that a fact?" Gorias said, humor fading as both hands rubbed his beard.

Lira looked at De Balm then folded her nervous fingers in front of her stomach. "Others think the cult is racing a team from Nosmada's realm to the spot."

"Yeah, I hear tell of an enormous army traveling this way from Nosmada's citadel," Gorias admitted. "Hence your mercs outside. Dunno what they would want with Wyss' bones, though."

"Nosmada's army is led by General Tolin himself." Robyn grinned.

Hands returning to his knees, Gorias frowned and shook his head. "Tolin, eh? He's a sweetheart."

"Tolin has the heart of a dragon," Robyn said, small arms raised as the tiny wizard aimed at Gorias.

He thought for a long time. "It's soul, anyway." Gorias then contemplated why they all wanted this dead fellow, Wyss. *Dead men tell nothing, they say.*

Lira turned and watched a figure who entered the room. Though dressed in dark clothing, Gorias thought this person a female, sort of boyish, but sporting plump, generous breasts nonetheless. The echo of her boots distracted him as well as her figure.

"Anyway," Lira said, aiming serious eyes back at Gorias, "there are real necromancers amongst these foolish youths and they plan to move soon. Real evil will come from their acts. Amid all this troop movement, I cannot abide dangerous games."

"I suppose not."

"Tolin has an appointment with Mitre at the Foundry of Syn."

"Do tell?"

"We don't know if Tolin is involved in this plan to resurrect Wyss or not. He will not suffer these youths and will kill anything in his path that angers him. I worry our city will feel the brunt of chaos unleashed by these fools."

"You don't seem to be in a great hurry, Lira Rhan, or you would have killed these kids yourself. Why all the subterfuge?"

"The bogs are still partially frozen from the winter," she reminded him. "Tolin and his army will not be here for a week."

"Good point."

La Gaul looked into the dark eyes of the girl who walked to Lira. Her tied back hair ran very dark, but her skin proved milky white. Her boots came to her knees and thick hose covered her thighs up to her cut-off, bastardized breeches.

Lira went on to say, "There is evidence that a massive force of barbarian warriors are moving this way. It is the largest force of such monsters ever seen. They march south of the rugged Zenghaus Mountains."

"Proto-sword."

"What?"

Gorias rolled his eyes. "Nothing, sister, just thinking. Quite a tight spot this city is getting to be in."

"Mitre thinks the barbarians are coming to buy his weapons as well."

Gorias wondered if these tribes of Zenghaus were the same ones led by the son of legendary barbarian warrior Brock, who he met decades ago.

"The forces of Nosmada and these barbarians may use our back yard for a battlefield. I have other problems to deal with aside from their imprudence."

Gorias nodded. "Being in charge is never easy, eh? If you know who these cult kids are, why not kill them before they ride out to the bogs? Why doesn't your miniature wizard there cast a spell, roll some bones and find the answer? Is he not as strong as he looks or what?"

Enraged, Robyn was about to speak, but Lira said, "That's one part of the puzzle. Once they try to raise Wyss, all of them will be exposed." She paused as the young woman who entered stood behind her. "Magic does not solve everything, old warrior. They've slain a few minor nobles at varied whorehouses for their blood-spells. For that alone, they must die. Shavon could ferret them out and slay them, no big news story, no bad happenings as the town arms up for war. All we need is terror induced in the troops knowing we cannot get a handle on a few children adept at sorcery."

Gorias noted the young woman as her murky eyes sized him up. Her left eyebrow twitched when he nodded a subtle greeting. He thought the girl looked enough like Lira to be her daughter, but built sturdy and not made for feminine games.

"Chieftain wants them dead, quietly?" He thumb pointed to the ceiling as if to reveal the leader of the city.

"Who wants a dead bard around, leading the youth into his paranoid fantasies?" Lira said.

"True," he agreed, wondering if what the youths were after was Wyss' wicked blend of herbs he used to make the will of his followers like jelly. That was a lost recipe as well…

Lira shook her head. "It's madness, but there's a rumor that our Chieftain is descended from one of Wyss' many wives. If they have success…"

Gorias stood and all of them leveled their bows. "Yeah, who wants a famous old daddy around? I get your meaning. I have been the object of diplomacy before, Lira. But how do you know of this?"

Lira motioned for him to follow her. He did, and the guards kept close with their stare and bows. Gorias glanced down at Robyn, who took a step back from his looming form.

She walked to a dark curtain on the far wall and drew it back. They traveled past many a door. One open revealed a link to a barracks, another showed a kitchen. In time, a series of steps led them down the side of the castle. In an area invisible to the outside world stood a series of torture devices sprawled across a huge underground chamber. Gorias' noted many circular bulges along the walls and assumed they were cisterns. Near these gathering places for necessities of life, many a life ceased to be.

On one rack lay a stretched, stiff body of a young woman.

"She was one of them who told us much, but she was short of a few names."

Gorias bit his bottom lip. "She won't be short again." He glanced at the dwarf, who still leered at him. La Gaul wondered if the tiny wizard lived on a drug or smoked something to make his eyes stutter so.

Lira glared at Gorias, but he didn't show fear at the fate waiting those below. "Dislocation loosens the tongue, every time. I knew this would not bother you. You are a man of violence. It suits you."

"Still, how do you know all of their motives?"

The other young woman spoke up. "We have a novice necromancer on the inside." She took out a small piece of parchment and showed it to Gorias. "He stole the jewel of Wyss from Robyn, here in the wizard's collection. That jewel holds the very soul of Carlato, it is said. With it, they can restore the dead man, if they can get his body up and moving. If you catch and persuade him, this youth will surely tell you of their location."

Gorias coughed. "Can't believe there would be much left of him by now…Miss?"

"Kayla, Kayla Rhan." She never offered her hand nor did Gorias offer his. "Our young contact fled their company and is a rogue, but he refuses to aide in the stopping of their enterprise."

Gorias read the paper again. "I see what you mean. That makes it all the more binding, huh? Still, he would know where they are I wager."

Robyn sneered. "The novice was quite a student, but he had anger issues when he studied under me. This youth must die."

The name of the novice was Maddox. Gorias showed no emotion as he asked, "This is the one you want neutralized?"

"Yes," Lira said. "He must die and the jewels must be returned to us. He worked yonder in the Foundry of Syn, but magic was his hobby, as it were."

"Was he a slave driver in the foundry? I hear there are a great many prisoners there."

Lira's lips tightened. "The boy was a smith as well and oversaw the construction of weapons. The slaves are there in abundance. We certainly will not pay for such hard labor in the foundry. Do you think you can track this scoundrel Maddox and not cause a fuss?"

"Certainly," La Gaul said. "I would be able to go right to him."

Though not showing it, he knew the full name of the young necromancer causing them such trouble. Maddox La Gaul.

By the look in the eyes of Kayla Rhan, she knew it as well. Gorias had to ask himself why this girl never told the information to her mother or the wizard.

CHAPTER III

GRANDSON ALSO RISES

Gorias stepped close to his white mount and glanced up at the outside of the keep. The city chieftain resided in the most fortified and elevated place Khabnur possessed. Protected by stone battlements, curtain walls, towers, and such, this place would be the last to fall, he ruminated. From afar, the chieftain made requests. Gorias almost laughed, for this individual had never deemed him worthy of being looked at, yet Gorias was to perform his will. Digging at the dirk handle with his thumbnail, he wondered what it must feel like to be a god.

Lira watched him fidget with his belt, then stared into his old face and said, "If you cross me, you'll die."

The breeze ruffled his flowing gray hair. "We're all gonna die, sister." His voice carried a heavy note of sarcasm. "Some sooner than others, by Heaven." He stepped closer to her and whispered, "You see, I got something in my belly that's eating away at me. It isn't the blood disease of Nosmada, but it's just as deadly. So you and your damned dwarf necromancer can shitcan the theatrics. You can't scare a man who's practically dead."

He mounted up and Lira Rhan calmed, folded her hands, and said, "Sending a dead man to stop more dead men from rising again. Who is the fool here?"

Gorias grunted in the saddle and eyed Kayla next to her mother. The young girl watched him intently, emotionlessly...or was there something there? He touched his beard before winking at her. "Great thing about having nothing to lose, Lira: The world gets really clear."

"God be with you," she muttered and turned back to the castle.

He studied the distant ejecta billowing up from the Foundry of Syn, visible as an orange cloud in the darkness. "You're funnier

than you think," he said but was sure she couldn't hear him.

The hour turned after midnight when Gorias rode out into the rambling city. He reviewed the provided directions to the spot, outside Khabnur's earthen works, where sources claimed the youths were held up. Gorias also thought of how the guards viewed him in the castle. Years ago, the looks would have been of admiration or fear. Now, their looks registered as hungry--thirsting for his legend and to be caught up in his wake.

As he rode through the outer reaches of the city, he made his way for the southern sector. "This is where they say you once lived. Manure, true enough, but spies are probably watching my gray ass. I'm too old for games."

The rabble of mercs still clouded the doorways of shops and homes around the perimeter of the city. Some gave him notice, but many others directed their gazes down. If any thought of way-laying him, they decided better to leave him be. Gorias knew that, on size alone, few would start anything with him. Surely, easier prey lurked elsewhere.

Aside from these people, several itinerant peddlers and merchants set up shop in the streets. Business was business, even in the face of war.

Near the edge of the main city inner wall, he saw a metallic rack with its higher tiers full of flame. On this pyre lay a headless body being consumed. Gorias wondered if it was Shavon or some other persona being snuffed from the planet.

Just outside the city limits, he surveyed the earthen works and felt the walls of his mind closing in on him. Death scented the wind and he feared it as his own. His senses weren't so dull that he didn't see a figure in dark castle guard's clothes step out. The guard leveled a bow and fired. The missile struck Gorias in the chest and he reared back on his mount. With a heavy groan, he fell from the saddle and struck the cold ground. His horse backed off and three guards emerged from the evergreen hedgerow.

"He went down rather easy," said the guard who fired the arrow, doubtful of his luck.

A rough voice intoned, "Fool. He isn't dead yet, and probably wears armor plates under all of those cloaks." Gorias recognized this voice as Robyn De Balm. Footsteps came near as they closed in on him. "Do you see, old man, that not even a legend can stop my designs? Do you think I would let some pathetic puke steal one of my souls for no reason?"

"He doesn't move."

The dwarf secured the strap under his chin and ordered, "Drive your pikes through and finish him fast."

Gorias tried to rise up to disengage his two swords, but the guards quickly jumped forward and grabbed his wrists. His fingers trembled and he involuntarily released the two blades. He fell to the ground and they moved back, laughing at how they disarmed the legend with little effort.

On one knee, he held his chest and gasped. "Well, I never trusted in magic much, Robyn. I like the feeling of steel going into the flesh of another." He moved forward fast and grabbed the dwarf by the ankles. "But in a case like this, flesh will do. Deliverance will come."

Gorias sprang up and swung the body of Robyn De Balm. He smashed the dwarf's head into the nearest guard's face. Since Robyn wore a metal helm, the jawbone and nose of this guard crushed far back into his head. Arms flailing, face ruined, the man stepped back. Feet dancing fast, Gorias maneuvered the body of the dwarf around, inadvertently knocking a pike loose from a shocked guard's grip. His rage turning scarlet, he struck again with the dwarf, smacking the second guard on the left forearm so hard a bone there broke. As this guard clasped his injured limb, Gorias brought the dwarf around and up with an overhand arc, like he would a broadsword, and nailed the guard on the top of the skull. The man collapsed in a heap. Smelling brains, and unsure if they were that of the guard or the dwarf, Gorias moved on.

The third man remaining had his bow loaded. He drew back and fired.

Gorias held up the dwarf and Robyn took the arrow in his gut. He swung the dwarf once more but missed in his attack. The guard scooped up one of La Gaul's swords, handling it with awkward fingers. He moved the weapon as if the blade were longer, missing his targets. Still he fought off Gorias, who continued to wield the dwarf like a bludgeon. When Gorias made an uppercut move, the ankles of the small body cracked. He swore as he threw the dwarf at the guard and drew his dirk. The guard fumbled with the body of Robyn De Balm in his arms. That provided enough confusion for Gorias to move forth, grapple him with one arm, and stab down with the other. The dirk sank through the heavy leather coat of the guard, and he ground it around. Chambers of the guard's heart imploded and he died gripping Gorias' sword, in the embrace of a fable.

Blood gushed from the wound as he replaced his swords. He looked down at the guard and then at the bloodied, crushed skull of the dwarf necromancer. Pulling the arrow out of his chest, he smirked. "Never even hit my skin, you young prick."

Under his shirt, he adjusted his brace and the armored chest plate that no one could see. He turned to the guard whose face he'd broken in his initial attack. Gorias crossed his swords with little effort, removing the guard's head and the hand that held his broken jaw.

Alone in the road, he spit on the dwarf's bloody head. He stepped near his horse and stopped. The wind shifted.

"Step out, missy," Gorias said calmly, sword still in his hands. "We may as well get this over with."

From the hedge stepped the figure of Kayla Rhan. Though standing in a defensive pose, she held no weapon. "How did you know I was there?"

He sheathed a blade then gripped his saddle horn and said, "I can smell you. Serious, missy, you have an earthy quality. That isn't bad, it's just you."

"My name is Kayla," she said with strength, her hands on the handles of weapons concealed by the hedge and the dark.

"I remember who you are," he said. "Were you part of this band of happy idiots or did you come to watch?"

She took a step but never drew a weapon. "I followed them because I heard what they were going to do. Robyn's a swine and planned to double cross you."

"He was a swine," Gorias corrected her, returning his other sword to the scabbard. "He seemed like a fence sitter with your mom. He wasn't much in the way of darkest wizardry by a long shot. I took him more like dim fortune-teller."

"Hell of a dagger you have there. I thought it would pass through him."

Gorias patted the dirk on his belt. "Yeah, it's made of adamantium. Fairly rare stuff and one has to kill a hundred people to get some of it. It can cut jewels or other steel at will."

Her eyes never blinked as she testified, "I know who Maddox is."

He climbed into the saddle. "Oh? Does that mean I have to kill you?"

"We'll see, Gorias La Gaul. I know that Maddox doesn't have the ideals of Nosmada at heart."

With a smirk, he said, "You wanted to see just what I was going to do when I get to Maddox, eh?"

"You'd never kill your own grandson," she said, her hand resting on the strap of her lacquered leather quiver.

"I wouldn't?" Gorias sent her a mocking look. "You don't know me at all, missy, uh, Kayla."

"You'd be surprised what I know about you."

"Probably." He coughed then said, "I have to find him and get down to business. I thought I had time to get out of this hole, but now with you knowing this…" He paused and saw what passed for a smile on her face. "You never told your mother Maddox was my grandson?"

"Of course not," Kayla confessed. "I knew Maddox wasn't evil and that you would never slay him. I also know he switched the jewels with those the cult obtained. Yes, he really pulled one on the Cult of the Dragon and those in the society of Wyss. They'll not be raising Wyss from the dead."

"Then you can guess that your Ma won't be pleased with me when she figures out that I took her object of worry and killed her Mage."

Kayla kicked the body of Robyn and said, "To Hell with him."

"What's Maddox to you?" Gorias asked as he looked down the moon flooded streets for witnesses.

The girl shrugged and said, "Sometimes one finds a man interesting due to what he is or who he is…or what he's apart of."

"I'm not much any more, sweetheart."

Kayla smiled, her pale skin beaming in the night. "Inhumanly ancient and quite jaded? There's no sin in that, sir."

"Ya talk funny, hon. I'm somewhat past being fervent about terms, deary dear."

Gorias turned his horse and started to trot away. The girl jogged behind him like a trooper taking the field. He headed for the place he knew his grandson resided. Looking back at the castle, he wondered if he'd played his cards correctly, not exactly telling Lira or Kayla Rhan about his motives for coming here.

Though still cold the season was turning, but the night chills still gripped the warrior. The cold didn't seem to bother the girl running behind him. *Then again*, he pondered, *I got seven hundred years on her.*

The simple home Maddox resided in attached itself to a series of other hovels that formed a city block. Made of planks, the thatched roofed home appeared well sealed against the elements with mud and pitch.

When Gorias came to a halt, Kayla jogged up behind him. She sounded winded but looked invigorated by the pallor of her skin. He turned his head as he heard a great crash inside the home. While he dismounted, a small figure ran out of the front door and onto the muddy ground. This youth fell at the feet of Gorias' mount. Kayla drew out a slim rapier and sank back behind his horse. The person fresh out of the home was a young man, very slender, sporting long greasy hair. Dressed in russet pants and a horsehair tunic that a priest would die for, he whimpered and trembled, many words trickling from his lips.

Gorias heard more thrashing inside the house as he knelt by the youth. Brow furrowing, he realized the boy sang.

"What say you, boy?"

"Give me some wine for my mouth.
Let me have peace in my soul.
If I could get to the Mercy seat
God would bless me true, I know."

"Kid," Gorias grunted. "What's going on here and where's my grandson?"

"Who? Maddox La Gaul?"

"No, the bride of Methuselah, ya little jackass." He gripped the boy by the hair and lifted him up. The youth sported a broad face, lightly freckled, and only reacted in pain for a moment to Gorias' action. "Why are ya singing and running away?"

Tears flowed heavy and he wailed. "Because I'm about to die and as a young bard I always said I would die with a tune on my lips."

Gorias scowled. "Very dramatic. Who's going to kill you?"

In response, the sidewall of the home splintered into a hundred shards of wood. A rather large figure flew through the opening and slammed into the side of Gorias' horse. The horse bellowed and backed away as the body fell to the earth. This sudden action knocked Kayla to the ground, but she rolled to her knees in response to this blast. The form from the house turned over and Gorias recognized his grandson, Maddox. A big man for twenty years, Maddox sported the La Gaul frame, but was leaner than himself.

"Evening, son," Gorias said and drew the two swords from his backpack. "Deliverance will come."

Up on his all fours, Maddox glared through a mane of black hair at his grandfather. Though this cover shrouded his expression, his gaze screamed alarm. Maddox leather boots dug into the ground, but he never sprang to fight whatever tossed him.

Gorias needed no ringing gong to tell him where the danger would originate. From out of the home emerged a gigantic figure, fully two feet taller than Gorias' great height. This man, corded with muscle, bore a long beard snaking to his belly. His skin was scaly and red as blood, but his eyes glowed orange. Bald and wearing deerskin pants and vest, he swung a crudely made spiked mace to break his path clear in his exit.

The giant spoke in a deep voice, saying, "Stand aside from the son of a fallen son of God."

"Great."

Gorias ruffled out the sleeves of his overcloak. The boy who sang stared at his arms, and Gorias wondered if he saw the threads dangling near the handles of the swords. Stepping in front of his grandson, he put the handles of his swords together. They slotted jointly and stayed firm, forming one two bladed weapon.

He demanded of the giant, "Who is your father, shorty?"

Six fingers gripped the mace as the creature faced him. The two boys scrambled to one side as the giant yelled, "My father is Azazel. I am Hawkabel, vice Lord of the Nephilum at…"

The words of Hawkabel stopped with a groan, as Gorias twirled his blade and struck the giant between the legs. Gorias frowned, knowing he missed his target, even if he sliced the buckskin open. Hawkabel swiped with the mace in his right hand and reached out with his left. Easily, Gorias was disarmed and flung back into the dirt on his backside.

Hawkabel laughed as he put down his mace. He held the joined swords of Gorias in the middle at the handles, admiring the legendary weapons. "These must be the swords made from angels' wings." He looked away from the gleaming blades and down at the handles he held.

Maddox and the bard both stared at the same thing Hawkabel did. Their eyes traced the long thread back to the sleeves of Gorias as he sat up in the dirt. It was a simple maneuver when he yanked backwards. The swords disengaged from each other and the giant couldn't resist grabbing for the blades as they fell from his grasp. Unfortunately for Hawkabel, his six fingered grip made fists around the blades. When he did, Gorias pulled back even harder. All the warrior needed was a modest yank and the blades sliced through the digits of the giant.

At the same time Gorias reeled his swords back in, Maddox took a chance and grabbed for the huge mace of the giant. He had trouble lifting it.

Hawkabel went to his knees, staring at his hands. Only his thumbs remained and blood poured from his wounds.

Maddox reached into his leather coat and each hand emerged wielding a small knife. He leapt on the giant's back, stabbing him in the throat on either side. Hawkabel shrugged off the boy, sending Maddox flying, but the wounds bled like racing rivers.

Gorias rose up and gripped his swords anew. "Azazel taught men to work in metal and make weapons," he said as he stepped closer to Hawkabel. "You shoulda paid closer attention to him." He slashed down twice, chopping at the head of the giant near the wounds his grandson made. It took both blows to cut into the skin near the Nephilum's throat. Hawkabel jumped up, gurgling, roaring, and swearing sulphurously. Gorias made a move with his right forearm, almost like a punch, but the belly of the giant split open in the move's wake. The youths behind him gasped, not comprehending how he brought Hawkabel down to his knees.

He hacked a few more times at the throat, and then placed the swords side by side before he swiped. The head of Hawkabel hung off his body backwards, still attached by his spinal cord. Geysers of blood vomited in the air and they all stepped back.

Maddox looked at the bard. "Next time I want to go to the tavern, Tammas, listen to me."

Gorias sheathed his swords and stepped closer to the boy. "That sounds like my grandson."

Kayla stepped forward, focused on the forearm of Gorias. "How did you do that?" Though armor rested on his forearm, she couldn't get a clear look at what on it could cause such an injury to the giant. The material gleamed scaled and sported a bony outcropping.

Maddox pointed at the house. "The creature wasn't alone. His wizard came along with him."

"Son of a whore," Gorias cursed and maneuvered toward the breech in the house. Looking around, he saw no one. "Where in the hell is he?"

Tammas muttered, "Bedroom."

Gorias moved through the breech before Maddox could stop him. The old one bolted through the darkness toward a door with an emerald glow seeping from the cracks. He kicked it open and beheld a small man carrying what looked like a mirrored shield. The wizard held the polished surface at the shelves near what Gorias presumed as Maddox bed. On these shelves sat many pouches, now discarded. Beside these empty cases lay a scattered series of jewels.

A disembodied voice in the room said, "No, no, no, wait, the emerald one! That is the soul we require."

The ruddy skinned wizard then saw Gorias and his face showed terror. He raised his right hand and made a forked symbol. When he started to invoke a spell, Gorias roared and swung his swords from side to side. He removed the conjuring hand at the wrist cleanly, sending it to the shelves. The other blade slit across the throat of the wizard, trapping his spell in his wretched neck forever.

The polished shield fell to the floor, a rush of crimson gushing over the middle of it. The wizard fell on the bed, dying with a massive twitch and a rude breaking of wind. Gorias stared at the shield and saw that, through the shadowy depths of the glass, someone looked back at him. With a grunt, he planted a boot in the bloody mirror and the inner shield lining shattered.

Gorias emerged from the home with the dead wizard on his shoulder. He threw him by the dead son of the fallen angel. He peered down the street and saw a few figures peering out of hovels, soon to vanish from his gaze. One lingered, a tall slender man.

"Who the hell is that? He seems familiar to me." His mind raced as this figure slunk back into obscurity. Who was that? He couldn't place the body exactly. Surely not Ezran…

Maddox stared at the old man as he smiled. "Grandfather? You're still alive?"

"For a while yet," Gorias said, regarding the long-haired, smaller youth with his grandson. "Tammas the bard is it?"

The young man nodded with vigor, somewhat stunned by who he looked at.

Gorias slapped him on the shoulder. "I assume you both know Kayla."

The youths exchanged glances, but were non-committal on that regard.

"Well, how did ya manage to get a Nephilum pissed at you?"

"Long story, Grampa." Maddox gave Gorias a half embrace.

"Well, are there any more of him after you?"

Maddox shrugged. "They came from an advanced party of Nosmada's band. They knew I stole the soul jewels from that little wizard. They thought I had the soul of one they wanted from amongst Robyn De Balm's cache."

"Do you?"

Maddox shrugged, mimicking his grandfather's body language. "I may have a few, but not what they wanted."

Gorias glanced down the sparsely populated avenue. "Nice spot. Somewhat devoid of thugs, too."

Kayla studied the old man, even poked him with her bow. "You called him a Nephilum, not an ogre like Mitre Stillwell. They're nearly the same size."

Gorias nodded. "Nephilum claim to be fathered by fallen angels and have six fingers and six toes, see? Plus, they are always in better shape and harder to kill. An ogre? Well, I think they come from really ugly people, but that's my own theory. Mitre is just a freak. He told me his mother slept with a Nephilum, but I think she just fell for a line of crap. Let's go to the whore-house and talk about it later."

Tammas glanced at Gorias. "Can you still…"

He roared with laughter. "My back is shot, kid. But ya don't have to stand up for them to go down. Let's go. Sing me a song, youngster. I like ballads."

CHAPTER IV

BALLAD OF MATTY GRAUM

Far off to the south of them, in a forbidding fortress of Kanoch, Nosmada peered into a stone well. The waters stood still and up to the brim of the stone circle. The tall, black haired man noted the guard behind him and the bent figure beside him.

Hands on his hips, he said to the elderly woman, "You saw it, Zillian?"

She brushed back a silky, purple hood as a creaking voice acknowledged Nosmada's words. "From the Well of Sorrows, yes, I saw the gilded jewel through the shield. You see the boy Maddox indeed stole what is required from the wizard."

Nosmada scratched his dark beard and brooded for a moment. The torches on the walls illuminated his features and added to his fearsome appearance. His hawkish nose centered over unusually high cheekbones. His heavy brow hooded his features. His jaw jutted out nearly as far, creating a bizarre profile of a crescent.

He extended his hand and pointed into the Well of Sorrows. "You saw *him*?"

Zillian nodded and closed her eyes. In the pulsing light her butterscotch colored eyes opened to glow like fire. She growled, "Yes and a curse be on him. Well, not that a curse from me would be able to nuisance one such as La Gaul."

Nosmada turned to the tall man behind them. The muscle bound guard stood, blank faced, and looked back at his master. "Lannon? You know who that was?"

"Of course, Lord Nosmada. The myth himself, Gorias La Gaul."

Zillian snapped, "Why is *he* there of all folk? Why does he step into this path at such a time?"

"La Gaul," Nosmada said with a grim voice, but not with heavy malice. His nostrils flared. "We considered him as alive for certain. It doesn't matter. Gorias is old and near death. We have the troopers led by Tolin on the way to gather weapons from the Foundry of Syn. What can one old man do to us?"

Zillian glared at him and said. "I need not remind you how important it is we seize Wyss before his followers?"

He shrugged and turned from the well. As he took a few steps, Lannon gave him room to move. "It matters not if he arises in his dead flesh. What's he going to do, tell his secrets to La Gaul? Unlikely. If Wyss' worshipers carry out their mad plan, Wyss will fall into line with my order or depart this life again." He turned back to the stone circle and the lingering representation there. Scarlet splashed across the waters and the image of the old warrior faded. "Gorias La Gaul visiting his grandson at this time. Who would have thought?"

Zillian trembled, her skeletal body never calming as her hands slapped the side of the well. "If he slew the wizard of Hawkabel, then the Nephilum himself must be dead as well. How could the old one have done that in his sickly condition?"

Nosmada almost smiled, tilted his head. "He's resourceful, you know. Perhaps he was aided. We cannot see it."

"That is the story, my Lord. That Gorias has a great resource watching over him."

His blemished forehead full of furrows, Nosmada swung an arm out dismissively. "Bah. Such interventionalist thinking is madness. The old story about Gorias and Ezran Gavreel? Nonsense. If the ones on high were about stopping me, I'd be dead seven fold by now." He paused. "He slew the wizard with ease."

Zillian nodded, placed her hand between her sunken breasts, twitched, and then looked away.

"Didn't that wizard father children with you in ages past?"

"He was not alone in that regard. If he died that easily, he was a bad progenitor now, wasn't he? Still, there is one problem that still exists—that of Wyss."

Nosmada laughed and Lannon kept his jaw clenched firm. "Gorias is a fading dream and morning is nigh. I, too, wandered the earth for ages until I came unto this place and built it for my son.

After much travel, I failed to find what ailed my soul. Only here have I found the answer. I will not have my plans thwarted by this relic from a bygone era."

✲ ✲ ✲ ✲ ✲

Gorias, Maddox ,and Tammas packed their horses. They took the mount that the wizard of Nosmada rode and gave it to Kayla. Gorias heard the young bard whisper to Maddox, "He doesn't seem to mind me coming along?"

Maddox cinched up his bags and checked to see that his bow was on the saddle correctly. "Grandfather is a different sort. You may not want to come along, Tammas. Old La Gaul is tough, but he's fair. You may have better opportunities for adventure or just plain living elsewhere."

Tammas gazed at the hole in the wall and the pile of wood under the giant's body. He pondered Maddox' words.

Gorias ripped planks and added to the firewood already gathered. He struck flints under the straw in the pile and lit the monster on fire. He picked up the body of the wizard and threw it on the headless corpse of the giant.

Kayla gravitated near Gorias as if she wanted to help him with the task, but he never asked for aid.

Tammas shivered. "I cannot stay here if more of Nosmada's party is nearby."

"You're just a kid." Gorias coughed as flames licked the body of the giant. "Hardly worth killing. No threat from a kid who sings, huh? We'll see if we can change that. Good disguise you have as such a helpless guy, though."

Tammas looked at the small harp he strapped to his horse. "Um, yes, it is, sir," he said, trying to stand at attention.

Maddox pointed at Kayla, who brooded with her head down. "What good is she?"

"She carries a bow," Gorias said flippantly, drawing a few tired breaths as he looked from the fire to the daughter of Lira Rhan. "Girl, can you shoot and ride?"

Kayla Rhan nodded, her hands on her belt as if she were ready to draw steel and demonstrate her abilities.

"There you go," Gorias replied, trying to get comfortable in the saddle. "Mounted archery is a skill, son."

We made need such a skill?" Maddox's voice almost cracked as his face flushed.

"C'mon, men," Gorias said as he climbed in the saddle. He eyed Kayla and smirked. "Or, near as much to them as ya can get. We shall hit the Madam's house before we depart. If we play this right, we'll get some fabulous treasure and all the whores we can eat."

Maddox eyed his grandfather, confused. "Treasure? What did he say? Where are we going?"

"If you got the forces of Nosmada sniffing for you," Gorias said, glancing around, "does it matter where in the world I take you?"

Maddox climbed into the saddle, gripped the reins, and then shrugged. "I suppose not."

Gorias put both hands to his head and massaged his wrinkled temples, admitting, "I was just joking about the treasure."

❖ ❖ ❖ ❖ ❖

Crossing over to the southeastern side of the city, the trio set out for a small gathering of buildings. These buildings sat situated near a large well and a covered cistern. They possessed a stable, a sleeping hostel for lodgers, a small tavern, and a whorehouse. It was a business-like atmosphere in each establishment. A few linkmen lit lamps on their iron standards.

"Why, Madam Wilkens," Gorias called out to the woman on the porch of the brothel. "It has been eons."

While the party dismounted, the tall woman put her long fingers on the hitching posts. They reminded Gorias of giant spiders. Her voice rang deep, and showed advanced age even if her form did not betray her years. "Gorias La Gaul? I win the bet with Jacquee and Rudi. You didn't die in the valley of the vipers." She chuckled deep in her throat and swept back her long, lush hair. "As far as how many eons, keep that to yourself."

Gorias tied up his horse then placed a boot on the steps leading up to the porch. "A gentlemen never tells years, my dear."

"Since when did you become a gentleman?" she said, letting her head turn in the light night air. When she performed this action, none of them had to strain their eyes to see the sheen of her waving hair. The luster in her black as night locks almost glittered, making them stare.

"Never said I was. Just stating a fact. Sorry to arrive so late, but it couldn't be helped."

Madam Wilkens sighed and motioned for them all to enter her establishment. Her gaze rested on each one, reading them in full. When she removed her over-cloak, she revealed a shimmering taffeta gown. The edges were embroidered with golden swirls. The cuffs and neck were lined with delicate fur or lines of colored beads.

"I eavesdropped on one of the ladies and their pillow talk earlier. They said you were in Khabnur. Quite a crew you have."

"Some have greatness thrust upon them," he muttered as he put a large canvas bag down on her foyer table, placing his hands on his waist. "Some of us take what we can get. Any girls awake or clean?"

"A few. So how did you escape the valley of the vipers?" She smiled, reached out to him, and tapped the back of her left hand on his chest. There was a clacking sound when she did this.

"Stealth," he said with a gruff cough, turning from the bag that he never opened. "How's business?"

"Good, seeing as all of these mercs and outlaws are in Khabnur." Madam Wilkens sighed as he gave her gold coins. He waved to his grandson to go on up the stairs and pick out a partner. "We had an incident the other night over who would get Rudi."

"Yeah?" Gorias asked, leaning his hips on a large couch. When he reclined, the old man made a crunching sound that caused everyone to look at him, save for the Madam.

Wilkens nodded and glanced down at the opal ring on her left hand. "Yes. Three of those outlaws went outside and the shouting started. By the time the constables arrived, two of them hung up the third and well…"

A knowing sigh escaped Gorias, but Tammas appeared confused.

"What? What happened?"

The Madam and Gorias looked at each other, then both sighed. "They strung him up and gelded him. You really do need to get your naughty little ass out more, boy child."

"There's a lot of people raised in-doors, Madam," Gorias said. "I met a young puppy--Lemach was that his name? I forget. Anyway, I don't know if sunlight ever hit his belly. A real palace servant, never drunk on duty, but I guess that is what happens when there are too many people on earth. Even the weak have to have a purpose."

Wilkens smiled. "I would say so, Lord La Gaul."

He watched Tammas turn away, sit in the foyer of the whorehouse, and set up his small harp. The old man glanced at Kayla, who raised an eyebrow at him as she clutched her leather belt.

"Is that your racket, kid? Play for your supper, so to speak? I like your thinking, but I paid for you already."

"No thank you sir. I am a celibate," Tammas said, never making eye contact with La Gaul.

Gorias took off his cloak. "Well, isn't that something?"

"Does that disturb you?" Tammas' hands soothed the harp's edges.

"No. Never know when I may need a virgin for sacrifice on a trip."

Tammas looked up and did a double-take at La Gaul. On his forearms rested bluish colored armor guards with tiny ivory spikes sticking out….no…*nails*! Tammas gasped as he stared at the light body armor Gorias wore under his cloak. Kayla blinked at him, her expression flushed and confused.

The old man motioned to a woman with long red tresses down her woolen dress and said to Tammas, "What, never seen dragon's skin before?"

THRALL

"Are all the legends about you true?"

Gorias nodded at the prostitute then at Madam Wilkens. He winked at Tammas. "Damn, I sure hope so."

Kayla's pale hand reached out and touched the dragon plating, then she ran her fingers over the nail on Gorias' forearm — the object that obviously gutted the giant earlier. She swallowed hard, her eyes cloudy as if in a dream.

"Well, little sister," he said to her gently, trying to cut through the apprehension in her. "I don't know what there is for you to do here. If you prefer women…"

Kayla shook her head. "No, Lord La Gaul. If I preferred, I would go to the tavern off yonder and get a man. The mood doesn't strike me this night."

He nodded and headed for the stairs. "Call me Gorias." The big man never eyed the red headed whore who asked if she could call him that as well. "Yeah, what ever pleases you."

Kayla watched him walk away. Her chest rose and fell fast. Her hands tried to stay busy, as if her thoughts couldn't be suppressed save for action.

Tammas plucked a few strings, cleared his throat. "Do you think he was kidding about the virgin sacrifice?"

With a shrug, Kayla settled in. "One never knows. I'm not worried about it."

❈ ❈ ❈ ❈ ❈

Tammas settled in behind his harp as Maddox and Gorias disappeared upstairs in the house. He strummed and began to sing.

"I am a dark, way worn traveler
Wandering in this evil world so slow.
I have no sickness, no anger, nor fears
For this great end to which I go…"

The Madam smiled in approval and took up knitting a pillow casing as he sang. "You have a lovely voice, young man. Do go on."

"I'm going to die, to see my father
And all my family who have crossed alone.
I am just traveling all alone now.
I'm just striving to reach my home."

She hummed the tune as he strummed and, after a spell, the Madam offered to end his virginity for free. Tammas declined.

Tammas paused in his song. "You seem quite intelligent."

Madam Wilkens looked up. "For a whore?"

His harp dropped a little. "Oh dear. Well, yes, for a whore, if you will. How is it that you came to run such a place?"

"I was comely once. I decided I wouldn't spend my life busting my back or on my back. Time chews at all of us, boy, and I know the destination of whores. I didn't want to be strangled and put on a pyre for giggling at a less than endowed politician, so I decided years ago to save my money and go into management. This way, I pick and choose who I sleep with."

"I just wondered..."

She put down her needles and stared at Tammas in a motherly way. "Humor me, boy. How is it that fate finds you in the company of Gorias La Gaul?"

"I'm friends with Maddox La Gaul, his grandson. We have been drinking buddies for a few months."

"I assumed you were fodder."

"Pardon me?"

"Fodder. You know, some fool he brought along to take up a blade thrust meant for him. My mistake."

✶ ✶ ✶ ✶ ✶

Some time passed before Gorias shambled down the stairs and collapsed on a reclining couch near Tammas. Drinking from a skin of red wine given to him by Madam Wilkens, he waved at the young man and ordered, "Play me something I know, kid." He looked at Kayla who sharpened a dagger. Her jaw appeared locked.

Was it jealousy of the whores? He didn't know, refused to ponder it, and relaxed.

Tammas cracked his knuckles. "Are the ballads about you true, sir?"

Gorias snorted and stretched out, watching Madam Wilkens bring him a tray of wafers, nuts, and candies. "Hard to say. I never wrote any of them."

"How did you get those armored sleeves and plates?"

La Gaul touched his dragon's scaled armor then took a handful of walnuts in his hand and chuckled. "Sing me a good song and I may tell you."

Tammas nodded, fingering the harp. "There's one I've heard all my life and I wondered if there's any certainty in it." The boy cleared his throat.

"On the high and finest and greatest holiday
On the very best day of the year
Young Matty Graum walked to temple
The Holy word to hear.
And some walked in adorned in white
And some in crimson and blue
And then came in Lord La Gaul's wife
A flower amongst the few."

As Tammas played an instrumental break, Gorias wore a small smile, but never said a word. Kayla sharpened her knife, eyes on the old man, showing no emotion.

"She looked at him, he looked at her
The like had never been done.
And when she arose and took his hand
and bade him come along…
Well they tossed and they turned in the bed all night
Till they were fast asleep
And in the light of the new morning dawn
Gorias La Gaul stood at their feet."

While he strummed, Tammas saw the old Madam gaze at Gorias and smile. She shook her head as Gorias closed his eyes.

> *"Gorias said, get up, young Matty Graum*
> *And put your clothing on.*
> *I'll never have it said in the whole wide world*
> *That I slayed a naked man.*
> *Matty said I won't get up, I won't get dressed*
> *I fear so for my life*
> *For you have got two very sharp swords*
> *And I have nary a knife…"*

Gorias broke into a grin and drank more. His eyes remained shut. Maddox started down the stairs and stopped as he heard the song.

> *"Oh yes I have two very sharp swords.*
> *They cost me deep in purse.*
> *And you can have the better of the two*
> *and I shall take the worse*
> *And you shall strike the very first blow*
> *And strike it like a man*
> *I will strike the very next blow and kill you if I can…"*

Maddox adjusted his clothes and gaped at Tammas. He then looked at his grandfather, who was ready to roll off the reclining couch in hilarity.

> *"Well Matty struck the very first blow*
> *And he hurt Gorias La Gaul sore*
> *But Gorias struck the very next one.*
> *Matty lay dead in his gore.*
> *Well Gorias looked at his wife in her bed*
> *The rage and the hate saw she.*
> *Who do you like better now, he asked, Young Matty Graum or me?"*

Gorias chuckled greatly. "She had hair like a flame of hell, that one."

Maddox asked, "Who?"

The old man gestured at Tammas. "Your grandmother." He then made a fist and crushed the shells of the walnuts in his grasp.

"Very do I like your brow, said she
Very well do I like your chin
But I like Matty Graum in all of his gore
Better than you and all of your kin.
Well he took her by the hair of her head
And dragged her down the hall
And with his swords, cut off her head,
And kicked it against the wall…"

Gorias sat up on the couch as Tammas finished the song. "Heh, great song, kid." His eyes glistened, and Kayla broke into a smile as well.

The validity of the song wasn't a concern for Gorias' actions told Tammas the story. "How did you get the armlets and the armor? From what I've read, dragon flesh and scales cannot be woven. How is it you can wear those armlets and chest pates that nearly fit you perfect."

Maddox extended his arms toward the ceiling and yawned. "Hey Grampa, you ever get tired of questions?

"And folks wonder why I stay incognito so much," Gorias said, running his rough hands down the armor on his forearms. "Do you know what a wyrmling is?"

Tammas shrugged. "I guess it's a youthful dragon?"

Gorias nodded, fingers tapping the nail on the armor. "Good show, youngster. You think I slew only the older dragons of the desert years ago?"

The boy's eyes opened wide and Kayla stifled a laugh. Tammas' harp went flat to his lap. "You gutted and skinned a baby dragon?"

Gorias wore a frown. "Was I to spare them because they

were cute? That's the problem with the youth. They look so cute, and yet they grow into ugly assed grown ups. I wish the Lord would shorten our life spans to two hundred years. That way there would be less stupid people in the world."

Madam Wilkens threw back her head and laughed. "That's old Gorias La Gaul! He was ever the one to live for the moment and let all tomorrows hatch themselves in due course."

A few of the prostitutes walked from the area of the larder, carrying drinks for themselves. The blonde who had bedded Maddox peered out of the shuttered windows and said, "Madam! There are several of the leeches outside tonight."

The older woman stood up, placed both hands to her back, and groaned. "So let them stay there. We see them pass by in the night, as all do since the blood disease has gotten out of hand. They are but the fruit of dumb spirits. Forget them."

Gorias yawned. "Gotta hand it to the leeches. At least there are no bandits out on the prairie any more."

Maddox disappeared, heading toward the larder. When he departed, Madam Wilkens said to Gorias, "Quite a young man, that one."

"He comes from good stock."

She smiled. "I've heard Maddox is famous more as a thief than a killer."

"Oh, he's a killer, all right, just not for hire. He's content to travel, drink, and get laid. Can't fault him for that. Hell, I still kill men so I can do the very same thing. That's the difference--I must pay for what he gets by stealth."

"Some say you have developed a death wish this late in life."

"No, that's untrue. I have no desire to die stupidly. I'm weary of life, but not tired of living." Gorias gathered together all of the shells and leftovers from what he ate. Tammas watched him keenly as the old man carried these pieces to the hearth and cast them into the fire. Knowing the boy watched him, he said, "Some say it's an old taboo to leave anything the body has touched behind. I'd hate for a wizard to walk in here and make a fetish to use on me out of these shells. I may be paranoid, but I'm a live paranoiac."

Tammas asked Gorias, "Is it true you have been all over this Earth?"

"Most of it."

"Is it true life began here in Shynar?"

"Nearby, depending on which song you listen to. The scribes take down notes for the few who can read. Each culture I have found seems to think life started around here. I've walked over the Bosporus land bridge and seen the land of Kemet. The reclining statue of Bastet is quite a feat. Far north of here is frozen Zenghaus where the barbarians come from. Near to them are more savages in Asgard. Farther west is a civilized land called Albion."

"Are they wondrous lands?"

"Most are beautiful, even the deserts, but the people make them ugly. Most are bored, and make it dangerous with all of the devils they let tiptoe into this realm."

As Maddox returned, the blonde whore entered the room again. "Madam! Lira Rhan is outside with a dozen of her guards! There's a tiny one leading them, dressed in a bloody helmet. They're forming a ring around our house."

"A tiny one leading?" Maddox joined them at the window. His eyes registered fear as he stared at Gorias. "Grandfather! I swear it's the wizard Robyn De Balm!"

Kayla's mouth dropped open and she bolted towards the window.

Gorias threw back his head and sighed. "I knew I missed something before I went to see Maddox. I forgot to burn the damned dwarf mage."

CHAPTER V

RECKONING WITH DE BALM

Lira Rhan shouted outside the whorehouse. "We are aware you are in there, La Gaul."

Gorias cinched up his midriff belt, adjusted his greaves, and pulled on his long cloak. "Congratulations, lady. Do ya want a prize for finding me in a whorehouse? You want a real treat? I'm gonna use the privy next!"

Laughter rippled through the men outside and Lira Rhan responded with indignation. "Silence, you fools! Train your bows at the windows."

After rectifying his armor plates, Gorias looked at the bard. "She sounds pissed." He then eyed Kayla, who wore an expression of shock, her knuckles shown white from gripping the dagger in her hand. If anything, he took her feelings to be honest.

The girls of the house ran frantically, but not without intent. They were double-checking shutters and placing extra bars on doors, almost with military efficiency. When they opened a tall, wooden wardrobe cabinet and removed several flails, Gorias had to laugh. Each one brandished the weapons and the swinging spiked balls as if they knew what to do with them.

Lira Rhan addressed the house again. "You dare to double cross me? I see not the head of Maddox at my feet nor his soul jewels. I have it on good authority that the necromancer we sought is your grandson."

Gorias motioned for the Madam to get closer to him, as well as Maddox, Tammas, and Kayla. "You been eating mushrooms, sister? I ain't had time to double cross you yet. Come back in the morning and we'll talk again." He lowered his voice. "All locked up tight Madam? Good. I want a firm count of how many of those bastards are out there if you can."

As Wilkens departed, Tammas said, "Sir, you cannot hope to

fight your way out of here. There must be two dozen men out there. Maybe more if the mercs slumming around are with them."

"Kid, I never had that in mind at all. I want to know how many of them I have to kill." He faced Maddox. "Go up top and get your bow ready, you understand? They will force the doors down and come in quick. Kayla, you back him up when…if he misses."

The Madam returned. "There are a dozen regular palace guards, a few local lawmen, and three rough looking constables with the wizard. I can see a small group of outlaw mercenaries out there straggling. I don't know if that group is with them or just watching."

Gorias swore against his opposition. "Robyn is dead and Lira Rhan doesn't realize it. I'll stomp the brains out of the damned little piglet this time." He then addressed the woman outside. "What're you saying, sister? I'm on my way out of this damned paranoid town. Can't a man indulge in what he wants these days or should I have returned to the Keep for a piece?"

"Robyn has told me of how you planned to double cross me, and I have seen his wounds," Lira said. "We saw the body of the Nephilum burning as well. You have slain representatives of Nosmada and will now bring his vengeance unto us all. For that, and lying to me about your grandson, you must die, either here or on my rack in the Keep."

With a frown, Gorias flexed his stiff fingers and looked at the bag he'd placed on the foyer table. "Well, I'm waiting, sister."

Lira Rhan paused. "Come out and give yourself unto us, Gorias."

The old warrior laughed. "Want to pass me a bit of what you are drinking? If I have to die, so be it. Come and see me."

"You want it to be known you died in a brothel?" Rhan taunted him.

"I'd like to see your kitchen, Lira," he retorted.

"Is my daughter your hostage?"

He sized up the people outside through cracks in the shutters. Gorias focused on the insolent eyes of the undead wizard in the bloody metal helmet. "She must think I'm insane." He drew out both swords and shouted, "You want me, sister, come on and get me." After he turned to Kayla, he said, "What are you still doing in here? If you haven't joined Maddox upstairs yet, then your soul isn't in this, sweetheart. You better go back out with your mother."

Kayla shook her head. "My place isn't with her anymore."

Maddox stood on the stairwell and snorted. "To Hell with her, Grampa. She's nothing but a damned groupie." Kayla's gaze flared and she looked like she would slay Maddox as he spoke. "She humped my leg because I was your grandson. I get that a lot."

She drew her short rapier and held it to Maddox's belly. "Not by many who can fight like me."

"Save it for later, kids," Gorias snapped as he pulled the bag off the object on the table. This revealed a great helmet, replete with a visor composed from dragon scales. "Follow Maddox up there, Kayla, and watch Tammas' back."

Maddox looked down the stairs, blinked at the helm. "Gods. Grandfather, I think we can jump from the top story to the roof of the tavern next to the stables."

"I said getting away wasn't on my mind. Listen closer, son. Those sons of bitches gotta die. I'm too old to run very far."

"I know, but we'll need an escape route once the killing starts. You cannot slay them all at once. We can kill many from up here."

Tammas took up his harp. "I have never killed a man before."

"It's time ya started, kid." Gorias slapped the harp out of his hand. "Madam? Get your girls out of sight. I'll try not to burn the place down." He grabbed Tammas by the forearm. "They'll bull rush the front door and circle around the back. Go on up to the top of the stairs. When they come in, I'll nail the first ones at the knees. The ones after will stumble over them."

Tammas trembled and his mouth quivered, eyes wet. He gripped his bow and arrows tight.

"Now, listen to me! You have to shoot the next ones for me. Can you do that?"

He nodded and held the small bow in his fists. "Are you certain we can take them?"

The old man grinned wolfishly. "Certain as the grave, boy. Once you strike the next few of them bastards, some idiot will try to be a hero. Never you mind that, because I'll get the dumb-ass who jumps in. Just be ready to cover me when I start up the stairs, got it?"

"Yes, sir."

"Maddox will ace a few trying to sneak in the back, right?" Gorias called up the stairs.

"Just waiting on the rush."

"Good kid," Gorias said with growing apprehension in his voice. "Wish his father were half the man he was. Kayla, help him to make sure he does it right."

A great weight rammed the whorehouse door. The wooden bar across it held, and Gorias scrambled back to a position beside the door, both swords at the ready. He gave his helmet a hungry look, but simply had no time to retrieve it.

Tammas loaded up an arrow and waited. He stared at Gorias, who read his feelings. *He must think I am crazy down here waiting for them to run through.*

The old warrior balanced his swords against the wall on either side of himself, and then peeked out the shutters at the men getting ready to rush the door. Abruptly, Gorias grabbed the bar and lifted it. Two burly guards broke through, stunned at the lack of obstruction. They fell with a tremendous crash. A third man was on their backs pushing them. A fourth stood behind them in the doorway, stunned. This was the man Gorias smashed the door bar in to. The man's jawbone broke at the chin, and he stumbled backwards off the porch of the whorehouse, clutching his ruined face.

"Deliverance will come," Gorias said, almost laughing as he raised the bar and dropped it on the skull of the last man who fell on the others. The light helmet the guard wore bent in under the crushing blow, and Gorias heard the skull make a popping sound. Dying and convulsing, the guard floundered on the other two men as they struggled with each other. They screamed when they realized that the dead man on them vented his bowels.

Amused by their terror, Gorias dropped the bar and returned to his swords. As he timed it, a burly warrior ran in swinging a short sword and a small shield. A mercenary through and through, this hulking man hailed from the far northlands and was just the battering ram he had wagered on. His blows never caught Gorias, but he did spot the old warrior when he entered. Gorias simply put out a foot and tripped the feral man, staying out of his path of destruction. His boot hooked through the madman's ankle and this fighter went tumbling, as Gorias took a step and dropped his swords down, slashing twice, gouging open the necks of the two men floundering on the floor. While they gurgled in their own blood, two more men step up to the door brandishing small bows.

On cue, Tammas fired and his arrow struck the first guard behind Gorias. He hit him above the armor where the bare neck was exposed. This man jerked to one side, stunned in his lack of breath and coming death. The other drew back and fired where the arrow came from. He missed Tammas, striking the wooden stairway next to the bard.

He swiped down, removing the right hand of the man in the doorway. The palace guard bellowed in agony and clutched his wrist as blood gouted. The old warrior turned from this man and faced the berserker, who arose near the helm in the foyer.

He glanced at Tammas, not needing to tell him what to do. The small bard drew back and let another arrow fly. This struck the wounded sentry in the face and stapled a flaring tongue to his other cheek. In a fit of agony, the man's legs surrendered and he went down.

The berserker charged La Gaul. He swiped swords in front of himself, but it wasn't enough to ward off the powerful rush of the thuggish warrior. Never did the move make the crazed attacker stop an instance or flinch. Though he removed a portion of the berserkers' beard, the man still tackled him. Wrapping his arms around the La Gaul, the berserker grappled him in a bear hug. Gorias maneuvered their combined weight over into the path of the stairway and kept his arms up, hoping the bard wouldn't falter in his aim. The youth didn't disappoint and stuck a shaft in the spine of the berserker.

Though a direct hit, the wild fighter never seemed to make great note of it. Gorias slammed the handles of his swords down into the man's back, but the berserker refused to slacken his grip. Bracing his substantial legs, trying to steady his center of gravity, the barbarian entreated his god, Wodan, for aid. When the berserker performed this shuffling progress, Gorias let all of his body mass fall toward the floor, forcing the berserker to hold him up more, upsetting the balance. On top of this, he drove his calf up and into the wild barbarian's groin. This move caused the embrace to slacken. He couldn't strike with his swords to fine accuracy, but he moved his forearm across the face of his nemesis. With the dew nail of the dragon affixed to the forearm guard, he ripped out the Adam's apple of the berserker. His enemy stumbled backwards, gripping his neck. The savage looked amazed as his breath refused to come.

Additional men arrived, but they hesitated once the beheld the bloodshed. Gorias used their vacillation and ran for the stairs.

"Get your ass up there, kid."

Tammas already exited his position. Arrows flew from the guards and many struck Gorias, but glanced off the dragon's skin armor under his clothes. Gorias and the boy disappeared down the hall as the guards pursued up the stairs.

They found Maddox and Kayla on the second floor. Maddox fired several arrows before shouldering his bow, pointing down the hallway. "That way to the tavern roof!"

Kayla kicked one of the invading guards in the face, pushing him backwards onto the others who braved the stairs. She shouldered the bow and swiftly drew her rapier. With a stab that made Gorias turn and raise an eyebrow, she found a spot between one of the palace guard's ribs. After a grunt, the guard threw his last breath out before falling backwards into the hallway.

They ran. Gorias appreciated the fact his grandson and Kayla drew the fire of the men away from their escape route. However, they were young and stayed too long in their positions. They didn't come after him until he yelled at them to do so. He could hear the footfalls on the stairs and soon they would be overwhelmed.

When the two passed Gorias in the hallway, he stopped. Hearing the heavy footfalls again, he muttered, "We'll never make it out the window." He noted the opposing doors in the hallway and kicked one in. Within the room, a pair of brunette whores crouched behind the bed, each holding flails. "Tammas, cover me."

He went flat against the wall. Tammas and Kayla both fired arrows at the stairwell opening and tagged guards rushing into the breech. Gorias kicked the door open opposite the one he just trashed. This room was vacant.

Breathless, Maddox grabbed Gorias' forearm. "What is it?"

Gorias elbowed him toward one of the rooms and nodded for Tammas to get in the other one. "May as well clean them out."

Obediently and full of panic, the boys complied.

He faced Kayla. "Draw that tooth pick of a sword and stand by me. We want them to rush us."

Looking at him dreamily, the sturdy girl did as he asked and stood in a defensive pose.

"Now get ready…what was your name again?" He winked

The two guards in the hallway stopped, facing down Gorias. The warrior stepped in front of Kayla and held out his swords, then motioned for them to come forward. One of the guards turned and ran down the stairs. The other stepped back, but kept his face toward them. Teeth showing, he looked hungry, but lacked the courage to attack a legend.

However, the next one off the stairs did not dither. This stocky man wore thin chain mail and a heavy helmet. From his walrus skin pants and white furred cuffs, Gorias guessed him to have traded with the northerners, but his yellowy complexion betrayed him as not one of the barbarians from Zenghaus. Over his left forearm, this combatant held a small shield. Gorias' eyes squinted as he observed the hands of the man. In his left, this mercenary carried a huge fan made of steel. This was an illusion, though, for the weapon quickly proved to be a series of glittering metal tomahawks.

When he slipped one into his right hand and drew back, Gorias flattened on the wall and shoved Kayla across to the other wall. The first tomahawk flew between them. Kayla wore a look of shock, but Gorias never stood pat. Again filling the hallway with his broad frame, he charged on past the doorways. Raising his arms up to guard his unprotected face, he took the next two tomahawks in his armored forearms. Though well made, the small hatchets did exactly what they would do if they impacted on a real dragon—nothing.

Gorias attacked, swinging his blades at the merc. With a guttural yell, he slashed the air, knocking two more tomahawks down. The experienced warrior leapt back out of Gorias' range, went to one knee, and drew out a slender blade. With this miniature scimitar and with the small shield, he stepped up into Gorias' attack. Every blow he made the merc parried. Every thrust he tried to turn into a deathblow, the merc turned to one side.

Stepping back, Gorias kept swinging. His attacks were less refined and not as pointed. This made the merc think he gained the upper hand. Lusting for the legend's blood, the man pursued. After a few steps, he stood in the line of the open doors. Maddox shot him in the kidneys and Tammas pierced his cheeks, like he had done the man downstairs. The warrior froze from this attack. It was at this time Gorias stabbed both blades forward, sweeping away the reflexes of the dying man then piercing the links of his chain mail, breaking through to his heart.

The man fell and Tammas emerged from the room, saying, "That wasn't the most gallant display, sir."

Gorias frowned. "There isn't going to be an award issued later, kid."

Through the break in the attack, they ran down the hall. At a large window, they could see the landing and gap that led to the tavern roof.

Maddox joined them last and pushed through, wanting to lead. While he started to climb out on the landing, Gorias gazed at the people outside and said, "I think your count is off."

Maddox shrugged. "I'm just glad not many are around the back yet. Their numbers are thinned out because so many came in the front."

He jumped across to the roof of the tavern. Quickly, Tammas went through the window and out after his friend. Kayla stared at Gorias and the old one pointed for her to go on ahead.

Gorias was almost through the window when the palace

guards reached the hallway on the second floor. He holstered his swords as he pulled his leg through the window. Reaching to his belt, he drew out his dirk and stood to one side of the window. Listening for the footfalls, Gorias counted in his head and then stabbed through the opening, blind. The powerful roundhouse blow sank his dirk in the soft guts of one of the guards. All of the guard's air and some of his last meal ejected out his mouth.

Down the hall, the whores emerged, slashing into the mercs and guards with their flails. Taken by surprise, they died where they stood. Gorias holstered the knife as he ran, leaping across the expanse with the younger folk.

"Let's hear one for the battling whores of Khabnur."

Tammas whispered, "Why don't they shoot us from the ground?"

Gorias took a few breaths, watched his grandson trying to kick in a window, and shoved the boys to the side. He threw his girth into the wooden panels, tumbling into the upper rooms of the bar.

"Knows how to make an entrance, doesn't he?" Maddox said to Kayla. She ignored him as they advanced.

Dodging arrows from the guards on the ground, Tammas, Maddox, and Kayla stumbled through the opening the old man made. They assisted Gorias in rising up and he was laughing.

"Nothing like partying with this old man, is there?" he said and drew his two swords anew. Drawing them afresh gave the old man new life.

"Grandfather." Maddox suppressed a laugh. "You said Robyn De Balm is arisen from the dead."

They moved into the dark hallway and Gorias replied, "Yeah, sure looks like it to me."

"Are you sure you killed him?"

Gorias leered at the boy in the dim light from the moon filtering in the far window. "His head was a rotten tomato, son. He's one of the blood disease victims now. The little bastard is screwing me with his lies to Lira Rhan even though he's arisen from the dead."

Maddox pressed his point. "But since when do those leeches

experience free will after they become vampires?"

Gorias stopped. "Free will?" His face lit up. "The undead leeches are just that, normally--bloodsucking creatures who feed, fill up on blood, and march back to Nosmada."

Tammas asked, "Why is that?"

Maddox replied, "No one knows...or do they, grandfather?"

"They never talk much," Gorias said as he cautiously approached the stairway that led down in to the tavern. "Robyn was a damned wizard. Maybe he planned on his death. Who knows? Apparently, he had enough brains to deceive Lira Rhan into coming this far. Kayla, why join us over your mother?"

She bit her bottom lip and never answered. They were in such a hurry no words were waited for, nor given.

They descended into the tavern and saw several figures by the light of the raging fireplace. Several barrels lined the walls on the north side of the establishment and Gorias moved closer to these.

In this tavern stood Robyn De Balm behind three constables in grubby clothes.

"Come on a bit closer, you little prick," Gorias taunted the wizard, slapping his own bearded cheek with his right blade. "I killed you once, so step up for the final curtain."

"You erred," Robyn said in a voice that made skin crawl. "By killing me, you made me more powerful. Certainly, the vampiric life of a blood vassal for Nosmada is not for all, but I see great possibilities. Your swords are of no good on me or these constables now."

Gorias glanced at his grandson. "The twerp has a point. We don't have the correct weapons to kill them."

"I will not ask you or your grandson for the soul jewels, La Gaul. I shall take them from your dead flesh. You will arise and join the army of the damned."

Gorias backed away, shielding Kayla, motioning for the boys to stay to the rear of him. Maddox gave him a strange expression, curious his grandfather backed down from this challenge.

The three constables carried short swords and moved closer. They bore bloody maws and fangs in their undead mouths.

"Hey, Maddox, I ever tell you how to kill a vampire?"

His voice shaking, Maddox held his bow up and replied, "No, grandfather. I think you left that story out."

Robyn stepped up beside the constables and they were within two yards of the old warrior.

"Well, a wooden shaft in the heart, direct sunlight, and running water." He raised his swords and the constables stopped. "Or in this case, beer will do." He slashed at the small legs holding up the barrels of booze and they tipped down. Gorias then slashed at the top of the barrels and they burst, spraying stored up, pressurized beer on the constables. Under the spurt of the compressed fluid, the beer doused the constables and they started to scream. Their skin melting, they fell to their knees. Kayla drew back and started swatting heads from their bodies

The tiny undead necromancer raised his tiny arms and chanted,

"The supplication is made, dire mother-father of the scarlet Chaos!
I conjure the viper coiled at the base of your mind.
The serpent that coils around your black heart, dire lord.
Send your seed on bats wings to destroy the man of lore.
The enemy of all things dark, who fights with angels wings!"

"That's enough," Gorias said, on Robyn in a few strides. Cutting down with both swords, the arms of the dwarf flew off in an instant. With a swipe, Robyn's head became airborne and the tiny torso slammed down into the running fluid.

The head stopped rolling, but it never stopped talking. "I will call up the flames of hell and burn this city! I shall quench the flames with the blood of your children!"

Though an eerie sight, the babbling head of the dwarf wizard didn't inspire much fear in the group.

Tammas even ventured forth. "How can he speak, detached from his body?"

Gorias shrugged. "It's dead anyway. It doesn't use air like the rest of us." He smirked at the head still talking. "Go on. Shout to your black heart's content, ya freak. Now, we burn these bastards proper."

"Grandfather," Maddox said, staring at the ceiling. "I think the spell of De Balm worked."

The dusky shadows on the ceiling increased, and amidst this murky cover it sounded like rats ran overhead. At the four corners of the tavern, Gorias thought the ceiling curled down. But no, the angles bent sharper and leathery. When the first tentacle dropped and slithered near Tammas, the bard squealed like a girl.

Maddox cursed and drew his sword. As another slimy tendril dropped from the ceiling, Kayla moved toward the door. The swag belly of the horror swung down and blocked her path of escape. Out from behind this trembling gut unfolded six legs, insectoid in appearance.

Gorias scraped his swords together. "Don't know whether to crap or drink beer." He stabbed up into the ceiling. "Guess I'll crap in my beer."

"We have to get out of here!" Maddox said, chopping the tentacle off Tammas.

Kayla stabbed her rapier, crying out in a voice close to fear.

"Smart boy," Gorias murmured.

Maddox ran for the door and Gorias stabbed upward, over and over. Uncompromising in his purpose, he savagely swung his blades at the horror conjured from the realms beyond. Kayla tried to join the fight, but a tentacle thrashed her to the ground. Soon, it was clear that only the swords of Gorias La Gaul could damage this unnamed horror.

A segment of this shadowy evil detached itself and plopped on the floor. In moments, it started to rise and take a humanoid form. Not waiting to see the outcome, Gorias slashed across it many times. It fell back to the floor like minced up pudding, and again tried to re-form. Gorias slashed it again. In time, the energy waned and this creature ceased to rise.

After the great fight, the ceiling stopped its attack. The nebulous opening sealed and became solid.

Gorias took several breaths, trying to get his strength back.

He scooped up a mug off the bar and dipped it in the belly of a broken barrel. After drinking deeply, he wiped his mouth on the edge of his cloak. He watched Kayla arise, pick up a discarded short sword, and behead the last struggling constable, never wavering in her motions. The torso and limbs of De Balm sizzled to nothing in the tide of beer. Gorias stalked outside and the two youths flanked him.

With little breath left in her, Kayla asked, "What are your swords made of?"

There was no answer given.

Lira Rhan stood with more guards by their horses. A few mercs stood behind them, but they decided to depart at Lira's sigh. She wore a frown. "Where is De Balm?"

"He's back in the tavern, cursing every man who ever lived and promising to piss on every boy that is ever born."

"Damn you! Kill him!"

A constable stepped forward and drew back his spear. His stare met with La Gaul and he paused. Gorias' swords never hesitated and he thrust forward, stabbing him in the stomach and upper thigh, then he brought up the blades and sliced off the constable's hand holding the spear. When the man fell, Gorias drilled him through the heart.

As this man sank, Kayla emerged from the bar. She looked at the dead man and then at Gorias.

"Sister." He breathed hard as he addressed Lira Rhan. "Don't listen to undead wizards. That little sucker was trying to get you killed." He then related his version of the tale, how he killed Robyn and the constables, and they were undead. Lira Rhan's face registered some confusion, but she tried to put on a brave countenance. "Do you find it so hard to believe we were heading to a house of ill repute before leaving?"

Her frown grew deeper. "Your grandson is a thief and belongs on a slave caravan to Nosmada. He stole something the forward team of Nosmada wants. I find it hard to believe you don't want this as well."

Gorias leaned on the hitching post outside the tavern. "Ever make ya wonder why your wizard wanted to stop me so bad? He was on the take, sister. All them damned wizards are out for blood as bad as the vampire children of Nosmada. I don't trust any of them, and wish my grandson would knock off the necromancy lessons."

While Maddox bowed his head to these words, touching the poach on his belt, Lira raged, "But you must stop them from raising Wyss!"

Gorias looked at the castle and chuckled. "You know, I doubt petty politics are what Nosmada's men have in mind for Wyss. I have other things in mind, but I'll ride north to the bogs and stop them. I have some time. I think Robyn was in this for himself. Not some other deal made with men on Earth, that is."

A screeching echo made them all look north. Lira gaped at Gorias but the big warrior never looked at her.

"That isn't good," he muttered. "I think you have bigger problems than Wyss rising from the bogs."

Lira Rhan pursed her lips. "What? The army of barbarians ready to fall over my city in pursuit of weapons, just like Nosmada?"

"That's one thing, I guess. I was referring to that noise in the distance. The barbarians want Nosmada's army dead. You all may fall under their eye if they beat them to death."

"Why is it that the barbarians want Nosmada's forces dead?"

"Well, for starters, Nosmada's army thought they would teach a village of barbarians a lesson and chopped off their hands. That's stupid. They should have just killed them."

Maddox blinked. "What?"

"A barbarian can pick up a sword or axe with his other hand, too," Gorias said.

Another scream trumpeted in the night and a roar after it. A bizarre clucking noise followed this in the air.

"I think that's the voice of a blue dragon, in the direction of the ruins of Larak," Gorias said. "Its remains must have been a matter of convenience for the worshipers. There weren't many pieces left of that blue dragon. It was gutted and fed to the populace of a small village outside Khabnur."

"Oliverian?" Lira named the locale.

"Yeah, that's it. My mind is fading on names," Gorias said. "I suppose the Cult of the Dragon hid the bits leftover. By the sounds of him, though, he's pretty amused."

Maddox face flushed, and Tammas was full of terror. "The dragon is laughing?"

"Shut up, kid, and go get my helmet," Gorias snapped. "I'm too damned tired to walk in there again."

Lira Rhan turned to her remaining men and gave orders. As she did Gorias faced Maddox. "Anything you aren't telling me about these idiots trying to get soul jewels? Anything you're leaving out about the soul of Carlato Wyss?"

Maddox wiped sweat from his face and said in a low voice, "The soul of Wyss was gone already. I had to tell the cult something, you know? They can't tell one crystal soul carrier from another."

"Carlato was gone already?" Gorias said and looked north. "Interesting."

"What does dragon meat taste like?" Tammas asked.

"Rattle-snake. I've heard some folks say chicken, but I never could see that."

Kayla stared at the dead man at Gorias feet. "That constable worshiped you. I saw you two talking earlier. He became a man at arms because he wanted to be like you. He believed in you so." Her tone sounded mildly shocked, not preaching.

"I guess that'll teach him not to believe in men," Gorias muttered. "You should only have to face God once--after you're dead. No matter how much you worship a human, they can kill you at any time."

CHAPTER VI

TOLIN AND THE NARK

In the fortress of Kanoch, Nosmada frowned at Zillian's caldron. He peered over at his guard and confidant, Lannon. The brooding Lord found none of the answers he sought. He yawned, but never covered his mouth. He looked back at the Well of Sorrows.

"De Balm failed yet again," Nosmada grumbled, but his voice carried no surprise. "And I think Gorias is correct: De Balm lied even unto me. That's quite wicked, but fitting for one such as he, really."

Zillian limped around the caldron as bleary images of the exterior of the whorehouse and tavern faded. "It didn't surprise me that whelp Robyn prepared for his demise well enough to resist your spell." She clutched at her chest, winced, and then said, "Such lust for power is inherent in his kind."

Nosmada shrugged then looked in her direction. "Lust for power will break most alliances, Zillian."

"It was all I could do to conjure that image of the outside area, Lord."

"Bah." Nosmada dismissed her words with the wave of a meaty hand. "You call it magic because the blood sickness makes them come unto me. Calculated reason is why it exists, and pure power on my part." He paused as his hands turned to fists. With a dour expression, he faced the rocky walls around them before stepping into the emerald light emitted by the caldron. His features showed clearly, and Zillian gazed at him without flinching. Lannon swallowed, staying against the wall. Nosmada took a few steps away from them and ran his hand over the right side of his face, up to his forehead over the gruesome disfigurement. Few would see this indentation offhand due to his long hair.

Zillian shot Lannon a look and said quietly, "Supremacy and power is what it is all about isn't it, Lord?" She cleared her craggy throat as Nosmada faced her, hands behind his back. "He held those soul crystals for a reason. We never knew De Balm even had them. The little fool was plotting something calamitous of his own, dividing his faithfulness to you, Lord."

"I gathered that. Loyalty is a difficult thing to tie up. At least the rest of those carrying the blood are just vessels who don't challenge the decree. How De Balm defied me is a mystery, certainly, but I'm not all-powerful. Given enough time, most wizards can solve complicated riddles. The leeches still serve the spell and my purpose. Better mindless fools than rabble all of a different mind."

"They failed to kill La Gaul."

Nosmada shrugged, his left leg moving as if he were about to take a step, yet he remained still. "I expected no less. Lannon, bring me wine."

Nodding, he exited.

"Gorias will try to stop the young ones from raising Wyss from the grave," Nosmada said. "This is the task they have given him--Rhan and her lot. The Cult of Wyss don't have warriors, though they have guards. They'll fall easily to the grandson and the fable."

"What has the old warrior to gain by all of this? He's far from a virtuous man," Zillian said, laughing.

Nosmada raised an eyebrow as Lannon returned with a large flagon of wine. "La Gaul is a primal force. He goes as he feels led." Nosmada drank, and his eyes flared wide open as he appreciated the wine. "He probably seeks to straighten out wrongs from the hands of his grandson, if I were to guess. I'd never believe he's still living if I didn't see it in the caldron, but that's of no matter. Raise Tolin on the viewer, dear, when you have the strength, but make haste."

Zillian shambled to a small cage nearby and reached inside. She pulled out a plump cat and stroked its fine yellow fur. With surprising force, she snapped its neck and dug her long fingernails deep in its guts. Nosmada never moved a tad as Zillian ravaged the cat and deposited it in the caldron. Lannon's mouth tightened but he said nothing. The blaze of the soupy surface bathed them in aqua light and the bowl filled with the harsh visage of Tolin, general of

Nosmada's military forces, nearing the region south of La Gaul.

"Lord Nosmada," Tolin rasped in a deep voice, his dull tone close to inhuman. That was well, Nosmada thought, since Tolin no longer held the soul of a man in his flesh. When Tolin's cave-like mouth opened, Nosmada half expected flame to erupt. The long, imperious face of the general was made all the more hideous by the taunt, grayish skin pulled across his enormous skull, flanked by long dark hair.

"Your army will reach the foundry of Syn presently?"

"Within days, lord," Tolin said, curiosity flowing from his dire, orange eyes. Keeping as still as sandstone, the general gave no clues to his thoughts via his expressions. "You know this. Is there a difficulty?"

"Perhaps," Nosmada said, voice steady. Lannon moved so he didn't have to see Tolin any more. "Acquiring the weapons of Syn will strengthen our forces, thus aiding our purpose against the Northern barbarians." Nosmada explained what happened with Robyn, the soul jewels, and the presence of La Gaul.

At the latter name, Tolin's nostrils flared and his eyes gleamed with fanatical intensity. "Gorias…is here?"

Zillian gasped at the expression of hatred in Tolin and stepped back from the caldron. Her body quaked and she tried to stand firm. Lannon receded even farther from the room, fully filling up the doorway.

Unaffected by this, Nosmada said, "Yes, your old nemesis is near At the Foundry of Syn even now. There's great mischief afoot concerning Wyss and—"

"The Blue Dragon," Tolin growled, brows lowering. "Your words are appreciated, dark Nosmada. Our sentries have claimed to hear sounds like those made by dragons. The Cult of the Dragon has completed a program, it seems. It is like a predator sniffing for food, the sound. The elders in our camp claim this is the sound we hear from distant Dundayin."

"Hmm, near the great dried sea and ruins of Larak?"

"That is correct, Lord."

"The ensuing bloodbath with our enemies from the North

must be remembered," Nosmada cautioned Tolin. "We cannot be distracted by too many factors. It's important the carriers of the blood reach my citadel. It's imperative you attain the weapons of Syn, slay the barbarians, and return their blood unto me."

Seething, Tolin gritted his teeth. "I will not forget the duty I hold. Those louts of the North cannot be taken lightly. Yet, we must stop this new factor."

"Raising Wyss from the dead will only complicate matters for us," Nosmada declared. "La Gaul…"

Tolin held out his hands. Heavy leather gauntlets held the digits in check, fingers far too long for a normal man. "I can feel something is wrong. I feel my olden soul, that which was birthed in this flesh, now residing in another host."

Nosmada frowned, noting the terror in Zillian and Lannon. "That's of no regard, Tolin. You gladly took on this new life and mission, no?"

"Indeed," he replied, curling his fingers into fists, any pretense of tranquility now gone.

"Then we must decide on our course of action." Nosmada thought for a moment. "From what we gather, Gorias and those with him head toward the bogs where the Cult of Wyss has gone."

"Our forces are still days away from the foundry of Syn," Tolin said, fuming. "Intelligence reports the forces of the Northern barbarians are on the march towards there as well."

Nosmada glanced at Zillian then said to the caldron, "That's what the mage here has told me. Glad to see your pickets are confirming her words."

Tolin turned away then turned back. "What if my pickets or a small group were to ride ahead of our army? Such a small force could cover the ground fast and intercept La Gaul and the Cult of Wyss."

His features brightening, Nosmada nodded. "Excellent idea. Send your best. La Gaul is old, but he will —"

"I want him alive, Lord."

Nosmada frowned. "Now is not the time to plot common revenge."

72

Tolin's eyebrows arched. "You speak to me of revenge? If not for the desire for revenge, you would not be planning what you are, Lord Nosmada."

Zillian drew back from the caldron, a feared of the reaction of her master. Nosmada simply smirked. "And yet, it must be. Send your force."

The image in the caldron faded and he turned away from Zillian. The withered crone hobbled to her reclining couch to collapse. Looking at his mage, spent of energy, Nosmada said, "I will send up food."

"Many thanks," she croaked, touching her chest as she closed her eyes.

Lannon moved to one side as Nosmada turned to the door, stopping abruptly. He caught his reflection in the distant caldron. However small the image, he touched the right side of his face. Swallowing hard, he left the chamber.

"He was a great warrior once," Zillian muttered.

"La Gaul?"

"Nosmada. He probably still is a mighty warrior. He never seems to age…" She opened her eyes and gazed at her withered hand, then clutched her chest again. "All of the world grows more dank and dies, yet he endures unchanged."

"Can he attain what he desires?"

Zillian's words grew sparse as she fell into sleep. "We will see. For everything there must be an ending."

✦✦✦✦✦

As he walked down the line of supply wagons, General Tolin's mind dwelt far from his troopers. The divisions of his large force rested, but stood at attention when he passed. All of them were armed for their appropriate sector in the army, but with inferior weapons. He looked at the mobile siege engines they brought along and thought of the tasks before them.

One of his trusted captains stepped up to Tolin and saluted.

"Sir, shall we cut some riders from the cavalry and go about your mission?"

The dour visage of the general turned toward the soldier and away from the covered trebuchet. "Six out of a few hundred horsemen will suffice for our chosen purpose."

Captain Karter swiped a hand down his trim black beard. "Six will be plenty, General, but perhaps an additional six will insure against any mistakes. We don't know exactly what awaits us."

"I appreciate your confidence," Tolin's said, placing his hands on his belt. "My own rage will be sufficient, but you are correct. I would prefer the company of you and Tubal at least."

The dark haired captain nodded toward the line of men at attention. A thick built man made for fighting took a step from the line. His head was shaved, but his beard flowed blond and bushy. Trooper Tubal turned to make further selections to accompany them.

Along lines of men and horses, Tolin and Karter walked. "Once we are armed well from the foundry, the army will be unstoppable."

Tolin watched the distant eastern mountains. "We are better trained than any army on this planet." He pulled on the edges of his gloves and went on to say, "Stone flints and inferior metals will be cast aside for proper steel at the foundry. The divisions of pike-men and infantry will fight better with stronger weapons."

"Combined with our training, we'll not be stopped."

Tolin gave a nod. "Certainly not by an army of barbarian maniacs wiping their behinds on bushes."

When a young attendant brought General Tolin his mount, the hulking leader searched the animal then stalked to his tent. Returning to the line of troops, he carried a small wooden box. This dark box shone heavily polished. He strapped the tiny container near his bedroll. While he did so, the common troopers looked away from him, but Captain Karter stood near.

"La Gaul." Tolin nearly let a smile break his dark, craggy face as he smoothed his gloved hands over the embossed saddle. "I am overjoyed he is not dead."

Tubal's green eyes glanced at Karter, but he said nothing.

Captain Karter completed the thoughts in the general's mind. "Very good, sir. I know you would be disappointed if another hand slew him."

Tolin by no means acknowledged this as truth, but his agreement was obvious in his body language. Confidence, strength, and power surged in the big man as he climbed onto the horse.

General Tolin joined the dozen warriors Tubal drew off from the cavalry. They mounted up as well and headed out toward the northeast.

On their best horses, the skilled fighters drove across the plains towards the land of Shynar. The mounts would probably be ridden to death, Tolin surmised, but their death was the least of his worries compared with the pleasure revenge would supply. New horses could be found, he reasoned. All he could see was the coming night beyond the daylight. All he could see was blood.

❈ ❈ ❈ ❈ ❈

The foursome rode hard for the rest of the night and the better part of the day. The structured skyline and marble domes of Khabnur were behind them fast. Outside the city limits, countryside rolled in gentle slopes. Empty fields awaited the serfs, for most of the land ran too rugged to plant. In the distance the hills humped into larger mountains, but that would not be an obstacle for them. They rode toward a series of scant forests, away from the heavy savannahs of the south-lands.

Stopping every so often to shake off the billowing dust and to let the horses rest, Gorias said to Maddox, "At least they travel well."

Maddox ran a hand through his thick hair, looked at Tammas and Kayla. "I suppose."

The old man pointed in the distance. "One can see forever out here in the clear. Glad the damned leeches stay in while the sun is out, eh? There's a slave train headed this way, look. I think that's what the line of slow moving travelers is, anyway."

Maddox agreed, almost standing in the same pose as his

grandfather. "Yes, they make frequent runs down to Nosmada's citadel and other spots. They come from afar, the damned slavers."

Gorias gestured at Tammas and inquired of his grandson, "If ya don't mind me asking, how did ya get that punk kid affixed to your leg?"

"He's a nice fellow."

"Nice?" Gorias said the word like it had leprosy and even spat to show what he thought of the title. "The kid told me he never killed a man before today. That surprises me more than his virgin line, frankly. All the niceties in the world can't cover your ass in a damned brawl, son."

"He's young--barely twenty-two years old."

Between drinks from his skin of wine, Gorias said, "He seems younger. Perhaps if you dried him off behind his ears a tad he would look older?"

Maddox stretched, massaging his lower back. "I'm sure he never had a life like your youth, Grandfather. He grew up sheltered."

"Was he high born?"

"The opposite, in fact. His mother was a prostitute, and he doesn't know who his father was."

"You'll have that with whores."

Maddox nodded as he watched Tammas doing the splits to stretch his body out. "I guess that's why he knows so many songs. He grew up over taverns and whorehouses, listening to ballads. His mother oppressed him, held him down, kept him from the world." He smiled, not so much at the bizarre body moves Tammas performed but at the insipid expression of Kayla toward the bard. "Kind of strange, being what she was, she kept any of the world from her son. We met in a tavern. He pitched in to help me when no one else would after a few toughs came after me. Nimble little sucker, I grant."

"What about Kayla?"

"What's to tell?" Maddox said, turning away from their traveling companions. "She's the daughter of a powerful woman and grew up in a world of powerful men. She lacks a male organ and fights to get the respect of those who have them. Kayla likes to play rough. Like any kid who grew up in a castle, learning to fight, she seems eager to put it to the test. Kayla has more balls than most men I know, Grampa."

"And you got near her because of me?"

Maddox smiled, his features aglow. "You're a great help getting sex."

"Thanks, but a boy as handsome as you shouldn't need too much aid."

"Oh, I don't need help getting women, but being your grandson seals it. However, being Maddox La Gaul carries a curse as well as a blessing. Quite a few men want me dead out of spite or just to say they did it, understand? This has made me a better combatant out of necessity. That's why I never tell anyone my last name anymore and why Lira didn't know my identity."

"I see."

"They say the world is going to end."

"Who are *they*, anyway?"

"Folks, necromancers. Hell, everyone I know says they hear the world will end soon. I figure you have been all over it. What do you think?"

Gorias exhaled and rested back on his right hip. "I wish it would hurry up, sometimes."

"I wish my father were dead."

"Yeah, so do I. You see? Not everything I ever did was glorious."

"I just wish he didn't exist anymore…"

Gorias watched his shadow on the ground growing longer as orange light stretched over the planet. "Can we talk about something else?"

"Do you know this guy Brock who leads the barbarians Rhan thinks are lurking to the north of us?"

"I knew a fellow by that name centuries ago. He died rather well, if memory serves, but I wasn't there to see it. This must be his son."

"Was he a great warrior?"

Gorias smirked, spat. "He had his moments, but his folk see

him as a god. Yet, a god can die, huh? One would think that such a thing would mar his legacy, but not. Death is overrated. Life can seem pointless, but one must make it count."

"Wyss' life will count if he's remembered as such? I don't understand it."

"Wyss deserves to stay dead. I don't car if I'm forgotten after I'm gone. It isn't about fame. If the time ever comes to make a difference in the world and I turn my back on it, I deserve to burn forever."

They moved on again for a spell. After the day started to die, Gorias ordered his group to stop and rest at a small creek near the bogs of Cielo.

Tammas stepped close, haltingly. "Cielo, funny name for a place, no?"

"Not really." Gorias said, imparted a forbidding glance. "That was the name of one of our patriarch's daughters. She got lost out here centuries ago and they assume she died. Cielo's dad, well, he salted most of the area and cursed it. Plants now grow scarce, but that was a long time ago."

"Interesting." Tammas sipped from a silver canteen. "Was that patriarch any relation to our chieftain?"

"Yes. In fact, Cielo's sister was the grandmother of Carlato Wyss."

Maddox laughed and eyed the horizon. "That's ironic."

"Not really. It just is."

Though they had taken many a rest during the day, they all dismounted, shook off the dust, and tried to regain their ability to walk properly. Gorias went to relieve himself near some brush. Maddox joined him, still appearing hearty.

"You seem to know where we are heading," Maddox said, staring at the scarlet streaks across the sky.

Gorias concentrated on the sunset. "You got something to say, kid? Ya look like you're waiting for ghosts to bubble up from yonder bogs."

Maddox glanced back at Tammas and Kayla. "Were you there when they executed Carlato Wyss?"

Gorias shook his head. "No, but I know the area they used for it. It was a common sinkhole back then near the edge of Benedikt Canyon. There's a spot over that hill there where the ground is always wet, even in the winter."

Maddox stared, jaw agape at Gorias' words. "We are that close?" He didn't seem afraid and Gorias smiled at that. Maddox inquired, "Is there a force in the earth that stays warm and keeps the bog soft?"

Gorias shrugged as they walked back to the spot where the horses drank. "Could be, but Wyss is just as dead. There are forces that we don't comprehend below us and I don't mean from Hell. The earth shrugs, we could die in an instant. Immense and uncanny, the forces of the earth are nearly like that of a sleeping god. Its bile keeps the bogs soft even in the frosty weather."

"This quest of the cult--it's all twaddle, right?" Maddox asked as Tammas got to his knees and drank with the horses. "These idiots can't really hope to find Wyss' body?"

Kayla refilled her carafe in the creek, shot Tammas a disgusted look. "You're a necromancer, Maddox La Gaul. You doubt the resurrection of the dead or their ability to find a body via their magic?"

"Of course not." Maddox pointed his index finger at her. "I know what soul jewels can do, and what hides in them, but this pursuit for bones of a man long dead is nonsense. How can they hope to find a body dropped so long ago?"

"Wizards, damn their eyes," Gorias said and sat down against a tree to rest his back. He glared at them with eyes as cold as glaciers. "If they can find a portion of his bones, they can make a mockery of life. Something will come up, I mean. Something bad."

With a wave of both hands at the sky, Maddox said, "Many of them, the youths in the cult, are students of the Daemonolateria and know their work well. One even has a familiar demon that sucks at an extra teat. Serious, it's true. Kayla, I have no doubt about their ability…"

Mouth transforming into a scowl, she snapped at Maddox, "How could I ever doubt one such as you?" Stamping away from them, she slammed herself against another tree, slowly sinking to the ground as Maddox stared at his grandfather.

Gorias watched all of this casually then looked across the creek.

"Grandfather, you must understand…"

"I understand fine. Don't ask me to solve problems created by you trying to get some tail. All of that is old hat to me. It ceased to amaze me years ago what young men will do to knock off a piece of a woman. They'll even pretend to get in bed with monsters, act out ceremonies to invoke the less savory demons of the underworld, just to feel that soft skin on their body."

Maddox frowned sheepishly. "But…"

Gorias looked to Tammas. "Can you fish?"

The boy nodded. "I caught ten fish in an hour at the Jothdan River once."

"Impressive," Gorias muttered, giving him a mock salute.

"I scaled them myself."

"We have been followed."

Tammas was starting to stuff jerky in his mouth and nearly choked. "What? You said flames would keep the leeches off us."

Gorias groaned with dismay. "Yes, followed close since we left Khabnur. The fool thinks he is stealthy, but my nose knows, if you pardon my language."

Kayla dark eyes darted a glance between them with cat-like furtiveness.

Tammas peered into the distance as he stowed his jerky in a pouch. "The slave train at the breadth of the bogs beds down for the night. They strike fires as well. Who follows us? Is it a man from that train or a leech?"

Down on his knees, Gorias gazed over the creek. He drew out both swords and his traveling companions jumped a little. They stared at him, how he kissed each sword on the flat of the blade then laid them at each side. Behind him, he folded his hands and let his body lay back. Facing the distant sunset's glow, he took a deep breath.

He glared at the bard. "What? Can't a man have a private

moment with his own God? Ya can piss yer pants any day, ya know."

Shamefaced, the three turned from Gorias. Kayla twisted back and waited for the two to move away. Maddox drew his sword and told Tammas to fix an arrow. "We'll hunt the countryside once we get some bigger fires made for the night. The leeches won't come near fire."

Tammas said, "Good God, we're really going to sleep outside?"

Glancing around at the area, Maddox muttered, "Looks that way."

"You must think me a terrible person," Kayla said as she stood near Gorias.

"For being human? There are greater sins than youthful desire. I hold no anger for you. Hell, any woman who can fight is all right with me."

She knelt beside him in the vanishing sunlight. "My daddy used to tell me tales about you when I toddled." She laughed. "I can still remember that. The picture in my head of valiant Gorias La Gaul, killing dragons, and fighting the evil ones of the world."

He chuckled, then said in a harsh voice. "I must be some disillusionment, girl."

"Never, Lord La Gaul."

"Words have made me a fable. Words grind on and on and foster dreams in the heads of youths. That I can't stop. However, my heat will indeed stop soon. I used to think it a great honor that young men would so willingly throw their lives away if I would but lead them into battle. I once thought it a grand honor that a highborn woman, or even a lady who swept the stables, dropped to their knees or spread their legs for me. After a long time…"

"It's an empty bag?"

Gorias smirked. "No, nothing like that. I'm long past getting too passionate about asinine words. I wish I were young enough to do it all over again." Kayla laughed and Gorias did as well. "I'm not one for maudlin feelings, young lady. They're a waste of time, really."

They both started to rise up. "I'm not much of a lady, Lord

La Gaul." Grinning, she gave him a mock curtsy.

Gorias saw the look in her dark eyes. Kayla's plain features smoldered as her gaze danced over his aged face. *Simple words,* he thought, *could make her love me more or hate me forever.* "You're strong and determined. I find that beautiful in any woman."

Kayla's face flushed pink.

For a moment, he felt evil…but only for a moment.

When the two young men returned, she put on a stern face and stepped closer to the nearby grove of trees. Her stance grew unyielding, almost more masculine in the presence of the two youths, he noted.

"Grandfather?"

"Words can do more than blades." Gorias picked up his swords. "What is it?"

"We can find no one around. What's your plan for the night?"

He watched Kayla retrieve a length of rope from her horse. "Well, the bogs of Cielo are just over the ridge. They crest out then give way to what the desert folks call the Slough of Despair, or the less dramatic Canyon of Benedikt."

Tammas nodded and scratched his scalp. "I know a song about it."

"Spare us, kid. I ain't that tired. It's called that because there is a sheer fall down from a great swampy area. It's an unlikely feature, an abrupt desert plain so close to the bogs. It was like God cursed the ground and refused to let it prosper. Anyway, once night falls, we shall sneak up and see if those assheads have found anything."

Maddox gestured toward the grove. "What's she doing?"

"Fishing," Gorias said.

Tammas was wringing his hands. "Is the yonder desert the worst one you have ever seen?"

"There's one out beyond Jericho, past Kemet, that seems to go on forever," Gorias said. "That one is the armpit of the gods."

Kayla extended her arm and leapt out of sight.

Maddox armed up his sword. "Aw, man, now what?"

Gorias walked behind Maddox and Tammas to the edge of the grove. Maddox had stopped his quick movements when he heard a struggle.

"Got you, rat bastard!"

However, Kayla didn't wrestle with vermin but a skinny man. Her rope had lassoed him by the arm. When she leapt on his back, the robust girl easily forced him down. She yanked his ankles up together, completing the hogtie move.

Tammas trembled, feet shifting, and slapped Maddox on his shoulder. "Help her!"

The young man hesitated, mainly because he could see what Gorias soon voiced: "She's doing just fine on her own. It looks like she caught our spy, by Heaven." When Kayla dragged the tall man out and threw him down into the dim light, Gorias declared, "Or should I say, Michael Galenson?"

Greasy black hair flew apart and a pale man glared at him. "Huh? How do you know me?"

"Ya were the bar tender when I killed Shavon, ya punk assed freak. I never forget a face. You'll pray in Hell that ya can forget mine."

Kayla slapped Michael's face down into the dirt then picked up his skull by the hair. "Who sent you?"

"Piss off, child."

Kayla drove her knees into his back and punched the base of his head. He screamed out and received a mouthful of dirt.

Gorias said with approval, "Damn, she swings like she means it."

Michael's bleary eyes leered at the men. None made a move to stop Kayla in her actions. They all stood deathly still.

Kayla rolled Michael on his side and kicked him in the crotch, twice, hard with her pointed boot.

Screaming, Michael rolled and wailed loud, "Gods! I think she burst my sack! Oh gods!"

Gorias glared down at him. "They were just occupying space anyway. Better answer her." He shook two fingers toward Michael's crotch. "She ain't mine, and I could care less if she kills you or maims your skinny ass."

"I ain't telling you anything."

"I believe him." Maddox sighed.

"Me too. I think he needs additional inspiration to talk."

"What sort of hero tortures people?" Michael screamed, still writhing.

Gorias' long hair shook as he laughed. "I never said I was a hero. Shoulda thought of that before ya started to spy on a professional killer, punk. Ya think because I'm old I'd be easy pickings? I killed my first before you saw the light of day, and I'll slay more once your miserable self expires."

✥✥✥✥✥

The night came at last, and the four travelers stared at Michael Galenson, staked out spread eagle on the spent winter/spring turf. Tammas and Maddox held raging torches, while Gorias stood between them.

Kayla crouched like a cat ready to strike as she whispered near to Michael's ear, "One of them is coming. They are sneaky pricks just like you."

From the ground, he looked between his legs and screamed.

In the distance lumbered a form. It approached from the direction of the Canyon of Benedikt. To anyone unaware, it was a drunken man stumbling in the night. But the light of the torches showed the face of the stranger, ashen and gray. This stiff limbed leech sported red eyes surrounded by dark circles. Arisen and hungry for blood, it blinked at the four then focused in on Michael.

"They drink blood until they are full," Gorias said. "Then they head on down to dark Nosmada so far away. What for is the mystery, but hey, it doesn't matter why Nosmada has invoked such a spell, huh? You look like a tall cold brew to him now. What say ya talk to us?"

Michael screamed and wet himself as the leech staggered forward, nearly to Galenson's feet. "Stop! I will tell you!"

Maddox was about to move forward with the torch, but Gorias slapped a hand on his shoulder. "I haven't heard dick yet, son. A name, Michael."

The leech went to its knees and placed a cold hand on the stake near Galenson's left foot. Mouth open, drool dropping from its fangs, the creature prepared to feed.

"Mitre! Mitre Stillwell!"

Kayla leapt, throwing a shoulder into the side of the leech. The creature flopped over and she cartwheeled away from it. Tammas prayed as he stepped forward, waving his torch to keep the leech at bay. Indeed, it respected the fire and stopped. It appeared bemused as to what to do next, yet its gaze returned to the helpless one staked out.

Gorias walked to Michael and knelt. "Why would that damned freak of Syn want to know what I'm doing? What could it interest him? There isn't great cash to be made from it."

Michael hesitated, then looked at the drooling leech and whimpered, "It was he that Robyn De Balm dealt with under the table. They swapped items often and—"

"Stillwell and the deserts of Dundayin. Damn my slow mind!" Gorias' head snapped back like a fist hit him.

Maddox's stare drilled into the face of his grandfather. "What do you know about that?"

Gorias eyebrows lowered . "What do you?"

Shaking all over, Michael squealed. "C'mon, man, let me go!"

Kayla kicked Michael in the ribs and told him to remain quiet. When she did, a small pouch rolled out of his clothing. Tammas snatched this up and it easily opened. Inside were dark green herbs.

"He was easily bought, ya see?" Gorias said pointing at the herbs. "Addicts usually are."

Maddox ignored this revelation. "I've heard the old ogre was an adventurer before becoming overlord of the workers at the foundry."

"Foreman sounds better, but go ahead. What else do you know of Stillwell?"

"Mitre will deal with anyone. He's a backstabber, but ogres are selfish by nature."

"So are humans. Mitre Stillwell killed and took his wealth and that's why he relaxes now."

"But I know he traded soul jewels with De Balm," Maddox confessed. "They were both snakes and lairs. What fortune is there in that? Is it like an investment?"

Gorias brooded over this. "Then why didn't he pursue you when he heard the jewels were stolen from De Balm? If Wyss rises from the grave, he may reveal secrets exposing the ogre as compliant with his old ceremonies."

Observing everything the night might throw at them, Kayla said, "Maybe Mitre knows better. That's why he isn't worried."

Gorias focused on Michael. "Is that it? Why does he want your skinny ass watching me?"

Michael rambled, "He wants to know what happens to you. I'm just watching. He wants a front row seat for the show. He doesn't want anything going wrong when the army of Nosmada, led by General Tolin, gets to the Foundry of Syn for their weapons."

"Tolin, eh?" Gorias said in a quiet voice, different from the confrontational one he had used. "Yet Mitre doesn't fear exposure at the rising of Wyss." Gorias ire rose. "It was Mitre who probably stole the Carlato Wyss soul jewel from those maniacs hiding in the desert of Dundayin, then he substituted it with another. He worked that area years back. I cannot see him trading that article to De Balm, but, damn, of course that is it! He didn't! The old mutt isn't worried, for he knows Wyss isn't in the soul jewel those fools got from Maddox."

"Damn." Maddox glanced toward the rising land where the bogs lay.

Tammas spoke up, "I wonder who is in that jewel?"

"Indeed," Gorias said, suppressing a yawn. "And I wonder where Wyss is?"

"Mitre was drunk one night and said he sold the Wyss jewel to the Cult of the Dragon on the edge of Dundayin years ago," Michael went on to say. "He thought it was a great jest, or at least that's what he told me. These cultists of Wyss are idiots and want their hero to arise to lead them to a golden age. What they obtained from their remnant in the desert or the Cult of the Dragon isn't their lord. That's all I know. Now, let me go like you said!"

With a laugh, Gorias took the torch from Tammas. "I never said that, ya nark."

The leech lowered its head and the teeth bit into the veins in Michael's calf.

"Die like all cowards should, groveling in the dirt," Gorias said, and then told Kayla. "When the leech is done with him, chop his head off and burn his pathetic ass. He isn't worth me killing him twice."

Michael thrashed and screamed as if on fire already. Kayla watched safely by the fires, ready to carry out her orders.

"Can she handle it?" Maddox asked Gorias, an eyebrow raised to emphasize his doubt.

The old man gazed at the edge of the bogs. "I told her to, didn't I? We need to get over there. I have a terrible idea about all of this, son."

Tammas trembled as he went to the other side of the camp by the fires. He held his hands on his ears. "How long can he scream?"

"As long as it hurts."

Gorias eyed the moon imparting light over the shroud of smothering vegetation. Distantly, he could hear the bellow over Dundayin. He knew what it was. He had a bad idea of who it was as well.

CHAPTER VII

HELTER SKELTER

When Lannon heard the voice of his master cry out in distress, he left his assigned position with haste. Though it was forbidden to follow Lord Nosmada down the southern most hallways in the fortress of Kanoch, Lannon discarded his orders. The cry sounded as one of weakness, not an emotion usually assigned to his mysterious Lord. The sound of Lannon's leather boots on the stone floor echoed and squished, for the dampness of these caverns grew more tepid and dank the deeper one traveled.

Unsure of his own safety, he saw the huge form of Nosmada, splayed half in and half out of the place prohibited by most eyes. Lannon had indeed been to the Chamber of Redemption before, but it was at the request and by the lead of Nosmada and Zillian themselves. To screw down his courage, Lannon swallowed hard and then ran forward.

"My Lord, what ails you?" he said, kneeling and helping Nosmada to sit up. Being a large man himself, Lannon still struggled to pull the heavy weight of Nosmada level.

Hand to his scarred forehead, Nosmada blinked his eyes and then glanced back into the circular chamber. For a second, he realized Lannon was away from his assigned post and in a forbidden sector. In that instance, Nosmada also smiled and shrugged off the obvious offense to protocol.

"Help me up, Lannon," he said in a low voice. "I was reading old bones. That makes me ponder on the past too much. I'm glad you are here."

With great effort, he pulled Nosmada to his feet. The heavy boots of the dark Lord shifted as he stood, but in a few moments, Nosmada gained his composure. Lannon peeked into the chamber of Redemption and swiftly looked down. He noted that there was a small rocky disk in the middle of the chamber raised up.

With a half smile, Nosmada reached out and pulled a small lever on the wall. Rapidly, a stone circle, not unlike a mill-stone, rolled to cover the entrance.

"Assist me back to my quarters so I may lie down," Nosmada said, more as a friendly request than an order. It was so he could lean on his guard with his full force and Lannon obliged.

"It's not far, Lord," Lannon lied, knowing their trek back to the sleeping room, just off Zillian's conjure chamber, was indeed a long walk.

"You are a good servant, uh, soldier, Lannon," Nosmada said. He seemed intent on not degrading the guard who served him in his darkest quarters.

Lannon replied, "You have always been a just Lord, sir."

"No matter what they warned you of before you entered my service?"

With a half grin, Lannon said, "Working for you is a joy in the world, not a curse. Men at arms fear me, women give me a second glance. I comprehend my place in it all, sir, never fear."

"A lesser man may falter at such a time or become sloppy. Do not give in to foolish pride, Lannon."

"I will try to stay on the narrow path, sir."

"Not just any man can witness what Zillian conjures in her caldron plus look into the well of my chamber of Redemption and remain sane."

"I try, Lord," Lannon responded, trying to banish the slithering, chittering terrors he glimpsed moments before. "I'd like to think I were made of strong timber."

"Being relation to Zillian helped you get this position," Nosmada reminded him without rancor in his voice.

"I'm here to serve, Lord," Lannon affirmed, his gait never slackening.

"So you are," Nosmada groaned, gratitude in his voice.

After several minutes, he deposited his Lord on a plush bed. Though the chamber was stone and stark, barely lit by lanterns, the plush bed ran quite sophisticated and the mattresses looked comfortable.

Just as Lannon drew away from his master toward the door, Nosmada muttered, "Take wine and food to Zillian. The poor lady is so weak."

With a bow, the tall soldier departed and did as his Lord asked.

Zillian already reclined on a couch, nothing fancy like Nosmada used. Then again, being so small and frail, she practically became lost on the small, elevated mat. Lannon went to a knee, raised her head and said her name. Her eyes flickered open and he offered her the wine flask. The old woman drank of if greedily and let her lay back down.

"It is nearly over, young man," she murmured, slipping out of lucidity.

Lannon stood. He took a swig of the wine and said with a certain stiffness, "Nearly."

❊❊❊❊❊

Though Michael Galenson's pyre made a rather large pinprick of light in the night, Gorias and those with him never worried about discovery. They moved on fast, skirting the northern edges of the bogs. They searched for the lights seen by Maddox on an earlier night patrol. Soon, more torchlight shone through the barren trees that hemmed in the bogs. So many of the skeletal trees shared roots there was a jungle density to that side of the territory.

They crept close to the ground and used the brush for cover. Maddox touched his grandfather's shoulder and whispered, "Who are the dozen skinny guys with bows around them? Security?"

"Or what passes for it," Gorias said, watching Tammas run back up the hill. "Easy pickings, but what would you say their number is inside that guard detail?"

Maddox frowned, throwing out his right hand in a gesture of disgust. "More than I thought. There a great deal more members down there than when I was near them. Then again, I never was privy to every associate list."

Gorias looked at Tammas and said, "Nimble as a goat you

are, kid."

Tammas said nothing, while Kayla said, "Weren't you in with them in the first place, Maddox? Isn't that how they got the jewel they thought contained Wyss?"

Maddox scowled daggers at her then faced back into the utter blackness around the bog. Clouds drifted in, blotting out the stars, but one beam of light came from the main fires of the cult. Maddox said, "They claimed a jewel. I never saw that many people at any one meeting. I thought they were a dozen kooks. There must be another thirty people inside the guard ring acting as cult members."

Gorias showed no signs of anxiety for this number. "Most are cowards. They'll run at the first sign of terror." He then turned back to Tammas who clung tight to his bow, notching an arrow.

"What?" Tammas gritted his teeth, genuinely surprised by the look. "Never doubt it sir, I am with you."

Gorias thought, *Yeah, that's what worries me.* "I think they may be more attuned to fright than I first thought." He squinted at the ring of torches then raised his spyglass. A beam of green light lanced the night, emerging from the ground. "Damn."

Maddox had a tinge of panic in his voice when he asked, "What is it?"

Gorias handed him the viewer. Pensive for a moment, he then revealed, "Well, we are too late for the arising of Wyss, such as he is. Take a good look."

Up from a partially thawed bog stood a humanoid shape illuminated by the torches, bonfire, and a green light bleeding from the figure itself. Glistening from the wet, sparkling from the errant ice crystals, the thing from the bogs stood and looked side to side.

"By the elder gods," Tammas said, the confusion in his voice bordering on anguish as his arrow rattled in his bow. "What is it?"

Kayla's eyes narrowed at the image, and she asked Gorias, "Is it Wyss?"

As he somberly studied the seething mass of muck and weeds, Gorias said, "Hard to say. They must have known where to drop the jewel, do the spell, or how to call him up. The fragments of the Daemonolateria say some can use that document to order up a husk of flesh. Only, though, if a soul is ready to occupy the body."

Maddox nodded, watching the green glow pulsing. "And it doesn't have to be the original soul."

Tammas' hand shot to his chest as if it constricted in sudden fear. "I thought our souls left the planet when we died."

Gorias nodded, wondering what chaotic visions filled the head of the bard. "Normally, they do. If some prick of a wizard is nearby, or swimming in the ether-world, they can grab a soul and keep it hostage. Or if you're a real jackass of a cult leader, you can arrange for a jewel to be set up for the moment of your death. That way when you do check out, you escape the noose...or bog as it were. I doubt this is what Wyss, or whoever is in that mass of muck, had planned for resurrection day."

Clad in a long, formal gown, the figure moved only an inch to one side before stopping. All about the character oozed mud and clods of dirt, glittering wet mosaics of dead grass, bone and blood. Amid the ever-shifting face of soggy peat, a profile took shape. With monotonous regularity, the green radiance endured.

"If the body is inadequate," Maddox said, certain of his knowledge of the ceremony, "the form recalled will gather unto itself a structure familiar, that of a human, from other human bodies. In this case, a golem of mud is being created from so little real tissue mass."

Gorias gestured at the feet of the creature. The frosty bogs, smattered with fresh blood, gave off a gentle steam. "I would guess something died to add unto that mess, huh? I wonder how many followers took a dive for their leader."

Maddox's face flushed, showing shame. Be it his participation in this arising, or knowledge of the mass murder it would have taken to make it happen, his emotions showed as his confidence waned.

Many of the cultists went to their knees, enthralled at the rising. Although a quantity of them wore flaxen robes of brownish hue, most were clad in regular pants and tunics. Ten of them worshiped gleefully while at least that many drew back, unsure of their devotion.

"Reality will get the best of them," Gorias said, watching the crowd near the shape of a fiend incarnate. "The hard-cores will stay, but we shall soon see who the real religious folks are."

The being from the bog moved forward a step. What passed for a mouth opened. A flood of slime and dead bugs flowed out. There was no sound, save for a distant, liquid gurgle. The leader of the cult raised his arms in evident relief he was alive.

Tammas features turned a shade closer to green as he touched his stomach. His eyes, round with horror, never blinked. Kayla elbowed him in the ribs and Gorias thought the youth would vomit.

"Steady on, kid," Gorias whispered and managed a half smile amidst some exhaustion. "The thing doesn't have vocal cords yet. Look close now, it'll get some."

Stretching long limbs of mud and bloody bone, the creature clasped the shoulders of two of the willing worshipers. They stood close, mesmerized by the spectacle. Like a plant grabbing a fly, the arms of the entity folded in and held the two people close to its bosom. As one of the cultists read from a parchment in the torchlight, probably the Daemonolateria fragment, a lighter emerald glow bubbled around the two men. They screamed in agony as they folded into the arisen thing, their robes rippling around the other muck of the being as their tissues broke down.

Maddox swallowed hard. "Like melting candles. Good God, that's horrid. It sounds like woven baskets full of meat breaking down."

Gorias quipped, "And you want to be a necromancer? Take a good look, son. It sounds so great in theory, such an act, but it isn't so much fun in practice, eh? See how matter can reform from more matter? Quite the deal, for one cannot get something, or someone, from nothing."

"Their leader, the guy near by the arisen one, is named Zeren," Maddox said, pointing at the man to avoid any confusion. "He looks set in all his glory."

Zeren cried out in joy, worshiping his new master.

While the two bodies disappeared, waves colored an aqua-green flowed over the form from the bog. This color surged into a hue of scarlet then back to emerald. The legs quivered and the outline shook as its body mass increased. It drew in, growing tighter, shedding soil almost like fecal matter. While still a monstrosity, the personage gradually took on a more human contour.

A few of those kneeling fell on their behinds and soon scrambled to their feet. When these people ran, the guards turned and shot them in the buttocks with arrows. Kicking and screaming, they were taken back to the spot of the arising.

Zeren, holding a fragment of withered parchment, called out, "Thus be any who would flee their destiny."

The guards threw these three people to the arisen figure, who caught them up and lifted their bodies like rag dolls.

Gorias thought the thing rickety, and that it may have broken from the bodies' impact, but the new individual proved made of sterner stuff. In a moment, these sorry people too deliquesced into it. Again, blood, muscle, and now skin began to spread over the form. The worshipers that joined into the shape conformed and were no more.

Brow puckering, Maddox whispered, "Zeren always was a hardcore bastard."

"Wyss needs guys like him, and so do all gods or they cease to be. Zeren returned his obsession and idol to the planet. He doesn't look old enough to have known Wyss. Possessed and obsessed, he is the dark prophet of his god. Ain't he lucky?"

"Come to us," Zeren said. "Lead us, Lord Carlato! We will be your servants in this new, terrible world. Show us the means of righteousness."

The figure of mud took another step and looked at the speaker.

Frowning in concentration, Gorias muttered, "You see how brave the leader of the cult is, son? He stands pretty far back from the action, by God."

Kayla offered, "Someone must be in charge."

Tammas asked, "If he is in charge, why do they need Carlato?" His voice was nearly caught in his throat.

Maddox glowered and never spoke. However, Kayla asked

Gorias, "What do they need him for really? Is it just stupid hero worship of a leader? What?"

Six women were brought forward, all in white robes, cowls, and hennins replete with thin veils across their faces. They were offered, two by two, to the arisen one. After the first two were absorbed, the others tried to run. They soon added to the figure and, in turn, added to the new man's humanity.

"Well, those looked like bridal robes. They probably thought they would be vessels for Wyss' children. They gave him new life after all." He disengaged his twin swords. "So I guess they cannot be totally disappointed."

Kayla paled, but wrestled her fear down. Still her manner was one of calm defiance, leaning back on a hip, teeth clenched and chest thrown forward. She touched Gorias' shoulder, then drew back and persisted. "What do they want Wyss for?"

He stared at the edge of his blade then back at the distant glow of the slow approaching army of Nosmada. "That isn't Wyss."

Tammas stammered, nearly dropping his arrow, "You mean they have the wrong body from the bog?"

Gorias shook his head. "No, that sort of looks how I remember him--skinny, lean and long faced--but the soul isn't Wyss, like Maddox said. I just wonder who they got in return."

"The tales of his debauchery and sins in the bygone days are legion." Tammas replied. "Who could be worse than Wyss?"

"Lots of people," Gorias said, his patience starting to crack. "Common folks aren't seized by wizards, witches, or necromancers when they die. It's usually a personality of power. Whoever it is in that body, they must die. I have let this go on far enough."

"But Gorias..." Kayla started to say.

"You care for their lives? I fear the chaos if I don't slay them all."

"No, of course not," she said with a shrug, looking at the being solidify. "I still do not know why they want Wyss."

"The Daemonolateria."

"Wyss knows where the full translation is?" Maddox spoke up and laughed. "So what? To take a chance of raising him from the dead on the possibility that—"

Gorias cut him off. "Carlato was the son of a worshiper of Lilith--*daughters of the heather* they are called. They never wrote anything down. Their history is oral tradition, boy. The fragments can still cause a bad way of magic to work or make a demon dance, yet how can one believe them? A demon can make one think they know where the real text is and lead you into your doom. They are lying bastards. It's what they do."

"Lillith," Kayla said, her mind turning the name over and over.

"You see," Gorias said. "Wyss used the Daemonolateria frequently and knew it by heart. Do you hear me? *By heart.* Wyss could dictate the book out to a scribe. He doesn't need to find tablets or a fragment held hostage. The bastard has it all tied up in his brains."

Tammas said, "I have heard of that book. If they raised him from the dead with a piece of it…"

Gorias shrewd eyes glinted in the dim light. "The full translation we had on this world was the trick of Asmodeous, kid. He did it to reveal too much and many avenues to Hades. It was done in hopes of a damnation of all the earth to satisfy Lillith. Yeah, she's supposed to be the daughter of the Devil himself, but don't get me distracted explaining that. Wyss was such a selfish prick, he never got around to destroying the world. I won't take such a chance that he'll be that slothful now."

Maddox grabbed his forearm as the old man tried to move forward into the clear. "Grandfather! Surely this isn't worth our time. If this arisen man isn't Wyss, then who cares? To hell with them!"

He pulled his arm away from the younger man. The others were stunned at the violence of his act. "I'm a selfish man. One has to be that way in order to survive. But there are some things I cannot let pass."

"He's just a damned crazy wizard…" Maddox started to say, but his voice fell, becoming lower.

"Maybe," Gorias said. "But he could be worse."

Confusion set on all their faces.

Gorias motioned to the guards, fixated on the manifestation. "There're gaps in the lines now. They look more worried about desertions. I'll go in straight ahead. The direct approach usually screws them up. Tammas and Kayla, cover my flanks with your bows. Maddox, come in behind me if you so chose." He turned and looked over his back. "I have the worst feeling tonight, almost as if…" He stomped ahead.

Tammas fixed the arrow back firm and Kayla did likewise.

Maddox pulled out his broadsword and followed in his grandfather's wake.

More cultists fell under the embrace of the glowing persona, consumed unto nothing. The guards weren't doing their duty, for the amazing sight tainted their attention. Gorias whistled quietly through his teeth and a guard turned from the exhibition to face him. It was the last scene his eyes ever recorded and they carried it away, through the air, as Gorias sliced his head clean off.

The guard next to this man broke from his confusion, about to raise his bow. Gorias slashed up from his left, striking low, breaking the bow in half and cutting deep into the man's hip. The right sword of La Gaul aimed at the neck, but buried itself in the shoulder until it struck bone. The guard screamed as he withdrew and transfixed his swords at the man's neck. The screams stopped.

Terrible cries continued to rend the air from the bog as the two attacked. Maddox swiftly impaled a guard, with his sword still affixed on the risen master. He acted fast to assault the next guard, who was occupied with keeping cultists from running away. When this man turned to face Maddox, an arrow from Tammas' bow struck his Adam's apple, and he went down with a wet gurgle.

Kayla paid Gorias the same compliment, but her shaft went to the heart of a guard who faced La Gaul. Gorias kicked him in the groin to knock him off balance, sending the guard to the ground. The final obstructing man, facing down Gorias and Maddox La Gaul, backed up into the ring of confused faithful who remained. Unfortunately for him, he walked straight into the reach of the personality from the bogs. In short order, he was added unto the solid body of the man.

"Ho there! We are breeched!" Zeren shouted and raised his spear in warning. "Hold fast and…"

The leader's words caught in his throat as he fell to the ground. In his back were two arrows. This confused Gorias until Tammas and Kayla came out of hiding fast.

Gorias looked to the risen man, who indeed started to resemble a muddy version of Carlato Wyss, then down at the lip of ground behind him. The thunder of hoof beats grew ever nearer and the old warrior shouted, "Get down and take up defense, fast!"

Confused, Tammas and Kayla searched for cover just as half a dozen horses broke over the ridge. Soon, they were joined by half a dozen more horsemen, all bearing men in light armor and ready for war. One of the men held the blood red standard that carried a familiar insignia. It was an "X" in a circle.

"Nosmada," Gorias muttered hotly, naming the emblem of the dark lord. Glancing back, he found the thing that was once Wyss continued to stare at him. It grinned. La Gaul looked over at the two-dozen frightened cultists and at the thirteenth man who joined the military force.

This man wore a tall armored helmet, for his skull was oblong and inhuman. When he raised the visor, the dark, grim features ate up the firelight.

"Tolin." Gorias, gripped his sword handles.

The response, though, came out of the mouth of the thing that was Wyss. It was a sound from across the gulfs of endless space. These were words uttered by raw semblances unaccustomed to speech. "Yes? You called me by name…father?"

From atop the horse, Tolin leered down and his teeth shown like a wolf. He managed to open his maw and say the words, "Hello, indeed, father…"

Maddox's bewilderment mounted. He glanced at Wyss, then looked at Gorias for answers.

The old man's look of confusion turned to one of resignation. He crossed his swords, showing no fear, and said, "Deliverance will come."

CHAPTER VIII

REUNIONS AND DEPARTURES

In the face of such an incredible threat, Gorias La Gaul knew the play to make. Amid the imminent military danger, utter confusion of his comrades, and terror of the cultists, he turned and faced Carlato Wyss. With a fast move his swords whistled, chopping off both of Wyss' arms at the shoulders. A look of confusion and pain came into the newly formed eyes of the arisen. Those in the cult gasped. Even the troopers of Nosmada paused, transfixed by the image and the very presence of the aged warrior in his dragon plated armor.

The panic was high. A few dozen remaining cultists arose and charged away from the bog. They tried to run past the thirteen men under the standard of Nosmada, but their attempt proved futile. If anything they confused the troopers, who stabbed at them with obsidian tipped lances and bronze khopesh swords. One of the faithful fell to her knees and shouted to Wyss for deliverance.

Tolin's mount reared up and the front hooves flailed. One hoof caught the woman in the back of her skull. Her head fractured as the hoof scooped out brains. While she collapsed Tolin's mount righted itself then treaded on her back, proving her prayers insufficient.

"Shoot, for God's sake!" Gorias shouted at Tammas and Kayla as he still faced Wyss. As these youths fired on Nosmada's troopers, Maddox scooped up a guard's fallen bow. He went to one knee and fired. His arrow didn't bounce off the soldier's armor, as Tammas and Kayla's did. His arrow struck a horse in the eye. The animal reared up just as the last of the cultists ran amongst the troopers. As this horse plummeted down, more bedlam reigned. The trooper yelled, his leg broken and pinned, his body soon trampled by sandaled feet.

General Tolin never hesitated and his mount thundered

through the line.

Maddox yelled for Tammas and Kayla to fire on the horses.

Tolin swung an object that hung low to the ground. This long bludgeon, a double headed morning star flail, connected with Maddox's left shoulder and knocked it out of joint. Pure luck dictated that the morning star strands hit Maddox, not the spiked head. This move sent the brash youth to the ground, writhing in agony all the same.

Gorias' stood aggressively in attack style, glancing back at Tolin, but quickly facing Wyss again. With great speed he again drove his blades down, chopping the man off at the knees. Wyss mouth gaped open and he fell to the ground as Tolin thundered close, a sinister look in his glowing eyes. The bludgeon swung again, but met empty air as Gorias dived and rolled, swiping with his blades as he fell.

As Tolin's mount came to rest, it bellowed and fell backwards. One of the hooves came off at the third phalanx. The horse bawled and fell, cut just above the short pastern. Full of rage, Tolin sliced the air with the morning star and fell off the horse backwards, onto the soft ground at the edge of the semi-frozen bog.

"Run, dammit!" Gorias shouted with fury at Tammas and Kayla.

The troopers threw nets on the last cultists and had already snared Tammas. The boy kicked and screamed, but still found himself a prisoner.

Swiftly, Gorias walked to where General Tolin fell. The general's legs were in the crisp edges of the bog. Tolin coughed as he stabbed down with the morning star, trying to use it as a means to pull himself free. Gorias stepped on the handle of the weapon.

Tolin looked up in to the face of La Gaul. His arched eyebrows raised in expectation of a coming death blow, and then a low growl started in his throat, like that of a blood mad tiger.

He squinted, hands resting on the handles of his swords. "You are not my son." After that simple statement, he kicked Tolin in the jaw with his heavy boot. The bone popped and the large man tumbled back into the semi-frozen cavity where Wyss had crawled out. Struggling in the open gap, Tolin couldn't get a handhold. Blood fury in his eyes, he sank into the embrace of Earth.

When he turned back, Gorias saw a trooper net the elusive Kayla. She slapped the helmet from the man's head, revealing this soldier's baldness. More nets fell, this time securing Gorias' grandson. Even in agony, Maddox kicked and fought like a wild dog, determined not to give in.

The glow had ceased around Wyss. Gorias grabbed the undead torso by the waist and jogged around the lip of the bog. The troopers watched him and failed to fire arrows at the gliding legend.

With a move that almost appeared to be magic, La Gaul disappeared.

❈ ❈ ❈ ❈ ❈

"Where did he go?" Tammas stammered from his restrained position in the nets. His words strained and tears lurked in them. "By the gods, he faded away."

Kayla's dark eyes glared at the edge of the bogs where the old man vanished with the torso of Carlato Wyss. "He knew we were captive." She whispered so no trooper could hear them. "Look at them trying to find the old man." Her face grew brighter, odd in her abject joy amongst the confined cultists.

The thuggish, bald trooper slapped her on the back of the head then went to peer over the lip of the bog, out into the lands beyond. One of the soldiers chided this bald man, for the girl gave him such a fight. He took the jabs with good nature and cursed them back in jest.

Several of the troopers also stared into the area beyond bog. They even held out torches and tried to perceive where the old man could have escaped to. Curses flew frequently and they returned to the bog.

"Captain Karter," the bald trooper shouted as he gazed at where the general sank. "Fetch rope."

After several minutes, the troopers pulled General Tolin free of the stiff bog. What he fell into was more of a hole than a bog trap. He stretched his tall frame and promptly slit the throat of his bawling horse. While he wiped off the slime, Tolin listened as the men told him of La Gaul's escape. He stomped to the brink of the deep canyon. His glare shot sharp knives out into the sheer blankness that dropped off into eternity. Soon, he roared at the sky.

Maddox winced. "The drop is almost straight down into that chasm. Grandfather knew what he was doing. He's very far from here by now."

"How can you be so sure?" Tammas demanded, confused at the taciturn response.

Recoiling from the pain in his shoulder, Maddox replied, "He never said *deliverance will come* before he jumped. He didn't expect to die that way."

"Why did he take the piece of Wyss?" Tammas said, almost weeping.

"Toughen up, damn you, or sing your death song. Tolin will kill any he cannot sell into slavery. You recall the slave train we saw? Keep your mouth shut. If we're lucky, they'll sell us to it."

Tammas gave a look of wary distrust. "Why did he take the body?"

Tolin stomped toward them, his face sinister and sardonic in the torchlight. He growled at his troopers, "The darkness is La Gaul's friend, men. He is far departed now. Damn him to Hades." He grabbed Maddox by the hair, twisted his head back so the boy faced him and demanded, "Why are you with La Gaul?"

Maddox pulled at the coins in his belt purse. "The old man paid us to cover his back. We're along for the ride…sir."

Blood fumes dancing in his eyes, Tolin snapped, "And he has used you well, pup. Damn you as well! What good are any of you fools but more food for the beast? You are but blood vessels for Nosmada's sacrifice. I shall dispense with you all, sucklings for La Gaul, to the damned slave caravan. We cannot wet-nurse prisoners or blood packages for the dark Lord." The roar of the general subsided and his muscles relaxed. "So close to the soul that once inhabited this shell, still, that matters naught to any of you."

As they were starting to be led away, Kayla leaned in and

whispered, "Would you explain something to me fast? What's happening? Is that wild man really General Tolin? Why did they both call Lord La Gaul *father*?"

"I can make a good guess," Maddox said, rubbing his dislocated shoulder. "General Tolin? That one is simple." He focused on the general retrieving gear from the fallen horse then strangely petting a small oblong box. "His last name is La Gaul. He's my father."

Kayla's eyes widened. "What? But he acted like he didn't even know you!" She fell silent, reading Maddox contemplative silence. "He never addressed you or even said your name."

Maddox nodded, but not with heavy conviction. "He hasn't been himself in years. In fact, I'm unsure who he is now. You see, Tolin La Gaul is said to have the heart of a dragon. Its soul, as it were. Wyss' figure calling Gorias father? I would guess a soul jewel switch landed the real Tolin la Gaul in the arisen flesh of the cult leader."

Tammas said, "That's crazy talk! That's the stuff of ballads and tales--men taking on the soul of dragons for unearthly compensation. Such a thing cannot be true."

"Yeah, insane just to say it, no?" Maddox said. "But he does have the soul of a dragon in that body."

Kayla looked at the bog with a frown of impatience. "Then where's the soul of your father, the real Tolin La Gaul?"

✵✵✵✵✵

Indeed, Gorias La Gaul had traveled far from the bogs. Sliding down the sheer edge of the canyon was an easy feat for a child, or many who used flat boards to ride the edges in the past as sport. For an ancient man and a reanimated torso, it was a rough fall. He remained stunned that the descent didn't knock him cold. He was on his feet at the base of the canyon and ran a quarter mile before collapsing. The darkness proved his ally, hiding him for a long time. He needed the rest.

The wind echoed in the canyon, howling like a traveling

spirit. While he sat, he talked to what was now Wyss.

"You tore me apart," Wyss said, barely audible. "How could you, Father?"

"Shut up."

"The spell is fading, and the life forces used to maintain me are waning fast. I can no longer absorb life, not even yours."

Gorias leaned back. "Oh, knock it off. I'd give my left testicle for a bed of moldy straw right now."

"But why, Father?" the hideous voice cooed from the cadaverous face.

"Because you need to stay dead, son. Simple as that. I never would have guessed the error in the soul jewels. What a grand joke it all is, to be honest. Makes me glad I'm mortal."

"They tried to raise Wyss from the grave and accidentally used my soul crystal," the torso said. "It didn't take you long to understand it all. I will grant you that. You haven't slipped far in your mind, remaining cognizant of the threats from beyond unknown voids."

"Well, I knew that you were separated from your flesh long ago. That was way before the bargain with ageless Nosmada. What walks around as Tolin doesn't even know who he was before, not completely anyway."

"I wonder if he realizes that young man by the bog is his own son?" Wyss said. "Poor Maddox. So young, so impetuous…"

"He's brave in battle, that Maddox, but he needs to grow wiser if he's to survive. That general hates my guts because of the dragon inside of him and an aura of his flesh he cannot seem to shake. I guess your childhood angst toward me lingers, eh?"

"Slaying all the dragons made you unpopular with them."

"I brought you along to make sure I was right. If you were human again completely, you would have died from blood loss when I cut you apart. You don't have long anyway, Tolin. Indeed, the spell fades."

"Then my soul will go free at last," Tolin said. "Committing a soul to a crystal as a necromancer is one thing, but the stasis is not pleasant."

"Silly of you. What did ya think to gain in such a bargain with Nosmada and his wizards? A new life in a better body?"

"The body of a dragon."

"Foolish of you to make such a deal," Gorias said, his heart hammering in his ears. "What's it like? What happens?"

"Nothing," the torso said in a desiccated voice. "Nothing ever. You have no sense of body, yet you dream, and you cannot speak. I dare not guess how long I was inside the crystal. One cannot count time. It is all like a nightmare, a very boring dream. By the looks of you and Maddox, it was years. Perhaps that is why any ingrained memory I have of Maddox is not in the mind of the general. My son was a child when I saw him last."

"Souls weren't meant for that form of stasis," Gorias said, lifting his head up to stay awake. "They're a part of you, not a bargain chip for demons and their plans for the earth. Those of the Elilum, Siqqusim, and the Teraphims belong in chains of fire, not on Earth. That book must stay lost."

"Vengeance can be a sweet thing, no? That is their plan, the devils and demons as you call them. The spirits are tedious creatures who get real joviality out of outwitting simple mortals. Their bargains are dust, Father. As the dire Teraphims lurking beyond are easily amused, mankind is effortlessly duped for their heart wants so much more than they should have, I know."

"Yes," Gorias said, his heart still thudding hard. "There's no bartering to be made of the afterlife for certain. The worms tunnel for the rich and the poor on the same day. It is all about what you did here that counts."

"Rumor is that God is going to destroy the world. I saw that in my dreamtime," the torso ventured.

He coughed, the hammering in his ears doubling in tempo. "I wish he would hurry up."

"There will be no escape for me now," the voice from beyond the grave said. "Once you do what it is I know you will do, my soul will go to Hell and burn for all eternity."

"Yeah, that's where bad people go when they die."

The torso shuddered. "Then I will see you there."

107

Gorias' looked at the sky and his heart calmed at last. "Well, I hope I never have to speak to you again. If I do see you, we will have plenty of company, son." He got to his knees and wavered when he tried to rise up. "Damn, can't let myself fall asleep."

Gorias drew his swords and slashed in the darkness. The head of a female tumbled across the chest of the muddy torso.

"Watch out for the leeches." The torso laughed. "I have to hand it to you for senses and stout reflexes. You still are in your element, but for how much longer?"

"Yeah, if I fall asleep and wake up dead then how stupid will I look?" He stood over what was left of Wyss, staggered and sighed.

Undead eyes stared into the face of the legendary fighter. "How can you kill your own son?"

"You're dead already. This is a bad dream in your crystal stasis, just remember that."

"No, not really. Return me to my flesh." The voice came out with eagerness. "Switch me with that bastard General who wears my old skin. Maddox could perform it. He knows how. I can smell necromancy on him. I care not that the general is a necromancer now that the dragon controls him. The general has power, I grant that, but Maddox could do it. If you really ever loved me, you could find me a new body."

Gorias was unaffected by the words. "Do I need to remind you just how a soul transfer takes place? It takes the blood and souls of thirteen infants to accomplish this. Thirteen on each end. I sure as hell am not gonna round up twenty-six babies just to put a mad dog back in his body."

"But the one who is Tolin has the soul of a dragon in him, and is far more dangerous than me."

Gorias looked back in the direction of the bog. "I'll get to him in time. You, however, don't deserve to live after killing more than that many babies, plus the thirteen the cult of Wyss took to make you walk again today."

"How can you say any of those babies were not worthy of it? What would they have been in life that was better than me? Abandon your hoary customs, Father, and listen to your blood. It is all in the blood and that is all that matters, from one generation to the next. Please do not put faith in silly gods no one else worships anymore."

"If one of those babies turned out to be a trollop, she would be better than a miserable sonofabitch like you," came the uncompromising words of Gorias La Gaul. "The only good thing you ever did was make Maddox, and I'm not so sure about him sometimes."

He raised both swords and brought them down, over and over, slashing and twisting, until he vivisected the torso into over a dozen pieces. A dank, moldy smell emanated from the numerous bits. Somewhere hidden in the mixture rested the bones of Wyss, rotten flesh, and the blood of infants. He kicked these parts away, stomping on the head, splattering the gray matter and praying to God his son's soul was indeed free of the earth at last.

"All things have their limits, Tolin," he said to the wind and gazed across the expanse of the stark canyon. "Anything else would be God." Wearily, he looked around, hands dangling between his knees. "Now how the Hell do I get out of here?"

✷✷✷✷✷

General Tolin La Gaul was true to his word. At daybreak one of his troopers rode out to meet up with the slave caravan bivouacked nearby. The general ate cured ham at sunrise, sitting by the largest of the bonfires fed well to keep leeches at bay. He stared into the dancing flames. Every so often, he let his enormous left hand rest on the tiny oblong box from his saddle. When the soldiers stepped closer to tell him news, he nodded and never spoke.

As he glanced at the leaders of the caravan of traders stopped near the bog, Captain Karter told Tolin, "The director of the slave convoy says they are lingering mainly because of the coming fight. They anticipate a high body count between us and the forces of the northern barbarians."

"Word travels fast."

"Quite. In the event of stragglers, they would absorb them

into their train and sell them to Nosmada at a profit."

Tolin laughed at this and said with a contemplative smile, "The depravity of man never ceases to amaze me. They are all meat at Nosmada's table, one way or another."

"Very good, sir," Karter agreed, hands clasped behind his back.

"Captain Karter," Tolin said as he placed his hands on his knees and arose. "You have no family, is that true?"

"That's correct, sir."

"You are smart. I'm full of twisted feelings and hatred because of family sentiment left in this flesh. Stay unattached to any bloodline. It is better for the mind that way."

Though he looked down at his boots, Karter soon raised his head and smiled. "The military is my life, General. It's all I have. I could care less for children or a woman to control me."

They walked toward the three captured with La Gaul. Transactions took place and they were sold to the caravan leader without any great incident. Tolin didn't regard the young ones for very long.

"Too bad La Gaul is such a bastard," Tolin said. "There is naught to be gained from holding these fools hostage in hopes of a valiant rescue. Gorias doesn't care about anyone but himself. Let them be thralls forever."

The three youths, long since stripped of their weapons, money, and mounts, had no choice but to go into slavery. Maddox wouldn't look at Tolin, but the other two did.

Greatly frustrated, one of the troopers searched the brush in the morning light. Two more soldiers emerged from the canyon, climbing up long ropes. Among them, Tubal called out, "Our ropes can't even reach the bottom of the canyon. If that ol' dog lived through such a fall, he's packin' arcane powers from another dimension, I reckon."

Lines in his face growing longer, Tolin grumbled, "He doesn't. I don't care what the legends say about his dealing with angels." The general stared into the canyon of Benedikt, asking the men gathering up their ropes, "What troubles you all?"

Tubal replied, "There should be anotha' hoss, General. We're missin' one from these brats. Three hosses are 'ere, but where in Satan's beard is the fourth one? Where's ol' La Gaul's horse?"

Tolin shook his head. "Damn, damn, damn." He looked away from the canyon and returned to the encampment. "Knowing La Gaul, the accursed animal is loyal. The man slips through my hands like any fable should, falling from a scroll of parchment like a story." His open hand tightened into a fist. "Damn him for all time."

"We coulda go an'do a search fer the hoss, sir."

"No. I have wasted too much time chasing that old man," Tolin said as he stared at the sky. Our duty lies beyond, getting the weapons from the Foundry of Syn. We must get rid of these young ones and go back to our forces."

Tammas looked at the soldiers then to the line of slaves. "Why don't they just kill us?"

Tolin mounted up on Maddox's horse, replete with his own saddle, roll, tiny box. "Why indeed? Can you guess, young pup?"

"We are worth more alive as blood donors for Nosmada's grand scheme," Kayla said with confidence.

What passed for a grin spread over Tolin's chilling face when he rode near her. "You comprehend much, dear, for all the good it does you." He stared at Maddox for a long time then pulled his horse away. Tolin ordered his men, "Barter for trail rations and let us be gone from here."

The grubby men from the slave caravan added Maddox, Tammas, and Kayla to their long train and led them away.

CHAPTER IX

RUSTY CHAINS

After climbing out of the canyon far from the bogs, Gorias rested and faced the sunny sky. He drank from his water flask and dug in his cloak for some jerky. Though he took a great many breaths, he still felt the exhaustion in his bones.

"What a rotten day to be alive," he said with a deep cough.

Gorias looked north toward the deserts of Dundayin, and could hear the echoes of what most dismissed as thunder. The warrior felt every year of his long life in his breaths, how protracted his recovery proved at this time.

He glanced up as he heard the snorting of a horse. "Well, look at that. Things are looking up." The white horse walked over near him to graze on some greenery near his feet. He grabbed a stirrup, pulled himself up, and yanked down his bedroll. Never did he unravel it, but he laid it in a bunch on the ground. Gorias returned to his backside and exhaled. His heart raced in his chest as he took another drink of water. His thoughts in order, he lay down and wished the day was over.

That's when he heard Ezran Gavreel say, "You are consistent, I will hand you that."

Gorias pulled the dirk from his belt. He looked hard, but only his horse stood near. For a moment, he thought he saw the outline of the gray man he knew from days of old.

Letting his head fall back to the bedroll, he kept his knife in his hand and said, "I expected to see you today, Ezran."

Then he fell asleep. When he opened his eyes, Gorias lay at a darkened place, years ago.

Ezran Gavreel looked down at him. "It seems every time I see you, you are covered in blood and gore."

Gorias rolled over and tried to arise in the dim chamber. He slipped on a mound of guts freshly unraveled from a rather obese man. Dropping his sword, he quickly picked it up. The midsection of the broadsword was jagged and broken off.

"God dammit." He looked around the tavern, blinking as blood ran from his scalp. Staggering from the final blow of the fat man...the bartender, that was it. Gorias knew that man had served his last drink.

"On the contrary," Ezran said from far above La Gaul. "God bless you."

All around the tavern lay corpses of men and fighting women, slashed open either from crotch to sternum or across the belly just below the ribs. On the walls several people hung, nailed upside down. Their heads were removed and their blood drained into large half cut whiskey barrels. Gorias peered up into the high ceiling of the tavern and beheld Ezran. The man cloaked in gray levitated, bearing himself up on silvery, glittering wings.

"I killed these damned fools," he said, waving at the disemboweled crowd in the tavern, "because they needed to die. Never has such a group of souls deserved to be separated from their bodies more. I tell you the truth. The folks on the wall, well, the sons of bitches running this place killed them for some ritual before I got in here. If you're something so damned powerful, you can see I'm telling the truth."

"I am Ezran Gavreel," the floating being said. "You have lost your sword in this fracas."

Gorias glanced at the broken blade. "I'll get another."

From behind his back, Ezran's hands brought out two long, gleaming objects. They glowed like lightning. When they ceased to pulse, the sheen ran akin to steel, but not unlike that of a mirror. Ezran dropped the objects and Gorias instinctively caught them. In his hands for the first time were his twin swords, made with grips that fit his fingers so well it was as if they hugged his very soul.

"God bless you, Gorias La Gaul." Ezran smiled and disappeared. "You will need it."

No sooner did he have the swords than the doors to the tavern opened. A rather slender version of the ogre, Mitre Stillwell, ran through the doors and swiftly closed them. Gorias helped him with the heavy bolt and went to the window. A company of men followed the ogre, probably a few dozen in number. They wore heavy body armor and carried crossbows.

"Well thanks for bringing all the fun," Gorias said to Stillwell.

Mitre snorted and grabbed a half empty beer from the bar. He downed most of it and tried to get his breath. "This is as good a day as any to die." He spat out some of the brew, for it was tainted with blood. He gawked at Gorias then at the mug. With a shrug, he took another drink.

"I reckon, but I think deliverance will come," Gorias said while studying his two swords.

The door burst open, showing a flood of fighting men, and Gorias sat up at the edge of the canyon.

After rubbing his eyes, he watched the sky. The sun had moved and a few hours had passed.

"Time I was leaving," he said, climbing to his feet.

※ ※ ※ ※ ※

Nosmada rubbed his forehead and frowned at the fading images in the caldron. Tolin La Gaul grew fainter. The words of Nosmada's general still echoed in his mind. From their ferocity, Nosmada was shocked they didn't echo in the chamber as well. His index finger traced the furrows on his forehead. The familiarity of the scars there made his fingers quake.

Zillian's hands quivered from eldritch magicks as she lowered her arms over the stone caldron. The ancient woman reached for a cup. Lannon aided her and placed the container in her hand. With great difficulty she drank of it before saying, "La Gaul is harder to kill than a greased serpent. I fear if I cut off his head he would rise again, and not as a leech."

"Which La Gaul?" Nosmada said. "Truly, having Tolin in my service leading my armies is a great thing. It's also a better situation for us that the dragon in his breast was a wyrm-ling. The young dragons aren't so wise, but still run on instinct."

Nosmada smiled "Tolin follows the ways I set out for him

and keeps in line. Imagine if he were an elder dragon in the flesh of a man? Such a soul convergence would never work."

Zillian chuckled, making her stomach ache. Lannon helped her to stand by placing his arm around her feeble back.

"I'd have never believe the oldster could elude a force like that." Lannon swiftly said, "I'm sorry I spoke."

Nosmada shrugged it off. "It's of no matter, really. Soon, we will have enough for the last sacrifice. This business with Wyss is proving to be a costly annoyance."

Zillian dipped her fingers in the cup and touched her forehead with the water. "Do you think it will be enough?"

A look of eerie satisfaction spread over Nosmada's face. "It's all about the blood. In the end it will suffice."

Lannon helped the mage over to her couch and she collapsed, sucking in air fast.

Zillian reassured herself with a question. "What more trouble can a feeble old man be, my Lord, no matter what his cunning? He cannot hurt you here."

Nosmada nodded and looked at Lannon before he let his focus rest on the wrinkled old woman. "You speak words of truth." He stared at his right hand. His fingers trembled, and they would not stop shaking.

✵ ✵ ✵ ✵ ✵

The slave caravan stretched on for a half mile. Horses and carts carried minor articles of value in the rear of the train, but humanity came as the principle trade of those in the billowing robes.

Yoked together with loose chains linked to leathery collars around their necks, hundreds of people walked in file. Their rhythmic gait happened naturally for those in this snake composed of human flesh. Another set of chains let their feet take strides, but these links were heavy. This way, fleeing would be unlikely, and for a long distance it would be impossible. Their hands linked together from manacles at the wrists. Over time the weight of it all drained the life from these slaves.

Tammas and Maddox found themselves yoked side by side, but Kayla resided in the rear with other female prisoners. Whenever they turned to look back, one of the mounted guards snapped a long whip near their heads. Once, this action removed the ear lobe of the man next to Tammas, sending droplets of blood across the youth's face.

The slave traders were businessmen, plain and simple. Many of them wore baggy clothing that traveled better than most in open spaces. Each man wore a turban cloth tied about his head, save for some of the guards dressed in light armor in case of attack by bandits. They had a wrap of cloth about their throats that easily substituted for a facemask against the dust. These handlers held little toleration for speaking amongst the slaves.

After noon the caravan rested for a half an hour. Slaves and animals were watered, fed a wafer-like square the guards called "bread," and they moved on.

"We're making terrible time," Maddox mumbled to Tammas, looking at the men who rode horses up and down the line. His shoulder ached terribly, but he fought off the pain as best he could.

"I guess we should consider ourselves lucky." Tammas almost stumbled. "Many caught by foreign armies are extinguished at the end of a rope."

"Shut up."

Eying the guards, Tammas disobeyed his friend. "There are several of us and so few guards. I only counted a couple dozen. Surely, we could overpower them."

"Good that you're thinking like a warrior. You may have a future in you yet."

Tammas managed a frail laugh as he walked in sloppy tempo with the others. "If I am liberated to fight again, I shall take you up on it. I am trying to sing as I go, to myself. The words are fleeting, though."

One of the lookouts paused and gazed down at the two youths. With defiance, Maddox said, "What, no talking?"

The guard shrugged. "Talk 'til you die, slave. I could care less than a damn. Hatch all the plots you want. I care not. Perhaps tonight you will be the one selected to give to the leeches for a joke."

Tammas face flushed, but Maddox showed no trepidation. His chin set and teeth were clenched. A strong resemblance to Gorias La Gaul crept into his features.

They walked for another hour and a half until they reached the base of a gradual hill. One of the guards called down the line. "We better stop them now. They will have an easy time climbing that hill with better rest."

Before the group could begin to sit down, Maddox heard a metallic, scraping sound echoing over the hillside. He wasn't alone in hearing this. Many of the guards called out to each other or cursed at their gods. Soon countless slaves shouted and pointed at the crest of the ridge.

Maddox patted Tammas on the thigh. "Look there. Deliverance will come."

The name that spread amongst the curse words thrown by those in the caravan was *Gorias La Gaul*.

On the edge of the distant hill loomed a huge man on horseback. He held up two gleaming swords, crossing them several times before charging forward.

"It is like a dream, or a song," Tammas said, blinking to make sure what he beheld was so. "To be saved in such a way!"

"We aren't out yet," Maddox cautioned as many behind them stumbled against their bodies. "Gotta hand it to the old bastard, he knows how to make an entrance."

While the slaves buzzed with talk one of the guards laughed. Yet another asked, "Where are his reins? In his teeth?"

Though Gorias wore his helmet, indeed the visor stayed up to allow the reins in his mouth. There was a slit in the visor, but Gorias wanted them to know who approached.

Maddox studied the guards who stared dumbfounded at the old man charging them alone. He shot Tammas a look. "Two dozen of these pricks, you say?"

Down the line, far in the rear, a commotion erupted. Screams among the women and many watchman registered panic. One shouted out, "She broke his neck!"

"Sounds like Kayla," Maddox said as he gripped the chains in his hands. "I like her line of thinking."

Since he couldn't loop the chain around the neck of the guard on horseback, Maddox grabbed the horse. Although pointing parallel to the caravan, the guard gaped the other way. Favoring his good shoulder, Maddox pulled. The guard fell off his horse toward him. Tammas looped the chains around his fists and smashed the guard's head after the man plunged. Surprise spread across Tammas' face at how easily the guard's head caved in under the crushing blows.

A rousing cheer went up from the mass of slaves as Gorias charged the main body of guards.

"He's mad," Maddox said, letting the horse go free, his expression one of astonishment. If any other man tried such a stunt as Gorias, Maddox would've yawned and started guessing how soon he'd be in his grave.

A group of four guards derived great merriment out of the charge until many of the slaves shouted out *"La Gaul!"* Uncertainty set in and the handlers decided to fix bows. All down the line, slaves followed the example of Kayla, Maddox, and Tammas by draping chains over the nearest guard's neck. A dozen guards died, thrashing and venting their bowels. Those remaining stepped way from the slaves who refused the conformity of the snake-line discipline. One charged Gorias on foot, along with many on horseback. A few of them turned their mount and moved behind the caravan.

Tammas swung at a fleeing horse, missed. "What are the guards doing?"

Maddox held his shoulder. "They're running. Keeping beaten men in chains at bay is one thing, fighting Gorias La Gaul is quite another, no matter how old."

The action came so fast, the young men in chains thought La Gaul missed the two guards who rode out to meet him. Since the arrows fired bounced off the invader's stomach and breast, they came at him with swords drawn. Gorias, reins still in his clenched teeth, swirled his swords and stabbed at the men. His weapons snapped back to his chest so fast that the men tumbling from their horses looked to ricochet off Gorias. One of them rose to his feet and looked down in astonishment as his intestines unfolded. No matter how hard he tried to push, he couldn't make his guts get back in his body. Another lay on the ground gagging loud, clutching below his neck.

Four guards stood at the front of the caravan, over a hundred yards from Maddox and Tammas. They brandished pikes and small shields, preparing to gore La Gaul's mount. With a suddenness of a man shot out of the saddle, Gorias flew to his left, hit the ground with a slide, and his horse pulled up, avoiding the serrated pikes. His large frame slid to a stop at the feet of the bewildered pike men. With a thrust between their legs, he swiped his blades through the groins of the two nearest him, splitting them up to the seam of their buttocks.

One of these guards threw back his pike so fast he skewered the man behind him in the face. Grabbing at the object lodged in his face, the man dropped his weapon and stumbled into the fourth guard. By the time the other freed his pike from the maw of the dying one, the tension in his legs were such from the earlier low blow that he collapsed.

Gorias threw a dagger into the guard's throat. Falling to his knees, the guard watched Gorias stand tall. The fable ran a luminescent blade through his opponent's mid-section. La Gaul held him up with the sword long enough to retrieve his knife. Then he let the man drop before he faced the cheering mob of slaves. Quickly, he beheaded the other man he'd slashed. This guard, busy holding his manhood together, never even fought back.

Two of the guards rode up on horseback fast. The one on the left threw a small misericorde at Gorias. He deflected it with his left sword, his lips peeling back from his teeth in a scowl. Another threw a heavy axe that did impact on Gorias' head. His helmet tumbled off, but the ancient warrior wasn't injured. His mane of gray and white hair flew free.

Two more guards approached, riding fast after the others. One of these men had demonical eyes and the face of a fighting man. Ever the one to set his own rules, Gorias went to his knees just as these men arrived to clash with him, stabbing his swords into the bellies of the horses, trying to avoid the blades of the guards. This sent the riders airborne, but Gorias couldn't get his swords free of the horses' bellies with great haste. One put his hoof on the fallen helmet as it stumbled. The helm never gave an inch and the hoof slipped, sending the animal into worse torments as it hit the ground.

The other riders were on him fast. Still on his knees, Gorias released his swords, waved his cloak off himself, and stabbed his forearms forward at the horse's cannon and tendon. The attackers' blades stabbed at his shoulders but glanced off his armor. One slid against his scalp but never made a cut. The riders didn't comprehend what Gorias used to slice the legs from the horses, but the guards soon headed downward. The dew nails of the dragon on his armor had slit through the flesh and bone of the animals like spoons in gravy.

He rose up, wrenching his swords free from the horses as two more guards rode in and came to a halt. They seethed at Gorias, but he returned a casual look. "Well, are ya going to die in the saddle or get off yer horses? Sit on your ass and bleed, for all I care, because yer gonna die."

The guards pulled back and ran, beating their mounts to a gallop. Even the ones on the ground who still watched did likewise, save for one. He pulled a long broadsword from a sheath on his dying mount and held it high. His glittering eyes belonged to a warrior and he wasn't about to flee.

Maddox held Tammas by the shoulder. "That man will never give in or run. Look at that bastard's grin on his face. He is too stupid to realize he is dead already."

Gorias didn't make a move forward, but waited for the man to rush him. However, this guard made no dive into the jaws of death. He circled Gorias in a defensive stance, both hands on his broadsword pommel. From what Maddox could see, the double-edged long-sword was heavy, probably crafted in the Foundry of Syn. The way he held the weapon showed he knew what he planned to do with it.

Gorias watched the guard close, aware of what Maddox saw

in this opponent. Usually content to let the fight come to him, he swished the swords and countered the movements of the guard.

The aggressor said, "Dragon scales, hang my ass pink! You really are La Gaul, his own damned self." There was no fear in his voice or eyes when he spoke. His recognition swiftly turned to determination and blood lust.

No mouthy bravado came from the one man who certainly had lived enough to use it. "Deliverance will come."

The heavy blade swung to the right and the guard was met head on. He slashed around the other way. Again, Gorias blocked him smartly.

"Nimble for an old cuss." the guard said, chuckling. "That armor will make me rich!" He made a bold thrust, aiming for Gorias' heart. The deathblow didn't arrive, for Gorias slid to the left with the elegance of a dancer. However, he didn't have a chance to drop his swords on the back of his attacker. This was what the guard assumed he would do, but the death strike proved a ruse. With great force, the assailant struck Gorias jaw with his left elbow. He let the weight of his sword drop against the scaled armor. Briefly he hugged Gorias close, avoiding the stroke of the two swords. The guard reached down to bring up his sword into Gorias' armpit. If he found a crease in the armor, the old man's arm would be off.

While the guard still embraced him, La Gaul slammed his head into his opponent's as he drew away. A wet pop echoed when the guard's nose burst like rotten fruit. The sharp jolt of pain and spray of blood was enough to confound his planned dismemberment of La Gaul. It also gave Gorias a moment to step away then attack anew. The heavy blade did strike, but the move came off blunted by Gorias' head thrust.

The old warrior wasted no time. He slashed on either side of the man, who proved a dexterous fighter that warded off the attacks by the swords. Not one to pause over the gory figures of his dead comrades, the guard stepped on their lifeless chests and moved away from La Gaul.

Gorias snapped his sword's together at the handles and kicked at the guard's shin. Stumbling badly, the powerful warrior regained his footing and faced him. Gorias used moves like a man fighting with a quarter-staff. In a frenzy of blind desperation, the guard swung his great sword in an overhand arc, connecting with the center of the false-staff weapon. Too late, he read the eyes of Gorias, for this was exactly what the old one desired of him.

The handles disengaged their connection, but it wasn't the blow of the broadsword. He twisted in his wrists, taking the terrific impact of the sword in the dragon skinned armor on his chest. The two blades snapped up, connecting on either side of the guard's ears, cleaving into the skull. The momentum of the heavy strike carried both men down, but it was Gorias who shrugged the man off. The guard laid still, the top half of his head rolling away.

Many cheers went up from the mob of prisoners as Gorias gazed down the line. He then proceeded along the procession, slashing his swords through the outstretched chains of the nearest captives.

Tammas said with glee, "The chains are made of iron or steel. Your grandfather's blades must truly be made of angel's wings!"

Maddox sighed and didn't look at his friend. "Be quiet. You have been smoking Galenson's herbs." He noted Gorias' blades never destroyed the broadsword, so he doubted their invulnerability.

Gorias' horse followed him as he walked toward his grandson. He said nothing as he slashed through their bonds. He handed the swords to the two youths.

"Free the rest."

Maddox gripped the sword, admired it for a moment. "Why?"

Gorias smirked, taking a great many breaths. "Because I said so."

"Any other reason?"

The old man paused, leaning one hand on his horse. "Yeah. It'll piss off Nosmada."

Maddox started to run then stopped and came back, almost as if to embrace his grandfather. Gorias reached out and the youth thought the old one meant to hug him. Instead he gripped Maddox shoulder and arm and popped it back into place. The boy screamed in agony.

As Maddox sucked wind and tried to recover, Gorias drank from a flask.

While Maddox rotated his shoulder as best he could, Tammas asked, "Where is Wyss…um…the thing from the bog?"

"Where he belongs. I made sure of it. Now go on."

The boys went to the front and started to work their way backwards. One of the prisoners retrieved the keys from the cart in back and the act of freedom moved quicker. Tammas gave Gorias one of the swords back. Whether it was the presence of the keys or the youth's fear of using the blade, Gorias never asked. While this jubilant act of freedom happened, he stalked to the rear of the caravan.

✿ ✿ ✿ ✿ ✿

Kayla stood over two dead guards and smiled as Gorias walked close to her. He slashed at her outstretched hands, landing a delicate blow, and Kayla's face glowed. "I knew I could count on you, dear," he said quietly. "Too bad you weren't closer to the boys. My job may have been easier."

"It's good to see you here," she admitted, arms almost reaching out to him, but she held them back.

"Hell, after last night it's good to be anywhere."

Kayla stepped closer to him, her body gently bouncing off the frame of the fable.

"Evening is coming soon. These maniacs have the right idea," Gorias said, motioning to the slaves wildly going through the carts bound for Nosmada's citadel. "Re-supply yourselves and cut horses from the guard stock. If one of these slaves gives you any mouth, cut it out of his skull." The three gaped at him, astonished. He added, "I may be a liberator, but I ain't no priest. I'm better at killing people than I am at being polite. Now get to it."

Gorias stepped close to a cart. Many short swords and spears were already gone from this wagon. He took out two steel blades very much like his own and walked toward his horse. Climbing back in the saddle, he exhaled. Clearly winded by the experience, he trotted away from the caravan and rested.

Doing as Gorias requested, without the need to kill anyone, the three soon returned on horseback. Kayla even had her original mount that once belonged to the wizard of Nosmada. Tammas complained a guard had his, but the beast must have fled. Gorias knew the animal was the one with white stockings he gutted earlier, but said nothing. Many of the newly freed men dressed that particular horse for meat as they spoke.

He pointed at the large weapon strapped to Maddox's mount. "Son, I see you have the last guard's sword."

"Yes. I'd like to use one more often. Mind you, he had a hard time giving it up."

"Oh?"

"Yes, his death grip on the sword was so tight I had to chop off his fingers to get it. Still a powerful weapon, no?"

"Yes," Gorias said, rubbing his beard. "At least he died well."

Maddox shifted in his saddle, trying to get steady. "Well, I don't know what comes next. I guess you stopped that damned Wyss from living on, right?"

Gorias looked in the direction of Khabnur. He watched billowy clouds emitted from the Foundry of Syn. "Not sure what the move is for the rest of you, either. As for me, I think I have an ogre to see." He stared at his hand then towards the open field.

"Are you going to ride in there and confront Mitre alone?" Maddox said. "You are crazy! The Foundry is underground, save for the exhaust towers. I wager there's a way in for sanitation, or an escape route of some kind, but that's all unwise chatter."

Gorias gave him a severe look. "You're the only one talking about it. If ya ever calm down, ya could be dangerous. That isn't what I had in mind. Not exactly, anyway."

Maddox laughed. "That band of troopers from Nosmada's army is probably waiting over the hill for us now."

"I agree," Tammas said.

Kayla said nothing. Her black eyes focused on Gorias. She had her hand over her shoulder, counting arrows in her leather quiver.

Gorias said, "Shows how damned young and dumb ya both are then. If they gave a beggar's toss about getting at me through you, they would have staked you all out in the desert for the leeches to get. They wouldn't be trailing this caravan like so many green hunters. No, you're just as good to them in the slave caravan. Tolin is a bastard, but he understands how important I deem various things. You would have all gone to the same place."

"What do you mean," Tammas asked, a confused look gripping his face.

"You think you were off to be house servants? You think these leeches are filling up on blood and walking to Nosmada for the hell of it? You can walk there just as easily and donate your blood."

Kayla nodded. "What does Nosmada want the blood for?"

Gorias frowned, keeping his attention on the fields. "I don't think I quite grasp it yet, but I got a really nasty idea. Anyway, no. You three and me, Hell, we're the last things on their minds. Well, maybe not Tolin's. I'm sure I'll be walking inside that skull for as long as he breathes, maybe longer. Now, I have a score to settle with Mitre Stillwell."

Tammas asked meekly, "Doesn't he run the foundry where Tolin and the forces of Nosmada are going?"

Gorias looked at the smoke from the stacks in the distance. "Nothing gets by you, kid. Yeah, I need to find out just what Mitre is doing in his spare time. If I ride hard, I may be able to make it in and out before the forces of Nosmada get there in a few days. It's taking his army a long time to march there because their force is so large. I wager they are a day or so away now. Their pickets and rangers must be out, so watch yer asses."

"Are you going to tell my mother Wyss is no longer a threat?"

Gorias looked at Kayla as if the idea was alien to him. Minutes ticked away, wheels turning in his head, until he said at last, "You know, I just may have to see Lira Rhan one more time. I think her and that army of mercenaries may come in handy after all as this falls together."

Tammas started to say, "About this Tolin hating you so

much…" but Gorias cut him off.

"Maybe legends shouldn't have kids? Maybe."

"Grandfather…" Maddox fell silent as the old man looked off at nothing.

"He grew up away from me," Gorias said, gripping his belt. "Learned to listen to idiots and lying tongues. It happens. I couldn't be there to hold his hand forever. Long ago, when I did, he thought I was all that there was on Earth. Evil separated us forever. Folks want to know why I kill the bad guys. Well, I'll never get to hold that little hand again because of evil." He looked at Tammas. "Kid?"

"Yes sir?"

"Sing me some old dirges, if ya will. They help pass the time on a hard ride. My memories fade off if I sing them to myself."

"Very well. Any requests?'

"Preferably one without me in it."

Maddox jeered, "You really want him to sing?"

"Beats having him talk. He's detrimental to good conversation."

Tammas sang;

"One last kiss upon thy lovely dying lips.
Allow me this, my love.

All of our torrid lives, through hardships and strife
Blood and lust, war and peace, heaven and hell
We endured it all…together.

Alas, no more…you must confront the dark warrior, death
alone.

He might not let thee past unmolested.
He might desire a fee of thee, because he knows me so well.

We both know the power in the dying so well.
He may fight me someday to relinquish his title
Whisper to him, tell him you love me. That should repulse him.

127

Go now, my queen, into the land of eternal afternoons
Await thy warrior there
And prepare him a way."

In time, the sound of hooves drowned the boy's voice out.

CHAPTER X

FOUNDRY OF SYN

Tolin and his troopers rode hard, driving their powerful mounts onward. The steeds, bred from the lower outlands of Xylon, were much larger than common horses. From eating the long olive grasses of Xylon, the horses lathered up at a slower pace and they endured the beating their riders imparted with ease. The group skirted the edge of the Foundry of Syn, giving the sprawling underground locale a wide berth. Their pace slackened when they reached the outer defenses of Khabnur. When he surveyed the earthworks, pits, and other defenses of the city, Tolin smiled.

They paused at the outskirts of the city of Khabnur to water their horses. Numerous mercenaries appeared and sized up the troopers.

Karter said to Tubal, "Several of these killers, professional and amateur alike, cluster in the outlining neighborhoods."

After splashing water across his face, Tubal rubbed his eyes and nodded. "Lotsa boardin' houses and brothels hereabouts. S'natural spot for them."

The riders traversed the gate of the outer most wall of Khabnur. An enormous door made of logs and tick iron rings, the gate was held shut with a locking timber.

Karter studied it. "The first obstacle in case of a siege."

Tubal wiped his mouth on the back of his hand before replacing his gauntlet. "General, those hired mercs musta really be ruthless men, fer sure, for they dunno fear of an army carrying the mark'a Nosmada."

Tolin ground his teeth together as he looked back at the city of Khabnur. "They are a filthy rabble, but every man not fit for service, or backstabber with balls enough to fight, is around that city. Hired killers, bah. La Gaul has guts, they are a newer breed, afraid of their own stiffening pricks. It would be like trying to root out an army of rats. Even if they are not well armed, they will bite. The come in here for the trade routes all intersect at Khabnur."

His bottom lip turned in, visibly worried about the gathering mercenaries, Tubal wondered aloud, "So, no need to care too much 'bout them at our backs 'er flanks?"

Tolin shrugged and faced forward. "No. Like I said, they are rats trapped behind walls. They are not an army, nor would they have the courage to fight, certainly not to attack us. These men are here for defense, nothing more. Their backs against the wall, they will fight a defensive struggle. There are many of them, I grant that."

"Perhaps a few of us should go for some drinks deeper into the town." Captain Karter said. "Once we pull recon, we could see what the true tenor of this rabble is, eh?"

Tolin looked to Tubal. "Take a few men with you and do as Karter said. Report back to me by midnight."

Tubal saluted, promising, "Yessir! I'll find out if they're smellin' their own piss or just tightenin' up their asses."

These three men detached from the group and returned to the city. The rest rode beyond the city limits to the southwest.

One of the troopers pointed North of Khabnur and said, "Look, the army of the west pitches camps. Their fires must be huge to make such a dent in the sky. We must be wary of their patrols."

Tolin's hands balled into fists and he swore mightily. "They have advanced faster than I thought possible. Truly they will overrun us before we reach the foundry."

Captain Karter cursed the barbarians. "Those damned barbarians from the North, they're too stupid to be afraid."

"The primal mind doesn't know fear, men," Tolin said, reining his horse back. "If there was ever a great need for necromancy to aid our cause it is now. I will not be re-routed by a few thousand idiots in bear-skin kilts."

The troopers lined up with stern obedience and they spoke as one, "What be your will, General?"

"I must contact Nosmada with Zillian. In a case this desperate, I must invoke my right to inquire after help." Taking a few breaths, he calmed down. "I am sure they will see it my way. Go attain what I need."

The troopers nodded and Karter rode forward a little. "Since the city wall is well guarded up to the first curtain wall, we will attain the sacrifices from where no one will miss them."

Tolin nodded, hand on the tiny wooden box on his saddle. "Go raid the nearest whorehouse. Who will miss them?"

* * * * *

Several hours behind Tolin and his troopers, on the opposite side of Khabnur, Gorias and those with him rode toward the Foundry of Syn. Since it was still daylight then, though growing overcast, they couldn't see the fires of the barbarian army north of the city. Gorias looked in that direction and felt uneasy. When the young ones stopped to look at his ragged expression of perplexity, he motioned for them to press on toward the foundry.

One passing by would almost never have known a complex existed beneath the earth, save for the rows of smoking stacks belching fumes. Like a bizarre buried animal, the Foundry of Syn let its presence be known from the smoke, ash, and grumble given to the skin of the planet. Each of the travelers placed a cloth around their mouths as they slowly rode onto the desolate plain where nothing grew. The paths and usual dirt roads gave the foundry grounds a distant pass.

"I have always wondered why there's no fence around this place," Maddox said.

"Why would there be?" Tammas replied, rounding on him. "Is someone going to break in?"

Even their horses shied away from the vibrating ground. This sensation increased every so often the closer they drew to a series of boulders set away from the stacks.

"They designed it this way so no major force could just take away the stock," Gorias said.

From behind rounded boulders, the sound of stone grinding on steel assaulted them. Annoying enough for all of them to cover their ears up, the sound went on so long, Maddox looked at his grandfather, who quipped, "This has gotta stop sooner or later."

They stepped around the rocks, finding a long ramp grading down into the earth. From out of this dark gap emerged a metallic helmet, far too large for a human to wear. The gigantic helm covered only a portion of the oblong skull this creature bore. An ivory horn pointed straight out each side of the helmet. It had dark green skin and black fur across its back and down its legs in uneven spots. So frightening was the thing that walked up the ramp, all three youths stepped behind Gorias. Maddox alone crept out, appearing somewhat hang-dog.

"By the gods." Tammas faltered as more like this creature stepped from the hole. "What are they?"

Gorias rubbed his beard, studying the creatures who were a tad taller than himself. Each one of the pair, thickset at the waist, sported a huge upper body and rangy arms. The legs were squat and out of proportion, but they gave steady support to the corded muscles covering them. Their skulls resembled a steer in many ways, save for the horns were smaller and curving out from floppy ears, like tusks across a piggish snout. Fat lips parted, revealing what looked like canines rowed across the abrupt mouth.

"They're Minorcs," Gorias said, palms resting on the ends of his swords. "They are crossbred from Orcs and Minotaurs. They make good guards but lousy pets. Mutts like their boss."

The three wore a communal look of confusion. "But..." Kayla said. "Mitre looks nothing like that!"

Gorias nodded. "That's because Stillwell isn't really an ogre."

"Excuse me?" Maddox said with a laugh. "That doesn't make sense. The few times I was inside the foundry, they said these things were *bugbears* or some such thing."

Tammas agreed. "The songs about Stillwell all claim him an ogre, for a hundred years or more."

"Trust one who was there, all right?" Gorias said, with an eyebrow raised. "Stillwell is a crossbreed. He's half Orc, half Bugbear. There aren't any around these parts for thousands of miles, so he gets away with the jape."

"I know an Orc is a large, fighting man, but I have never

seen one," Kayla said. "What's a bugbear?"

"A big, ugly bastard, cousin to an ogre, kinda what Stillwell looks like," Gorias said. "These Minorcs are the result of rape and class warfare afar off. There'll soon be very few pure blooded sectors in this world."

The Minorcs never attempted to speak as the travelers talked. They leaned on their spears and looked them over with swinish eyes.

Hands in the air, Tammas said, "Then why does Mitre call himself an ogre?"

"There really aren't that many ogres around to argue the point," Gorias said, "and you know that's the truth. I wager it was because being an ogre sounded better. Being a bugbear doesn't sound as tough as *ogre* in a tavern or a brothel, now does it? By the looks of these Minorcs they are gelded, eunuchs if you will."

Kayla almost laughed, but restrained it as she eyed the hideous beasts in guard uniforms. "Why do you say that?"

"They're more bloated in their legs and midsections. Plus, you don't hear them talking, do you?" Gorias pointed out with a wave of his huge hand.

Maddox steadily thumbed his new sword's pommel. "Why is that?"

"When they cut a Minorc's sack, he looses the ability to speak. Don't ask why, because I don't know. If it were up to me, they'd do that to a generation of humanity and make the world a better place."

The Minorcs of Syn made no advance. Thick and cruel in their looks, these guards appeared as unforgiving as any human tough they had ever set eyes on.

"Ho, travelers! State your business or die," came the gruff voice from behind the lead Minorc.

When the enormous, one-eyed head became visible, the four humans put on a brave face. The gigantic head pushed through the Minorcs, revealing that it was floating through the air. Gorias took steps backwards. Long tendrils flowing from the head of this one-eyed creature looked like heavy strains of hair. On the end of each strand an eyeball blinked and observed.

"Easy, kids," Gorias said, no fear in his tone. "That's a Beholder. You think Michael Galenson was a nark, those damn things are really hard to shake."

The leathery, almost reptilian, flesh of the Beholder tightened around its mouth as it opened. Rows of fangs decorated its huge maw. "State your business," it said, "or the Minorcs will destroy you, old man, and enslave the children."

Maddox took a step toward his grandfather, who called out, "I'm here to see Mitre Stillwell."

The Beholder's main eye leered at him, while the other eyeballs looked over the three. Strands moving in snaky symmetry, it growled, "Master Stillwell sees no one, save for at his invitation. Move on or sell your youths as slaves to the foundry."

"Tell him Gorias La Gaul would like a brief audience."

The Minorcs exchanged glances while the Beholder dropped the serious expression then burst out laughing. "Shall I tell him the all-father Adam has stopped by with a bushel of apples? Can I say that Gilgamesh has danced past in search of eternal life while I am at it? Mitre will be thrilled in any case."

Hands flexing, Gorias sighed. "The Beholders are short on mirth, too, kids. I guess that's what you can expect out of wizards making trouble with flesh and bone experiments." He quickly drew out both of his swords. The lead Minorc nearly fell to his backside. "You can tell him I would like to talk with him, briefly, or I'll feed your ugly assed Minorcs to the damned leeches."

The Minorcs looked to their leader. Pondering this, the Beholder said, "Leave your mounts with Igao here." The eyestrands pointed at the Minorc in front. "He will tend to them. The rest, come below with me. I will see if I can talk to Mitre."

They dismounted and handed their reins to the one called Igao.

However, when they pulled their bows about themselves, the Beholder said, "No weapons in the foundry whatsoever. It is the law."

Gorias waved to the young ones and they disarmed. He

placed his swords back in their holsters. "It would take too long to disarm me, shorty. You'll have to take me on in as an honorable man."

The lead Minorc gave a shrug and the Beholder said, "You pull a weapon out, you are as good as dead in here anyway. All of the guards are armed Minorcs and my brethren, the Beholders, watch everything. There is but one way out of the Foundry of Syn."

The lead Minorc then produced a bag from under a metal plate that covered his pants pocket. He took out small, waxen plugs and offered them to the strangers.

"It will help your ears," the Beholder explained. "Day after day, one will go deaf from the noises."

As they inserted these devices and walked down the stone ramp, Maddox wiped sweat from his brow and said, "Perhaps we should wait outside."

The Beholder regarded Kayla, who held a defensive pose, and said, "She should, at least. There is no call for an unfamiliar one amongst the workers."

Her nostrils flared and she shot back hotly, "There are many women enslaved below, no?" Her index finger stabbed at the Beholder.

The Beholder studied her up and down with its strands before saying, "It would be ghastly for them to see one as hygienic and handsome as you. I sense you have an egg ready to drop any time. Others will sense this as well."

Tammas rolled his eyes toward the stone ceiling in the tunnel, but Maddox couldn't resist a laugh. Kayla leered at him and Gorias sighed. Kayla was considered no great beauty whatsoever, but compared to what toiled below it would be too much of a distraction.

"Kayla, Maddox, you go on and wait outside. Tammas, come along with me."

Maddox then pointed at his own chest. "You meant me, right?"

The old warrior extended his index finger at Tammas. "I want the kid to come along. It'll be a pivotal experience for him. Maddox, you two go outside and try to keep from killing each other."

Her face long and hurt, Kayla folded her arms under her breasts as she turned away.

Maddox, confused at the finality of Gorias' words, shook his head as he left. Tammas wore a stunned look.

"Maddox will understand in time," Gorias said.

Down flat stone steps they went. The grind of gritty hinges echoed, and the heat blasted them in the face. Heavy footfalls of the Minorcs dulled as the sound level began to rise.

Tammas folded his hands and tried not to tremble. "Like stepping into Hell itself."

Gorias winked, the clang of armor in his ears. "I think that's a little different. Smell is about the same, though."

When the stone door slid closed behind them, the difference between Earth and Hell blurred. All along the left side of the descending ramp hung polished weapons, a gallery of what they produced below all inserted into finely honed stone slots. Heavy broadswords, short staves, daggers, axes and lances decorated this wall of fame for the Foundry of Syn.

Another Minorc guard stood at an opening of two smaller doors. He eyed the people coming toward him and took down a heavy link chain that sprawled over the entrance. Passing him, they descended a series of steps carved into the sandstone surroundings. Off to their right the great cavern crawled forth. A sturdy metallic rail kept them from falling over into the expanse. Gorias touched it and felt the heat stored in it.

Tammas rubbed the sweat from around his eyes and looked across at the churning pots of molten fire. "How do they feed such a thing?"

Gorias waved a hand at the many stout men near the ceiling, who worked cranks for the ventilation billows, and said, "I would guess there's a mine farther down, no? The raw ores and whatever it takes to fuel the torches or facilities are brought up from there."

The Beholder gazed at them with the strands in the back of its head and never answered.

The set up painted out eerie and truly effective. A deadly symmetry to it all, Gorias thought, like a spider's web. However,

Stillwell's office didn't lie in the middle of the plant. They walked away from that and along the side of the massive production floor.

Noise reigned, for the grinding and hammering didn't stop. Countless workers labored in the ungodly heat, barely clad in loincloths. Sweat glistened on them and they frequently drank from heavy containers. The Minorc taskmaster walked a catwalk above them. A Beholder, identical to the one leading the two from the surface, watched a worker lean against a pallet full of sword cases. Staring at the taskmaster, some mental communication took place for the Minorc then unreeled his whip. The lash struck the worker on his back and he screamed. No one around seemed to notice this nightmarish display save for Tammas and Gorias.

After several minutes, Gorias drew his leather flask and drank from it then gave it to Tammas. As the youth drank, he noted many workers stared at him. Quickly, he handed the flask back to La Gaul. "That was wine!"

"It's great for the blood," Gorias said. "Quaint place."

"Yes."

"Feels like one could expect a dagger in your back at any moment, aye?"

Tammas rubbed sweat from his eyes but didn't reply.

The Minorc unlocked a door in front of them to let them on to the next catwalk. His keys were so small they were nearly lost in the huge fist.

Down farther they walked until they reached the main level of the foundry. Their breathing proved hard and the acrid aroma grew more powerful as they walked across the lines of men hammering out swords. Many women sat, wrapping leathery bands around handles.

Amid these workers toiled an usually tall man, probably as big as Gorias. He honed blades on a grinding wheel then used a small wet stone by hand. The vents from above washed air over him. When he looked up, they saw this worker had but one eye. His left eye was ruined and healed over, his mouth locked in an eternal grimace. The muscle bound man kept to his task, but his eye told a tale. Gorias asked his identity.

"That is Noel," the Beholder said. "He was one of Mitre Stillwell's best supervisors back when he let humans do that task. However, he fell out of favor with the ogre."

Tammas leaned in to get a better view. "How so?"

The Beholder whispered, "You know how it is with two big men. Mitre has a manhood complex, as do all creatures born with a penis. Noel was a lover of great capacity, it is said. Stillwell thought Noel plotted against him. I don't think he did. Noel was smarter than any of them and would never let something as petty as a female stand in the way of his goals. But to make an example of him they put out his eye, cut out his tongue, and chained him down amongst the lowly workers. It shows the others what happens in the case of rebellion."

Gorias stared at Noel then the Minorcs. "It has to be a bitch being herded by a bunch of creatures with no balls. Just ironic, that's all."

They moved across the main production floor and up another flight of stairs before they felt cool air on their faces. After ascending a great distance, they were led into the offices of Mitre Stillwell.

The red-headed creature peered up from a clipboard in his hands. "La Gaul." His surprise turned sly. "I see you're here. You come to visit this person of great taste and wonderful discernment for the better things in life?"

"We must talk, you bugbear bastard." Gorias closed the door.

❖ ❖ ❖ ❖ ❖

Maddox La Gaul glanced at the entrance to the foundry and frowned. Hands on his belt, he spat, making no attempt to hide his displeasure at being yoked with Kayla. Kicking at nothing on the ground, he twisted as if an invisible hand slapped him.

The daughter of Lira Rhan, however, made no eye contact with Gorias' grandson. She cleaned the shoes of her horse and said quietly, "No use pouting. It doesn't become you, even on your worst days."

"Why didn't he take me with him?"

"Who knows?"

"It doesn't make any sense."

"Perhaps you over estimate your importance."

Maddox raged on. "Tammas is a child and knows nothing about the world, much less keeping a straight face in the eyes of danger. Educational? Hah. Breathing every day is a new experience for him. You and he nearly pissed your pants at the sight of those Beholders. I've seen them before."

"Angry that those in the foundry cannot see you on Gorias' arm?" Kayla said, a hint of sarcasm in her voice. "One more chance to bleed the legend of Gorias dry and make your shadow grow longer? I think that's why you whine like a girl."

Now his stare blazed at her. In that moment, full of anger, Maddox La Gaul resembled his grandfather a great deal. "I'm glad I never saw anything in you. You're just a hanger on with no imagination."

"It's true I searched for your grandfather in you." There was no sadness in her tone. "You have a great deal of road to tread before you're a quarter of the man he is." She expected Maddox to snap back and gave him a fierce expression.

He looked off into the distance, far to the north, and said nothing for a long time. "Life is a teacher, girl. I have a long way to go. The old man is a lover of life. Well, he was at one time. I can feel what he feels in his blood--the desires, the wanton lust, and the eagerness to fight."

Kayla ignored his words. "I expected you to flee by now. There's a bad war coming."

"So what? Like you will die in it. You can always go back to mommy." His voice turned grim. "No, I must stay with the old man until the end. Running away isn't an option."

"Do you fear Gorias hunting you down to kill you?"

Maddox raised an eyebrow. "There's nothing in me that allows me to run. It is not in my nature, as useless as you think I may be for women and drink. There's a time when every man must face his destiny, son of man or son of gods. I've had my fun, but I'll answer the call when it's made, make no mistake. I'll fight and I'll die like I'm supposed to."

Kayla returned to her work, but this time, her pale fingers shook. For some reason, she couldn't stop this action.

❈ ❈ ❈ ❈ ❈

Tolin walked in a large circle in the dead grass of late winter. His lips worked in soundless curses and groans as his troopers whisper to one another, "Zillian refused his request." The troopers guarded a crude altar they had set up out of stones. On it lay the body of an aging prostitute who had been vivisected to obtain enough blood for Tolin's contact spell. The archaic scarlet designs in the grass and on Tolin's face faded with his sweat and with the tramp of his boots.

With a disagreeable roar, he placed a foot on the body of the woman and pointed at the other whores the men had brought. "You did well to bring enough of these along, men. You knew I might want to call out to the realms beyond if Zillian refused my request."

Captain Karter nodded, still at attention. "I have served you for years, sir. I know your ideas and desires, if not your perfected will."

Tolin pointed at the open space. "Lay the five out and dig a hole in the middle."

"Yes sir," the men said as one.

Still struggling against their bonds, the women were laid out at perfect angles, forming five points to a design that terminated at the waist of Tolin. The troopers then grabbed their tiny shovels used in making foxholes for long attacks. In time, they scooped out a basin by the heads of the women that ran fairly deep in the earth.

The troopers handed Tolin heavy gloves from his saddlebags. These gauntlets held sharp knives on each finger. Tolin howled to the shifting sky and slashed downward, cutting the throats of two prostitutes. He gouged the necks cross, causing the blood to spurt at him. The others screamed under their gags as he delivered their fates. He stood at the center of the five points of shooting blood.

When the words of his entreaty were uttered, the blood congealed on him like jelly. Soon, it fell off and formed into a scarlet mass. This blob turned an orangey hue and rose up like a serpent. Its density faded and transformed into a beam of light, arcing to the sky.

Far away in the North, there arose a roar that trumpeted across the land. It was greater than any horn of war and a sound unheard in centuries.

It was the call of a dragon.

CHAPTER XI

LANNON, MITRE, AND THE SUMMONING

Deep in the fortress of Kanoch, Lannon once again met Lord Nosmada near the Chamber of Redemption. This time Nosmada required no aid in walking. He moved with measured strides yet his legs quivered, appearing feeble. Lannon kept a respectful distance and slowed his pace so as not to out distance his master.

Nosmada asked him with weariness in his voice, "How is Zillian after speaking with the general?"

"Zillian is very weak, sire, as always after using her viewing."

Nosmada's face became more vital and rage rose in him, but his words remained steady as he said, "I wasn't planning for her to use her magicks yet. Tolin requested an audience and isn't powerful enough in his state to conduct such magicks. It took more out of my Zillian. Bastard."

"He sounds quite determined, Lord."

In his place of rest, Nosmada reclined and pondered his words. He told Lannon to go care for Zillian. Just as he was leaving, Nosmada said in a fatigued tone, "How long have you served me?"

"Most of my adult years, sir. Not all in your inner chambers, but for most of my life." Nosmada already knew this, but he answered him anyway.

"I contemplated your words to me earlier, but refresh my memory. What do they say of me in the outside world?"

Lannon didn't answer right away.

Nosmada smiled. "You choose your words carefully. That's wise and amusing unto my very soul. But be honest. Entertain me with words, good or ill, from outside these walls. I'm not likely to kill such a faithful servant as you, am I?"

"Oh, I don't listen to idle gossip, sire."

"But I wager they fear you in the taverns and halls because you work for me, no?" Nosmada offered in a kind voice.

Lannon couldn't help but smile. "True, sire, your patronage inspires fear, loathing, and love."

Nosmada laughed. "I can see the fear and loathing, but love? Oh, do tell. How does the accursed one of Earth inspire love?"

"It's an element of what bards call celebrity or being associated with legendary status. Since there are so many legends and tales about you, they think any man who serves you so long and lives must have favor in your eyes. I am not foolish enough to be that arrogant. I serve and go home. However, the young females in the taverns, or the girls that don't go to saloons, just want to be close to your aura, your legend."

"So." Nosmada laid his head back. "You get many women because they are caught up in my thrall?"

"That's about correct, sir."

"No wonder you serve me gladly."

"There are worse duties, sir. May I ask a simple question?"

"We shall see if I answer it. Go on."

"Have you ever met Gorias La Gaul? He's incredibly long lived, such as yourself…"

Nosmada shrugged. "Great age is no fantastic exploit in these times. Most are long lived in this day, if they don't end up murdered. No, I have never met Gorias La Gaul. He has lived but seven centuries while I have trod this planet much longer. I respect him in that there are so few like him on Earth. That barbarian king of Albion, far off from here, is like Gorias. They are both powerful bastards who care not for any but themselves."

"I see."

"Yet, they are hailed as heroes. It baffles one side of me, but the human side understands. People are frail and need something to believe in. If they refuse to put their faith in gods, they will put it in men. If not men, they will screw up their courage and follow a legend farther than any god can send them."

"Then what is your desire, sir? What is it that you want?" He added quickly, "If I may ask."

144

Nosmada looked at the ceiling. "It isn't about control, power and destruction. It's simple yet complex. It's all about blood, everything in life. That's one reason Tolin hates Gorias so." Nosmada opened both hands and gaped at his fingers. "You see, he hates him due to his soul--that of a dragon—and for exterminating his kindred. His own flesh hates him because Gorias sired him. Though he isn't always aware of that part of himself, it's an important element in it all."

"I understand now."

"Tolin's greatest sin is that he is *not* Gorias," Nosmada said. "Imagine growing up in that shadow? He certainly attained a different kind of fame."

"Why didn't you grant General Tolin his wish, sir?"

"Why? Because I didn't."

"Will he be angry and try to contact the dragon himself?"

"Probably." Nosmada turned over on the bed, saying, "He does wrong, yet I will forgive him."

"Permit me one last question, sire. Why would you do that?"

"I'm the only one who can. Forgiveness is better than punishment. A man punished is a man who carries vengeance to new and bizarre lengths to be, in the end, justified in his actions or to be forgiven. Forgive him and vengeance will not grow in his heart."

*****

Gorias sat across the vast table from the massive creature. Mitre Stillwell's one good eye looked at him then the young man who stood beside.

"Who are you, schoolboy?" Mitre said, sounding insulted at the presence of the youth.

"I am no one," Tammas said. "Just a bard traveling with Maddox La Gaul."

Gorias imparted a glance at the young man that almost showed pride in the words spoken by the bard.

"Bards." Stillwell snorted via his enormous nostrils. "I killed a bard once, right on stage, God Almighty." He glared at the ceiling as if answers were printed there to read. "Must be fifty, sixty years ago if it was a day."

Tammas lifted both eyebrows and said, "There is a song, a warning ballad for bards not to travel into the ice lands ruled by Gorm the—"

With a slice of a great paw, Stillwell cut him off. "Hangman. Yes, I know of the area. Gorm the Hangman ruled it with an iron fist. Fear of him never stopped me from charging the stage and ripping the fool bard's throat out."

"Why did you do it?"

"Not fear Gorm or kill the bard? I didn't fear Gorm because I was too drunk. I ripped the throat from the bard because I hated his song, and I was too drunk."

"I was shocked to see you in a position of regular authority," Gorias said. "You always did drink too much."

Mitre was very still, and then he stifled a laugh before saying, "Look who is talking, such a pure man. My work interferes with my drinking, that's certain." He cleared his throat. "So you come to my foundry to see me. You still have stones, old one."

"Yer no spring rooster yerself," Gorias retorted, lifting the cloth that covered the table. A look of surprise spread on the old warrior's face.

Mitre rolled his eye and sighed. "The little lackey is on break. I'm not a devil."

Gorias shrugged, glancing at the filmy curtain in the corner of the office. "I guess what goes on in a bar doesn't go on in here as often, eh?"

"They all serve me here,," the ogre said hotly, gripping the desk edge. "They are all my bitches if need be."

"And that's all this is for you?" Gorias said, his boots nudging the front of the desk. "Making stern weapons for the nameless armies who pay you and being overlord over all of these sad, wasted lives?"

Now Mitre shrugged then tapped the desk top with his right thumb. "It's a living. Some need to feel the chill touch of fear in their spines to perform well at anything. I'm just a provider."

"Not much of a life for such an adventurer," Gorias needled him.

"Things change." Mitre sent him a serious stare.

"Apparently. The great *Ogre* Stillwell, slayer of men, defeater of armies, deflowerer of virgins now sits, beats down the weak and gets oral gratification from fat little slobs."

Non-plussed by his words, Mitre took a drink from an enormous ceramic mug and said, "Just because you haven't seen fit to die yet, don't cast stones on the latter stages of my life."

Gorias leaned forward. "Let's cut to it, old bugbear. Why was that puke sniffer Michael Galenson following me? Why?"

"I think you know." Mitre belched, thumbing his drink. "Tell me about it."

"You didn't count on me showing up, did you? But you knew my grandson was a necromancer, or played at being one."

"He played at being your grandson to get women. A good racket if you can run it, I suppose."

"Anyway, you never counted on my presence in the coming affair. Old or not, no matter what your bluster, you didn't want any X-factors in your scheme."

Mitre's chuckle gurgled up from his belly. "This is fabulous, you old fart. What scheme is that?"

"Maddox named you as the dealer in souls. I can see your work a mile off. You swapped soul jewels with that damned prick, De Balm. He was always working an angle with the forces of darkness. Most little dicked wizards are."

"He's dead now, Robyn?"

"I killed him."

"Oh?"

"Yeah, a couple times. He worked one approach when Maddox stole the soul jewels. My grandson is still not the brightest star in the sky, but that's youth."

"True."

"You knew his desire to please his friends in the Cult of Wyss and you screwed him. Maddox never knew what he was doing, but could feel the spirits were wrong. He was double-crossed by the cult, but they humped the dog already, eh? You made sure that their dreaded master wasn't ready to arise from the dead by changing the crystals around long beforehand."

"My, what a story!" Mitre smiled. "Where's that little slob of mine?"

Gorias continued. "Wyss arisen from the dead, a beacon unto his servants, isn't what you wanted at all. Your dope fiend mole said you sold the soul of Wyss to the Cult of the Dragon in the desert of Dundayin long ago."

"So Michael told you about my dealings with those in the ruins of Larak," Mitre said. "There's no honor in a dope fiend."

"True," Gorias agreed, shuffling his boots. "I knew an arisen Wyss would be of no use as his old self to you. What I cannot gather is why trade that soul off to the dragon cult? Instilling such a society with such an article--there's no point to it beyond sheer cruelty against the world."

Mitre laughed heartily, a disturbing sound to anyone nearby. "True, old man. What good would such a cult have for the soul of Wyss? I mean really, they want the sentient dragons of old to lead them. What good would a doom cult leader do such folk?"

Gorias wiped sweat from his forehead and his eyes widened. "They don't realize it, do they? They think they have the soul of a dragon."

"My, my, you're still bright for a dimming star," Mitre said.

Tammas looked from one to the other and said to Gorias, "What do you both mean?"

Gorias stood up. "The dragon cult would have the time, resources, and will to try to raise a dragon from the dead. It would take a great many lives and a great deal of blood to perform such a feat. Once they had a body close to being reconstituted via their magic, they would need a soul for their creation. Yet there are no souls of dragons about any more, are there?"

Mitre said dryly, "Save for what walks in the breast of Tolin La Gaul."

"This is but a fable," Tammas said, trembling. "The tales of the Draco-Lich arising from the sands are as old as those about..."

148

"Those of Gorias La Gaul being a real person? We all know what manure those stories are, aye, boy? Tell me one about Mitre Stillwell, ostracized outlaw, making good on a sale of souls for a place to rest his weary head."

Tammas stumbled back, but Gorias grabbed his wrist. "Steady, boy. I see how it is, old ogre."

Mitre grinned wider, an elbow on the desk. "Judicious flattery will get you no where with me."

"To unleash that wickedness on this world, that is just evil!" Tammas stammered, setting his feet.

Mitre extended his arms out. "Come give me a kiss, boy. You have met evil incarnate this day. How's this for an adventure? Kills boredom, doesn't it?"

"I recognize what Wyss knows, old ogre," Gorias said. "You didn't want the Cult of Wyss to have him, but damn, why give that secret to the dragon cult…" His voice trailed off as it all came to him.

"Can you get it through your skull, old warrior, from one dying man to another? Perhaps for you, deliverance will come, but others have to make their own bridge."

"Come on, Tammas." Gorias snorted and turned away from Stillwell.

Tammas glared at Mitre and his glance stuck. When the big creature stood, it was a stumbling move. The filmy curtain in the corner of the office fell. The youth saw a metal ladder leading up into the ceiling, wide enough to hold three men, or a bastard bugbear posing as an ogre.

"It's too late to stop it now," Mitre said. "A storm is brewing fast. One from which no man can hide. We will all die, but even Nosmada will be my ever loving bitch in the end."

"I'd tell you to go to Hell, but that goes without saying."

Hands becoming giant fists, Mitre replied, "There's no such thing as a bloodless war, boys."

"You made a deal with Hell itself."

"Where's the adventure in throwing in one's lot on the side assured of a win?" Mitre said, not missing a beat.

La Gaul stormed from the office and rounded a corner. The Minorcs and Beholders gave him and Tammas a great deal of room. The two kept walking fast. Once, Gorias threw a shoulder in the direction of a Beholder nearby. The eerie creature backed off fast. A few times Tammas tried to stop Gorias to question him, but the old man held his tongue.

Crossing over the foundry on the catwalk, Gorias paused and looked down at the large one called Noel. The glistening worker faced up at him and stopped in his labors. Noel ignored the lash from the Minorc as their eyes met. Tammas peeked down at Noel then at the old man next to him.

Gorias said with acid in his tone, "Remember this day, Tammas. Remember it well, for it will matter."

With that, Gorias La Gaul left the Foundry of Syn, never to return.

❖ ❖ ❖ ❖ ❖

In the fortress of Kanoch, Zillian wailed in agony. She slumped at her caldron and wept. Her loud cries caused Lannon to open the door and summon their dark Lord Nosmada.

Kneeling beside the frail woman, Nosmada bore her head up and asked, "What was it you saw? Was it a nameless horror dire, a plan hatched against us? Tell it unto me."

"Tolin has gone against our wishes as we feared," Zillian said, her hollow cheeks void of any color. "He has called on his former self, reached out to his blood kin to aid in an act most vile. This will undermine our plans, my lord and savior Nosmada."

He stood, supporting her as he peered into the caldron. The evaporating imagery showed Nosmada all he needed to see.

"Damn them all," he said, but little venom lurked in his words. "Tolin knows not what commands that flesh arisen from the sand. He will damage my strategy in his haste. I need time."

"Her earlier visions of the savages from the bleak hills of the North weren't comforting," Lannon said. "That army is closing in on Tolin's forces and on Khabnur."

Nosmada grunted bitter agreement. "There are more of them than we thought. What can they do to our forces, really? They're better at butchery, not real battle."

Zillian stumbled to a chair. "My Lord, Gorias served our purpose in destroying what was Wyss, but even he was deceived. Wyss is more powerful now than ever. I can distinguish the mind of Tolin and it is clear to me, yet cloaked in darkest malevolence. The knowledge Wyss possesses will destabilize your plan."

Nosmada considered this. "You must seek out La Gaul, soon." He noted her feeble frame, the pain in her empty eyes, and he smiled. "Soon. I shall send for more blood. Some of my precious store can be used for this." He knelt and said to her gently. "What am I if I am blinded, dear woman?"

Facing the caldron, he concentrated on the fading image from the mind of Tolin--an image of the Draco-Lich, the undead dragon, as it descended on a village north of Khabnur.

CHAPTER XII

REVELATIONS OF THE OGRE

As Maddox, Kayla, and Tammas re-armed and mounted up, Maddox quipped, "That didn't take long."

"You're just delighted we came back," Gorias said. "Mitre is indeed a bastard, though not lacking rough mirth. Taking the foundry would be tough for one man, unless he had an army behind him."

He looked at the plumes of smoke and thought. Using his viewer, he checked far to the southwest. The fires of the army of Nosmada reflected off the gathering clouds. To the north, the fires of the barbarian horde shone plainly on the sky as well. He then peered at the sprawling city and frowned.

Kayla looked up at him, half serious, half in a dream. "Lord La Gaul? What is it?"

He shook his head fast, as if he cleared a slate. Lines of exhaustion brought his face down. "All laid out for them and no one can see it. It's hard not to think like a soldier, even after all these years. One always fights on the run and sees possibilities for battle. Anyhow, we have to go. We must make the city by nightfall. Perhaps the whorehouse will put us up for the night."

"Tammas is confused, Grandfather."

"You're telling me," Gorias jeered as he climbed into the saddle.

"Seriously, what's this all about?"

"Listen good, kids, because I think I can only say this once. Mitre Stillwell thinks everyone else is like him and shares his point of view. Not all of us are monsters obsessed with want. Anyway, he has everything he can want in this life, but look at him. He's getting older, weaker, and wants what Lord Nosmada wants."

"Which is?" Kayla asked.

"Immortality. While I think most regular folk want

immortality even in this putrid world, it is impossible to achieve. They want to live forever here because the afterlife scares the piss out of them, no matter how much they don't want to admit it. I think Nosmada and Mitre both want it but by different means. I think that Mitre has come to face that thing we all do after centuries of existence."

"And that is?" Kayla said.

Gorias winked. "Non-existence. He has seen enough to know his flesh is frail and his soul carries on after this husk is gone." Gorias held out his rough, weathered fingers and then continued. "Facing eternity unbound from his mortal flesh isn't a comfortable idea, seeing as the life he has led isn't up to anyone's definition of purity."

Maddox reined his horse in and they all paused. "How do you come by all of this? Because what you say has arisen from the soul of Wyss? A Draco Lich?"

Tammas offered timidly, "Perhaps you think your grandfather is putting his own fear of mortality on another?" Gorias shot the youth a hard look and Tammas swiftly added, "I said he may think it, not I, Lord La Gaul."

La Gaul smirked. "If you think I'm one from the days of antiquity, you're erroneous. Do any of you know how old Nosmada is? He's getting up there, for he was ancient when I was born. Yeah, that old. He's smart enough to realize death is inevitable. However, from the power over the leeches and his interest in Wyss, I fear he's up to a grand scheme that far dwarfs a military skirmish between his armies and those of the West."

"This is all over souls or fear of death?" Kayla spoke. "These men play grand games with lives and blood for their own interest in their soul?"

Gorias raised an eyebrow. "That's all you have, sister, in the end. Mitre? He's thinking about his as well. I don't know if creatures like Mitre, degenerate residue from a bygone age, have souls. Mitre thinks he has one and that's all that matters, I guess. Stillwell is more isolated in his way of thinking than a personality like Nosmada. Mitre is worried about himself alone. Nosmada thinks the world is not right without him."

Maddox wrinkled his nose and proclaimed the obvious: "Mitre is an ogre, or whatever, and thus egotistical by nature."

Gorias kicked his horse to a trot and gave the fading sun a glance. "So are humans, but all such things as Ogres or Minorcs are the flawed versions of human beings, son. Ogres are the freakish result of problems in human blood. Magic and sex? No good can come of it, no joke implied. That's how one gets ogres on this plain. Mitre is male, but he isn't a man. Nosmada is a man, believe me."

Tammas and Maddox exchanged looks and Kayla rolled her eyes at their reaction to his words.

"My father once told me that being born male is by chance, being a man is a choice. Big difference. However, this isn't a matter of personal responsibility, ability in the bedroom, or fighting. This is a deal for eternity or for control of one's eternal soul. If one can muscle that situation, my, but isn't that a manly task?"

Tammas drew back and fired at a passing leech. The shaft impaled the creature's head, almost ear to ear. "How can one muscle the afterlife?"

"People will try anything," Gorias said. "Some sell their souls to demons in exchange for earthly wealth or supposed control of human souls in the afterlife. They commit great acts of evil to create a dark mansion for themselves in Hell."

Kayla fired at a leech emerging from a ditch by the road and huffed, "Preposterous!"

"And yet," Gorias said, "it happens. While Mitre is out to free the soul of Wyss into the body of that arisen dragon, he knows a great evil will come of it. That's his bid for favor in the afterlife. Nosmada, well, his act is different. While perceived as evil, Nosmada has a different perspective than a back stabbing ogre."

"Why is that?" Maddox asked as they retrieved their arrows from the dead bodies of the fallen leeches. Kayla sliced off the heads of the fallen ones and bounded back to her horse.

"Because," Gorias said, matter of factly. "Nosmada has spoken to God himself. That would change anyone's view on the afterlife."

"Lord La Gaul," Kayla said gently as she looked up at the old one in the saddle. "There are great tales of who Nosmada is exactly. They say that isn't his name and he's a man with a great curse. Who is he?"

"He's..." Gorias started to say then coughed. "It's rather complicated. However, he isn't my concern. The madness of that damned ogre is. Would that I could've killed his fat ass and walked out of the foundry, but spite would not stop what he has set in motion. We'd have never made it out alive. He wants the *Daemonolateria* back in this world. It's his bid with the demonic forces beyond to curry favor. Yes, he made a deal with a lord darker than Nosmada."

"That book," Maddox said, "will only cause men and demons to dance closer together. The fragments of it around now are bad enough."

"You see, if Stillwell wants that damn thing back on this plain in full, he really has given up living forever in this world. He wants favor, a position if you will, in the dark realms of the afterlife. If I know him, the situation will be like the one he has now."

Tammas shook his head. "I am confused, sir. What do you mean?"

"He wants an arrangement of control, to be an overlord if you will. Denizen Lordship is the term for those condemned to Hell who serve the demons, torturing their fellow condemned. A supervisor over the lost souls here, and the sonofabitch wants the job in the afterlife."

"To allow an undead mage to return as a Draco-Lich, just to get the Daemonolateria back on Earth, thus causing mayhem and more souls to be damned," Kayla said. "What a bastard Mitre must be."

"He's the prince of them," Gorias conceded. "Mitre always was making a deal for his big ass. To get his version of support from the demon horde, to help fulfill their agenda for the twisting of humankind, Mitre will do this great evil. He believes their demonic rhetoric that promises he will be rewarded for his acts."

Maddox eyed his grandfather as they rode. "You doubt this?"

"Stillwell is a dupe. What fool would believe any deal struck up with demons would hold water off the earthly plain?"

"But why would he trust them?" Tammas said. "They are demons!"

Gorias laughed. "Good show, Tammas. There's hope for you yet. I shall buy you a whore for your great thinking."

The boy shook his head. "I need no sex to clear my head."

The old man sighed. "I certainly do. All of this thinking of unfathomable mysteries is making me hot down below."

"Grandfather, don't *you* have some sort of bargain with those not of Earth?"

"Well, I talked myself out of that one, didn't I. Angels are demons in better clothes. The demons despise this realm and all of us, but they are not all powerful or all knowing. They will do great acts, promise many false effects to further the spread of iniquity. The angels saw to it that the original texts of the Daemonolateria were destroyed via their servants. What remains scattered on this world is rewritten, badly transcribed, and perverted."

"If the angels are so great, why didn't they destroy it all?" Kayla said. "Why hasn't Almighty God stopped this in its tracks?"

As the many pickets of the hired warriors around Khabnur looked them over and whispered *"La Gaul"* Gorias said, "Fair question. The angels aren't omnipotent or omniscient, either. God, from what I see, lets his children on earth rise and fall by their own hand. That is freedom for you, eh? A parent cannot be a dictator. My son is a complete waste of flesh and air, so who am I to wave my prick at God? He watches and sees how we run the maze, I guess."

"Doesn't sound fair," Maddox muttered.

"No one said it was supposed to be. Don't be a baby. Life is awful and one has to do the best one can."

"Why would God be at such mischief?" Tammas said.

"Perhaps to see if his children deserve to survive in this world. Any man close to the earth will tell you that, at times, one has to fish or cut bait. Think on the theory this way: Hold your own baby in your hands and swear you would do anything for it, even die for it. The baby doesn't even know you by name, save for the sensation of your care. Yet you understand that it is a part of you, flesh and bone. You'll die for your children even if they reject you. That's how God is with us. Even if we give him the brush off, I wager he's always there. Does his patience have a limit? Sometime I think it makes him mad he made us."

After riding on for a while, they dismounted at the whorehouse of Madam Wilkens. Gorias looked up and held out his hands to restrain them all from walking forward.

"What?" Maddox asked.

"The door is open." Gorias waved then drew both his swords. "Something is wrong."

A few of the hired mercenaries walked up behind them cautiously, making no attempt to hide their approach. One waved as if to make sure they knew his intent was friendly.

"What do you want?" Gorias said.

The young merc swallowed and backed up, but the older man with him said, "We wanted the same thing as you earlier today, but the place is cleaned out."

Kayla drew her dagger and went to the open door with great caution. She pointed at the interior and the overturned chairs. "Struggle?"

Gorias pointed at the side of the doorframe then at the ground. Tammas turned and suppressed a wretch. Blood spattered on the fractured wood didn't tell the complete tale, but the fingers on the porch did.

"Looks like the Madam didn't want to leave," Kayla said.

Maddox glared at her. "How do you know it was her?"

She nudged the board nearest the fingers with her boot. "That's her opal ring. I saw it when Tammas played the song to Gorias."

Gorias opened the door to the building wide then gave the mercs a look. "Damned attentive, ain't she?"

Maddox followed him into the alcove and watched the old man replace his swords in the slots. "What now?"

Gorias sighed and grabbed the banister. "Lock the place down against leeches. Try to scrap up some food. May as well get some sleep, all of you. I have a lot to do on the morrow."

THRALL

The youths traded glances as Gorias climbed the stairway.

❀ ❀ ❀ ❀ ❀

Mitre Stillwell drank deeply from his oversized flagon. The bitter beer went down fast as he watched the Beholders feed. It was nearly time for the night shift janitorial staff to awaken. First, the Beholders satiated themselves on the sleeping workers' dreams. Little did the workers realize floating heads sucked the very essences of their sleep time from their being. They awoke weary and had to be beaten severely due to slow performance. These lashings led to more nightmares, thus feeding the Beholders more astringent mental bile.

The monstrous leader of the foundry mused not over the lives being crippled by his Beholder servants but over La Gaul. He knew he could easily replace the slaves, but ridding himself of La Gaul's memory was impossible.

"Damn you, Gorias," Mitre said and one guard gazed up.

He walked through the cooler areas of the production line, glancing back at the personnel in the foundry. Many of these areas and rooms were reserved for kinder crafting points on blades, special designs, and superior work endowed by artisans to the craft. The attendants here were younger girls or older women who still maintained enough beauty to be blissful in a superior's bed.

They all saluted or nodded, as this wasn't a place of punishment, but an area of refinement and precision. Those who worked here came from the outside or slept their way into a subordinate position. Mitre wasn't without recognition of beauty. He kept an avenue of the loveliest up here. Not that they had much to fear carnally from the old creature, his current state being what it was. All they had to dread from him was death, not molestation or even oral obligations. Stillwell had lackeys for that, ones who wouldn't talk.

Again, La Gaul walked through his mind. He cursed the old man for his very presence. "Why here and now? Bah, a curse on you, La Gaul, from all the demons in Hell and in the name of Almighty

159

God himself. You're a weathered, broken elderly man. You cannot stop my dreams or destiny now."

He stopped walking and talking, for if anything he was practical. It occurred to him that he was not fully convinced the old warrior held no threat.

Looking across the foundry production floor, he spat. "God damn you all."

❀ ❀ ❀ ❀ ❀

General Tolin rode back to his army. He understood their progress was measured and had inched along since he left, per his orders. However, he expected to find them more advanced than he did when Tolin rode west of Khabnur.

Reining his horse in, Tolin looked all over for his forces, knowing they were near from the firelights reflecting off the clouds in the distance. "Where are they? Why have they not advanced?"

"I'm sure there is a good reason, General," Captain Karter said.

"There better be." Tolin brooded and kicked his mount.

As he rode on, he recalled the dreamy communion he felt during the ceremony. A smile played on his hideous mouth, thinking of the tune in his head from the being who touched his mind.

> *"Father of the dragons is going to love you*
> *Fulfill your dreams, your nightmares too*
> *Give you an embrace that is going to last.*
> *Wrapped in his wings and claws so fast*
> *Now they all, fly on*
> *'Neath the moon, stars and the sun.*
> *They all fly on*
> *Searching for one more soul to be won!"*

They were a few miles from the army when the pickets met them. Karter pointed at the ground and sighed. "By the looks of it, they advanced a ways and had a run in with another force. Small, but enough to get their attention."

Tubal looked around as well. "A minor skirmish stopped the army from advancin'."

Tolin saw what they meant. There were large prints left by another set of pickets, feeling out the army of Nosmada. However, these prints were not those of horses. They were large, deep, and round.

"Barbarians," Tolin said like a curse word. "They probably would draw glee that one of their own is known unto the mind of Nosmada. Oh yes, blood kin of the aged barbarian fighter Brock is amongst them. What do they care if we kill a few people? They decided to ride south and arm themselves and attack us just out of spite. Don't they know they are walking into a bloodbath?"

Tubal dismounted, looking at the heavy tracks then at the general. "It is a good thing we have those steel weapons in Syn."

"To Hell with a bunch of barbarian dolts," Tolin said, looking north. "I have played a rather important card. I can feel lives seething out of the earth. Those damned barbarians always talk of their kindred and how everything is in the blood. We shall see about that, eh? We will see whose blood is superior."

In the distance, thunder rolled...or was it laughter?

❀ ❀ ❀ ❀ ❀

Ringing out a rag in a basin, Gorias finished his bathing ritual. Seldom did he remove all of his armor as he did now in the high room of the whorehouse. In-between swipes, he took draws from a tall flagon filled with wine. The scent of Madam Wilkens still lingered in her private bedchamber. He drank to this and to her memory.

Sitting on the luxurious bed, he looked at his armor all laid out on the dresser, cabinet, and floor. After he ran a rough skinned hand over his scarred chest, he realized how vulnerable he was to an attack without his armor on. Early in life he wore little covering. Now, he felt death close by without the dragon skin near to his own.

When a soft knock came to the door, he said, "Perhaps that

is death now."

The door latch clicked and the wooden structure swung inward. Gorias gripped the handle of his heavy dagger, but relaxed at the sight of Kayla Rhan.

Carrying a tray, she shrugged. "I wondered if you wanted some food. We found some jerked beef and nuts still edible." She sat the tray on the desk beside his armor. Pausing, she looked at the dragon skin then at him.

Gorias stood up, naked as the day he was born. "Thank you, sister."

She gave his body the once over. By the lack of trail dust and radiant skin, Kayla looked to have taken a bath since they arrived as well.

"You aren't too proud, are you?"

Gorias dropped to the bed and swung his legs back onto it. "I ceased being that way a long time ago, dear. I'm not quite dead yet."

She stood beside him. "Are you warm enough? Can I fetch you more blankets?"

He closed his eyes and sighed. "I'll survive. Damn place is getting mildewed. Like everything else, this house is rotting away."

"How is your back?"

"You mean from the ride here or for the ride I was expecting to get?"

She laughed lightly. "I never knew if you could do that much anymore. From what you said before, I mean, you were more of a lay back and enjoy kind, you know…"

"I enjoyed what didn't require me to use my back?" Gorias chuckled, jaw raised confidently. "It still works, kid. My back and everything else."

"I'm no kid."

The back of his hand touched her bare thigh. It was soft and his thumb rubbed it. She didn't draw away.

"That you are not."

She reached behind her neck and undid the clasp there. Her full breasts fell free, but not very far. Still youthful, they held their place as she shoved her tunic off her body. Sliding down her undergarment, she let her hands touch the sides of her waist. It was a peculiar move, but one performed to stop her hands from shaking.

Gorias watched her curiously, saying nothing.

She climbed onto the bed then placed herself between his legs. Her hands ran up his thighs. Her lips quivered and Kayla's arms shook.

"What are you doing?" Gorias sat up, eye to eye with her.

She leaned close to his face as one hand gripped his hard manhood. "Hopefully, not making a fool of myself." He touched her hand on himself and it stopped shaking so much.

"Easy, dear," he said gently.

Their lips met as her arm flexed, making him eager. Kayla's breath quickened when their tongues met. She looked down as she worked him and her eyes glowed. Kissing him again, harder this time, she pressed her nipples to his rough chest. His strong hands ran up her belly and to her bosom. She stroked his long self against her belly.

Gorias thought the tough, hard-edged girl felt as soft as silk in his hands.

He then lay back and let her do as she wished. Her dark hair splayed about his midsection. She groaned deep as if a climax came to her before any of it started. In time, she climbed atop of him and discovered if his back still worked or not.

❖❖❖❖❖

In the dead of night, sounds at the side of the house roused Maddox La Gaul. Bolting out of the bed, he grabbed the handle of the heavy broadsword he'd obtained that day. Slipping into the side exit of the looming house, he looked across the connection to the stables.

Heavy footsteps approached from behind. "You placed the mounts in the stables after we entered, correct?"

With a stifled yawn, Tammas replied, "Yeah. Why?"

"It's a tad more active out there than I care for."

Tammas watched Maddox with a frown as the grandson of

Gorias returned to the kitchen area. In this spot they had stored much of their gear. He put the huge sword down and reached for his own. After strapping this weapon to his side, he looked at his grandfather's materials.

"What is it?"

"Bring your bow and back me up," Maddox said, yet never made a move to the side door. Instead, he grabbed two handles out of Gorias' pack. Both youths blinked at the same time, half expecting to see the famed gleaming swords of the fable. Instead, these two swords, well made of steel and perhaps the same size as Gorias' blades, were common weapons.

"Why does he have those?" Tammas said, rubbing sleep from his eyes.

"I can't understand him all of the time. Come along. I can't swing a broadsword in a stable."

"Why..."

Maddox leered at Tammas. His blue eyes burned with the same fire as his grandfather.

Brandishing the two swords, he stepped lightly out the side door and crept into the stable. Glancing back to make sure Tammas had an arrow notched, he moved forward.

Between the slats in the boards, he could see two men inside. They were beginning to lead the horses out when Maddox stepped into the moonlight. Scraping the swords against each other, he said, "Deliverance will come."

One of the men was dressed in heavy leathers and armed. This one jumped at the surprise and went for his weapon. Before he could draw it out, Maddox slashed the air with the swords, striking the man's wrist. As the hand went tumbling into the straw and his scream split the night. His backstroke hit more flesh. Once the blade crossed the man's throat, he screamed no more.

The other man in the stable was much smaller and cried out in terror when he heard Maddox words. He fell beside Gorias' great white horse and broke wind. Terrified of his death, he vented his bowels.

"Not La Gaul," the man mumbled and stood up.

Maddox smiled. "There you are wrong." He turned to Tammas. "What is the crime for horse thieves?"

Tammas swallowed as the grandson of Gorias la Gaul continued to smile.

Once back in their rooms, Maddox settled in to rest. He knew that no one would disturb the mounts again, not after the warning he placed outside the stables.

Tammas peeped in. "Did you have to do that? Was it necessary to hang him up, headless, by the stable with the *horse thief* sign on his chest?"

"Yes."

CHAPTER XIII

RHAN'S REQUEST

Kayla lay beside Gorias all through the night. His huge arm wrapped around her while she nestled her head close to him, hand on his scarred chest. Certainly not the first time the warrior had held a contented young woman next to his body, but he found himself happy she proved true to her outward nature and never spoke a word afterwards. As with most females he knew, he assumed she'd want to converse and share emotions after the act concluded. *No, not this one,* he thought. She expressed her feelings and downright worship of him during the session. He then stroked her hair, thinking of how she burst into tears during orgasm, screaming out she loved him. He believed her. She was something he seldom found--something that scared him. But as with most things he feared, he would never stay close long enough for it to hurt him.

Damn, he thought, *she made me think of emotions after the act…*

Still, the arms of sleep came unto him and he drifted away. Deep fell the slumber, but his dreams were seldom blissful. Gorias dreamt he was a young man again, sitting in a tavern with the enigmatic Ezran Gavreel. While he drank bitter beer, the stranger Ezran downed honey mead.

"They are burning that beautiful woman at the stake," Ezran said, gesturing at the open windows of the saloon.

The tavern owner had thrown open the shutters to reveal an act of execution outside. A grubby man ordered many on the exterior deck to sit down so the tavern goers could enjoy the view without rising.

Beyond the high stake and pile of corded wood arose the serene mountains of Cilicia. The snow-capped peaks, a sight Gorias hadn't seen in centuries, looked down across the tangled growth of glens surrounding the edge of the hamlet. The stabbing stake couldn't spoil the beauty of those mountains. Gorias could feel cool wind on his beard.

"Oh, the black widow?" he said, watching the town guards drop torches and the flames spread. "She killed every husband she ever had and a few that never married her."

"The very same."

"She deserves to die."

Ezran raised an eyebrow and took a drink. "You slept with her?"

Gorias drummed his fingers on the table then nodded. "Of course. It was long ago."

"And you feel nothing watching her go to the flames?"

Gorias swished the contents of his drink. "I wish they'd close the damned shutters and block out the cold."

"Interesting set of ethics you have."

"If I cared for every woman who said she loved me, I'd have to grow an extra heart."

Ezran smiled. "That would give you one and a half then?"

"Stop right there or I'll tell you how much the mountains look like teats."

The curses then screams of the black widow sounded out while Gorias motioned for another drink.

Ezran reflected with curiosity, "I wonder why she killed so many men? Just to gain a living from their estates? Why then the string of murders of clients and others?"

An ample chested wench refilled Gorias' mug. "You ask so that you can tell me. She was a crazy woman. So many are, but then not many males of the species are stable, either."

"Most work at things in life, even if it is a bad thing," Ezran said. "Thieves, murderers, men at arms, or even farmers. They have goals or quests, you understand? They have rituals, strategies, and endings planned out. A free spirit as yourself, you must chart for the future at times."

"At times."

"Even an unbalanced individual keeps going after his or her goal to make life bearable. It keeps a person alive to keep fighting for something or someone. That struggle, that fight for a goal, is the point in their existence. Once they reach their goal many go to pieces, my friend."

"You think too much," Gorias said. "I'm at peace, even if that squirrelly cunt is afire out there. I'm making good money based on my victories and reputation. Someday, they'll come for me in droves. Ridding the world of bad men is good work and a task I'm not soon to run out of stock for."

That day faded, falling under the crush of many other days and other death screams. The choir of slit, gaping throats singing his name, was a familiar sight if not a favorite he awoke to often. Like the name of the smoldering black widow, these images grew fuzzy in time and faded until they lost their ability to induce emotion.

He awoke feeling himself in the mouth of Kayla. Her determination demanded he arrive as he soon did, somewhat angered he couldn't recall most of the waking act. Gorias blinked and fell back into slumber. It didn't last long.

A great many scenes flooded his dreaming moments. Centuries of life and many faces he wished would never return often assailed him. This time he awoke to a fully clothed Kayla Rhan shaking him.

"You must arise and get dressed," she said with desperation in her voice. "My mother is outside!"

"Damn, sister, I'm a little old to worry about a line like that."

Gorias coughed as he swung his legs out of the bed. In his nostrils lingered the smell of Kayla, the smoke of spent candles, and the mysterious scent of sawdust & stale ale.

Her hand on her belt, she wore a wry smile and said. "I will go and speak with her. Lira's guards are amused by Tammas morning songs."

"Glad someone is." Gorias he rubbed his eyes. "They wake me up. I prefer your method, though."

He donned his clothing and dragon skinned armor in thrice the amount of time it used to take him. He then washed his face, over and over. After going downstairs to perform his morning necessities, he joined the group outside.

Lira's sour frown showed her displeasure. The tall woman

stood with a compliment of guards bearing helmets, shields, and corselets, plus a half dozen hard-eyed looking men Gorias guessed as mercenaries.

Hands on her hips, wrapped in her usual aloofness, Lira Rhan glared at him. Her guards seemed to hold their breath as the legendary warrior strode out of the whorehouse.

"I am unaccustomed to waiting, Lord La Gaul."

"Yeah, and I'm not used to be roused this early without sex involved. If it's a fight you want, we may as well get it over with. Need I remind you of how your last visit to this place turned out?"

These words from La Gaul made Maddox and Tammas exchange a glance and nearly run for the whorehouse. Gorias could see by the lazy manner of Kayla that she had assessed the troops and felt no malice in them.

Maddox frowned at Tammas, who trembled openly.

Lira stepped away from her guards and looked at her daughter. "No need for violence. I see my daughter is alive after this venture with the Cult of Wyss."

Gorias leaned on the hitching post nearest him and sighed. "Nothing gets by you in the morning does it, lady?"

At his words, the guards and mercs broke into smiles. Truly, they weren't used to seeing their superior treated in such a way. Gorias wasn't positive if any of these men were amongst those who met him before, but knew what power his celebrity carried. These men would forget how tired Gorias looked and recall his taunts and armor more than anything else.

"I hear the rising of Wyss was broken up. For that, our leader is appreciative." Two of the guards brought forth horses laden with supplies and many bags. "There are goods and gold enough to make even you happy, La Gaul."

"Well, thank you kindly. It wasn't all us, but we will take the payment."

Lira stepped toward him. "I have heard the tale of the rising and how General Tolin and his men appeared at the site."

Gorias frowned, inhaled the damp air. "That so? How do you come by this information?"

"One of Tolin's loyal troopers drinks too much," she said, raising an eyebrow. "He let his tongue get loose and told the tale in town."

Gorias rubbed his chin, scratching the heavy beard there. "What the hell are they still doing away from the army of Nosmada? It isn't a wonder they aren't at your fore-gates by now?"

"They aren't that close yet. I wish you would have slain Tolin."

"Well, ya can't have everything, lady."

"The trooper also said he was afraid, for the general seemed at odds with the desires of his dark Lord Nosmada."

"That so?"

"Not as far as turning his allegiance against him, but having plans on his mind other than just the acquisition of weapons."

Gorias pondered this. "What else did he say?"

Rhan looked at the empty whorehouse, wrinkled her nose. "He said his general used a series of harlots for a sacrifice. This act disturbed him and his men."

"They ought to be used to Tolin's disturbing acts by now," he said, noting the sun in its climb up the sky was barely a handbreadth from the earth. He gazed at the door to the house and thought of Wilkens again. With a heavy sigh he banished her from his mind.

Rhan nodded. "I gamble they are, sir. But it is what else the trooper spoke of that bothers me."

Gorias observed the small crowd and how they listened with intensity. "You don't seem to care if these guys get drunk and tell how you were here at a house of dead victory girls talking with me, though."

"It is too late in the day for niceties," she said. "He said if the war with the Northern force does not yield enough blood for Nosmada's purpose, Tolin's army is supposed to liquidate this fair city. I think the trooper might have been here to plant a seed of fear so many would flee."

Gorias nodded. "What of your fine mercenaries there, sister, to protect you? These fellas make you feel warm at night or no?"

She frowned.

"Apparently not, eh?"

"We have an awesome number of men here, both hired and of our own. Many common folks have taken up arms and will defend the city if need be. I will not have the populace of the city slaughtered and bled like…"

"Like so many whores?" Maddox said.

Lira's face trembled. "We all know the fairy tales about Nosmada. What he desires and why is a matter of various disputes. You have been around longer than any of us, La Gaul. If anyone has studied or could understand his agenda or rationale, it might be you."

Gorias eyed the gathering dark clouds. "What of it? What are you getting at?"

"I have no doubt that the army of Nosmada will reach the Foundry of Syn and achieve better arms. That is a given. I also have no doubt the Northern forces will crash right into them with grand furor. Tolin's men will fend off this assault, even if the story about the son of the old barbarian Brock leading them is true. There will be blood for the beast. I see Tolin attacking our position behind the walls of the city."

"Why is that?"

"They are bringing artillery pieces and siege engines."

Gorias looked at his grandson and then at Kayla. "What is it you want out of me?"

"Though we have leaders of our small forces, there is no way the rabble of the mercs will follow them in any organized battle. The militia, well, will they really fight in the most desperate of cases?"

Gorias shook his head. "Oh, sister…"

"You must lead us, La Gaul. These men would follow you into Hell itself!"

"Sounds like it's where we would be headed, too. I'm a bit past that stage in my life. I'm no miracle worker, either. There'd be no time to train them to fight like an army."

"True," she conceded. "But they would fight in an assault behind you. They would go bravely into battle because of you."

Thunder rolled as the morning light faded away.

"There's no time," Gorias lamented. "And I really don't have it in me to lead such an attack, not even past Hell's waiting room. I'd get to die first for your chief up in his tower. That would be swell of me, huh?"

"The great Gorias La Gaul? Slayer of dragons, Nephilums, and deflowerer of maidens? You have no taste for war with simple humans again? Do you know what your presence on the battlefield would do to Tolin's army? If even a fraction of them would desert —"

"I think there's a greater evil beyond, near to the army of the North. A wickedness superior to Tolin's army. If what I think has happened has really occurred, you will have wished Carlato Wyss were in his old flesh."

"We have heard tales of a dragon there, heard it call out. You can slay a dragon another day. It will be no time before they will be at the foundry. Our slim hope of deliverance will grow with your presence."

"I'm not afraid, sister," he said. "We all have to die sometime. I've gone on far too long. The bards and hangers on want to be a part of my life and, Hell, even these men around you yearn to be a part of my death. I think they could find better work than that. If God shrugs his shoulders, urinates on the world, I'll be forgotten forever. That said, I think it's a damned shame so many forces are around here and cannot be coordinated to fight together."

She looked at him, confused.

"I need to go to the apex of the castle and view everything," he said. "That being done, I'll tell you my plans."

Lightning struck but Lira didn't move. "I think you better hurry."

As the rain started to fall, Gorias turned his craggy face to it and let it strike his beard. "On the contrary. I think a good rain may be just what we need."

❊ ❊ ❊ ❊ ❊

Zillian used a sturdy wooden cane to walk the long cavernous corridors in the citadel. Soon, the wood floor would vanish when the real tunnels in the rock began as she drew closer to the redemption place of Nosmada.

The elderly wizard showed a quantity of dread as she approached his inner dwelling. Lannon stood outside this place, giving her a minor shock. She guessed Nosmada had taken the soldier into his ultimate confidence and stationed him there. Zillian was wise enough not to intrude on him. Sitting down on a carved outcropping, she caught her breath.

Stone ground on stone as Nosmada shoved the door open to his inner sanctum. The chittering sound behind him ran steady, never ceasing. His long face didn't show anger as he beheld the old woman. His look was one of curiosity, if anything at all. Nosmada looked at Lannon, waiting for him in case he needed aide. This time, the dark Lord walked evenly as he left the Place of Redemption.

"Will it be enough?" Zillian asked as she heard the high pitched screeches from the chamber. She watched Lannon swallow and look back into the chamber as the door stayed open. The young man sweated, but kept his face stern.

"In time, we shall see," Nosmada said. "It has to be. I take it all on faith."

Lannon lowered his head at last, unable to fake strength over his revulsion any longer.

The towering lord closed the seal and patted Lannon on his shoulder. "What is it, young man? The presence of thousands of undead leeches, clinging to my inner walls like so many bats bothers you?"

"No, sir. It is that you can keep them there, under your power."

Nosmada laughed heartily and then regarded Zillian. "What is it?"

"An entire village, lost. The Draco-Lich arises, a winged predator still not whole. It has taken the lives of so many, but not in the way Tolin wanted."

Nosmada knelt. "What is it you say, dear?"

"The general invoked the Draco-Lich after it arose. He thought it would smite the barbarian army from Zenghaus. In my caldron, I have seen the army moves nightly and gravitates closer to Khabnur. The Draco-Lich took the first mass of lives it saw, not the barbarian army. The Lich is no fool. The barbarians would have fought back with all of their might. They always do."

"Damn him." Nosmada snarled, his placid demeanor evaporating.

Fear shredded Zillian's voice. "It's so angry, my Lord. The winged marauder has arisen from the dead and it's so hungry. A sprawling monster with a body like something out of a nightmare. It has fulfilled the frightened dreams of the folk of that village!"

"Calm yourself."

She persisted. "After so many years of suffocation under the sands by Larak, the blue dragon has arisen. Humanity will run like scuttling rats before his pitiless gaze and hungry maw!"

Nosmada gripped her shoulders, drew back his left hand to strike her, yet hesitated. Truly, a blow from him would kill her. He relaxed and tried to make her do the same.

Terror rippled through her body. Some words came out, but so hysterical burned her frenzy they couldn't be discerned. "You seek a vast sacrifice, my Lord," she said, calmly now. "I fear the earth is now in line for the Draco-Lich. It will seek out a sacrifice for the Elder Gods—and we are it!"

Above them, they felt the earth quake ever so slightly. After the words she spoke, Lannon's expression changed to one of confusion bordering on fear.

Nosmada dismissed this. "It's just thunder, so be at ease. There's a storm coming."

"I think there is," Lannon agreed.

❈ ❈ ❈ ❈ ❈

Walking amongst his lines of wagons, General Tolin cursed the falling rain. All of his troopers were sheltered under expansive tents, while Tolin stalked the tarp-covered lines of war chariots. His anger boiled hot.

"Damned hairy fools from the Hinterlands probably don't

175

even notice the rain," he said, swearing colorfully again. "It won't slow their gargantuan mounts much."

Captain Karter walked with his leader, directing him to come inside the officer's tent. "I think it may clear soon, sir."

"Your eyes do not lie well, Karter. Give it up," Tolin snapped back as he motioned for an infantryman to pour him a drink.

Karter peeked out the large flap of the tent. If anything, it rained harder.

"To be so close with a well trained force and to be held up by water from the damned sky," Tolin rumbled as he drank the contents of the cup in a single long shot. "Of all the conflicts, wars, and simple border skirmishes I have been in, washed out roads are the worst enemy of any warrior."

Tubal spoke up, "This rain'll slow da' barbarians as well, sir. All of their bluster can't navigate heavy mud."

"Will it? We shall see."

A young soldier whispered to another loud enough for them to hear. "I heard, as a lad, that an old hag once purchased a pouch full of good weather. They had to skin a virgin for this one shaman and..." His voice trailed off when he realized the general watched him. Both young men stood at attention, saying no more.

Tolin was about to speak, then gave them a dismissive look. He spoke to Tubal without looking at him. "The pickets say the barbarian army is the largest force they have ever seen?"

"Yes sir."

"Bah, they are but savages. They unite only under the banner of hating everyone else, even if this Brock could really be leading them. He is no La Gaul, just the barbarian with the loudest voice, strongest arms, and longest manhood. The trouble is, this time, it's me they despise. We will see who survives the fight between our superior arms and training. What do they have but ferocious resolve and wiliness?"

Karter declared, "They shall fall under your leadership, sir."

The rain came down in sheets. Tolin barely contained his rage, knowing that if this deluge kept up the advance of his wagons to the Foundry of Syn would be delayed.

"Would that I had a mace large enough to bludgeon them all into the accursed ground--Khabnur, the barbarians, all of them." He looked north and grinned. "Perhaps if my blood sees it my way, I shall have just such a tool, eh?"

"Yes, sir," Karter replied. "In the end, my loyalty is always to you, sir."

The general understood Karter was his and appreciated his words. His anger at the elements could not be quelled, though. "Damn," was the last word he uttered at the rain before closing his eyes and turning his face toward the top of the tent.

CHAPTER XIV

ARMIES AND THE VILLAGE

From the apex of the temple, where the majestic terrace made of bronze opened up to view the city of Khabnur, Gorias raised his scope. Kayla, Maddox, and Tammas pointed at the surrounding territories, easily viewable in the storm-dimmed day. The glass wasn't necessary to outline this area, yet he still used it for a closer look. Though a tempest raged, they still looked on, the wooden canopy offering good cover. In a few minutes, the rain lessened.

Maddox drew near to his grandfather. "What are we looking at here?"

"Well, let's think of this entire area as a huge wheel, all right? The City of Khabnur is the center of the wheel where all the spokes go around." He paused to wipe rain from his face. "Over there to the south-west, anyone can see the fires from the army of Nosmada. You can see the tents all lined up just so. They even have extra wagons. Fascinating."

Kayla nodded as she pulled her hood close. "They're in divisions and ranks. They may as well be labeled."

Gorias agreed with a grunt. "Yeah, there they all are for ya to see. There're great amounts of infantry, pike-men, archers, chariots, cavalry, even spots for artillery men and whatnot. I'm sure their ranks of tents house greener troops and veterans by rank and experience." He pointed to the east at the billowing smoke and belching flames from the factory. "Doesn't look so far from each other up here, eh?"

"Not really, sir," Tammas said. "Terrifying, in a way, to think such machinations of war are right at our feet, is it not?"

"It makes one think. All of them know their place and function, be it auxiliaries full of archers or slingers, or companies of engineers to aid in the machines of war. They are right on our ass."

"Those wagons, sir, confuse me. If those tiny boxes so

far away are indeed wagons. Why are they empty? Waiting for supplies?"

Gorias sighed. "Or booty from Khabnur. Look there to the east. Over there are the bogs of Cielo by the canyon of Benedikt."

Kayla pointed over to the northwestern glow. "What is that? The army of the barbarians?"

Gorias nodded. "I wager so. Hell, one can almost smell them on the wind the closer they get. Being subtle isn't what they're known for. Requiring blood for revenge and feuding, yeah, that's a barbarian for you."

"How many are there?"

"Thousands, I bet. I cannot believe they aren't the prime worry of ol' Lira Rhan. They have little to lose by destroying a carelessly laid out city like this. Then again, they have no siege materials, unless they plan to encircle ya and let ya all starve."

Maddox spat out rain. "Why are the fires in the northwest barbarians camps so large and spaced out?"

"They aren't orderly troops like those following Tolin," Gorias said. "They're barely clothed, I wager. Barbarians through and through, even letting their blazing fires smolder in the rain. They don't care if anyone sees them."

"Why so many fires?" Kayla asked.

"They dance, drink, and copulate around them in a real frenzy. It's primal and a good time if ya have a nice partner to attend with and are young enough to survive it."

She turned her head, peered out of the canopy and said, "What's that sound from over there?"

"Trumpeting."

Tammas frowned. "That is no instrument."

Gorias shot back, "I never said it was. The savages of the North don't ride horses."

The young ones all exchanged glances. Maddox was the first to offer, "Elephants?"

"Sort of," Gorias answered, nostrils flaring at the scent on the wind.

Kayla's brow furrowed as she looked to the north. "But

where's the Oliverian village in all this darkness? I should be able to see it. It lies to the north of Khabnur and I see no lights from it."

Gorias trained his viewer toward this locale. "The heavy rains earlier may have put out their fires or they have evacuated due to the coming conflict. It's day time so I doubt they would have need of a fire like the troops or savages do."

Kayla wore a worried frown. "Oliverian is a retirement village. Only the elderly live there with a few guardians."

The thunder rolled and the clouds billowed over them. "Beyond Oliverian in the realm of Dundayin where the Cult of the Dragon is quartered' Gorias said. "If the Draco-Lich indeed has arisen…"

"What?" Tammas demanded.

"Maybe," Gorias said, rain running from his soaked beard, "we need to go see the leader of the barbarians. This ain't the finest idea, but it may be a shot to spare the city. Kayla, you ought to stay here."

"Why?"

He raised an eyebrow. "They are barbarians, dear, an army of them. Respect for female integrity is non-existent. Half the reason Lira Rhan keeps the mercs is so if the barbarian horde survives the war with Tolin the savages won't rape her women and burn Khabnur. No amount of threats of female bravado can save ya and a song by a bard about Gorias La Gaul can't help, either."

"Leave me in Oliverian then," she requested. "There are a few oldsters I know there from my volunteer days."

"Yeah?" Tammas said.

Kayla nodded. "There was an aged lady there with a scarlet spider tattooed on her back. Rumor had it she retired from being a famed sorceress centuries ago. She used to tell me tales."

"About what?" asked Tammas as Gorias and Maddox rolled their eyes to the dark heavens.

Kayla stared up at Gorias and no more words were required.

Gorias turned and spread out both arms out as if to embrace the territory. "Look at this set up? It'll be a grand slaughter if Tolin gets properly armed. Hell, him armed as he presently stands will be a crap sandwich for all."

"But isn't he coming to take the arms away, back to Nosmada for some greater attack?" Tammas said.

"I think that the men with Tolin aren't armed as such," Gorias said. "They have wooden, obsidian, or bone weapons or primitive bronze arms. The art of being a blacksmith is hard to come by in their sector of the world. It's a rare craft. However, the Foundry of Syn will be their strength. They'll receive better arrows, swords, and shields. The barbarians are well armed with clubs, stone tools, and hard-ons. Usually, that's enough for them to get by. However, against a trained army with steel, well, no." He waved his arms as if to dismiss the city. "All of these mercenaries, damn, if they just had a show of force Tolin's ranks would flinch. Most of the mercs are armed with steel acquired abroad."

Maddox looked at his grandfather with intensity. "What are you thinking?"

His face toward the billowing smoke from the foundry, Gorias said, "Such a waste to squander so many lives. But it's all about the blood, son. Tolin wants more blood for his master, no matter how conflicted he is within his heart."

Tammas spoke timidly, "Sir, who exactly is this Nosmada?"

The words fell like a dead rat, and Gorias waited a long time before saying, "A man with a lot of murder on his hands. He wants something that I don't think even a god can give. He'll take down countless lives in search of it. Come along, you all. We need to ride before the rains start up heavy again. The sun is poking at the clouds. There's enough light to ride by now"

✦ ✦ ✦ ✦ ✦

When the rain slackened, Tolin extolled his captains to start assembling the wagons. Though they knew this wasn't the proper action in such weather, they obeyed fast. As they brought the carts out from under their heavy canvas covers, the rain started to fall again in earnest. Tolin went into a frenzy, but soon stopped his actions. He leered at the well-traveled roads getting wetter still.

Stomping a boot and forcing the wet soil down, Tolin looked to the sky and cursed God to his face.

Captain Karter motioned for the men to return the wagons to their places and they complied, glad that he would take the brunt of General Tolin's wrath.

Approaching Tolin, Karter bowed and said, "Sir, perhaps we can just detach the men and march to the foundry, carrying a round of the weapons? We shall cast away the weapons we have when we obtain the new ones. Who is there to assail our machines left behind? The barbarians have no use for them, and we can leave enough men to dig in fast in case of such an attack."

Tolin brooded silently.

Karter pressed on. "The carts cannot pass on these roads. If we detach a great score of the army, it can march in the roughs beside the road or in the lesser ruined places."

"I am vexed unto my soul, such as it is," Tolin spoke words hemmed in blood and fury, but his seething hate was quelled under his heaving breast. "Something as simple as water is stopping our advance."

A trooper added, "And that of the Northern forces, sir. They cannot move forward, either."

Tolin's anger appeased. "That is true. We must wait. Time is not on the side of those barbarian fools. They are more than a minor worry, but a cancer to be dealt with. The festering abscess that is barbarism must be destroyed and bled for our master. There are so many more of them than us. That doesn't concern me, due to our abilities. They marched right unto my door for the bleeding. Nosmada will be pleased after the victory."

Karter gave him a nod. "You fear not those behind the walls of Khabnur?"

"Not really, once their walls are knocked down, they will flee," Tolin replied. "They will overrun their Paramour who sits in his castle."

Tubal approached, bowed low. "Sir, Zillian has contacted us. Lord Nosmada wants to know of our situation."

A bemused look locked on Tolin's hideous face and he gave

a grunt as a response.

Walking toward the tent that held the mirror communicator, he said to his troopers, "Yes, men, I would tell that fragile little bitch of my condition."

They all laughed as their leader stepped into the tent, swaggering, and stood at attention before the mirror. The grim visage of Nosmada glared back at him. Tolin showed no fear.

"Report, General," Nosmada ordered.

"We are stuck in the mud, Lord Nosmada," Tolin said. "The heavy rains come and not all of our sacrifices can stop them. Our carts will be stuck if we try to move. The timetable will simply be stretched is all."

Nosmada nodded. "More days? There's no other way, I see. At least the barbarians cannot attack you."

"Not very effectively, no."

"Any news of La Gaul?"

While the wrinkles in Tolin's forehead rippled, his temper didn't explode. "The old man is nowhere to be seen, Lord. Perhaps he got his gold for services to Lira Rhan and departed. That is his usual way of operating, is it not? Indifference is a trademark of La Gaul's."

"Could he be an issue?"

His teeth ground, but Tolin said in a curt voice, "That is the question, is it not? He is but one man. I have thousands. What could he do to me?"

"Indeed. One man can make a great difference, but La Gaul is past being a real threat."

"That is our sincere inclination."

"Zillian senses the presence of the Draco-Lich."

"Really?"

"It's far to your north."

A great deal of snide remarks regarding Zillian sprang into the mind of the general, but he let it pass. Invoking the presence of the Draco-Lich was a swipe at him for his practices.

"Let us hope the undead dragon does not like the rain, either," Tolin quipped, causing his men to struggle to maintain their straight faces.

Nosmada's eyes narrowed. "Petty personal conflicts cannot interrupt the grand diagram. I'll not have my moment stolen because of a damned egomaniac and personal business. If this Mitre is really behind all of this…"

"Why would you think that?"

"Zillian isn't omniscient, but she sees a great deal darkly."

Tolin wrenched his hands as if Zillian's throat were in his grasp. "What is it you speak of?"

Nosmada related information concerning Mitre Stillwell and the exchange of soul jewels.

Tolin's face never betrayed an emotion. "Stillwell is a grubby monster. I would take pleasure in removing his ego before I eradicate his life."

"Did you know," Nosmada spoke in a kindly voice, "that the Draco-lich never attacked the barbarian force? No, he found sustenance elsewhere."

"Lord." Tolin smiled. "Sometimes one has to scramble eggs to make them edible."

❀❀❀❀❀

After the image of Tolin faded, Zillian staggered back into Lannon's waiting arms. He let her recline on the bench and she gasped heavily, hand between her withered breasts.

"Curse him for all time," Nosmada muttered bitterly. "He plays little boy games…child games with *ME!*"

"He cannot help himself," Zillian said. "I do not hope to defend him, my Lord, just explain him. What was once Tolin La Gaul is a loyal warrior."

"Because Tolin bears the soul of a wyrmling dragon, yes, yes. Curse me again for trusting in such a man for so long. Who would guess such a thing would all come to a head at once?"

Zillian shrugged her tiny shoulders and looked at Lannon. "Like the aged tale of the woman nursing a snake back to health only for the snake to bite her and kill her. Tolin can do no less than his nature asks. He's a dragon, after all. Did we expect manners and stable behavior?"

"The blood of the caravan and that gained in Khabnur will be what fills the void of my soul," Nosmada raged. "He won't stop me now."

Nosmada left cursing, but Lannon knelt by the aged woman. His hand on her cheek, he watched as her hand stayed in the folds of her robe, attached to her chest. Lannon blinked, for he thought he saw something between her breasts move under Zillian's fingers.

✿ ✿ ✿ ✿ ✿

The rain increased as the four rode out of the last set of walls at Khabnur, but Gorias insisted they set off for the village of Oliverian anyway. They rode off the beaten path and away from the muddy roads. The dead plants from winter provided some turf for their mounts. While Tammas and even Maddox groused at the deplorable conditions, Kayla pulled her rain slicker close and never said a word.

The rain lessened at times, but continued steadily as they rode into the edge of the village. No signs of life offered themselves to the party.

Gorias said to Kayla, "It has been ages since I rode through this area of Shynar. What sort of community did you say this was now? Full of older folk?"

"Yes, to a degree," she said as they passed the first of many mundane cottages. "Many of the older people retire here, but it isn't just a group of elders. There are many warriors who laid down their swords and decided to settle here. Quite a few aging Prelates as well have come to contemplate their gods. These wouldn't be easy pickings to casual raiders. The lady I knew with the scarlet spider tattoo could conjure magic in her most ancient of days. The old men still were full of piss and vinegar."

"I know how they feel 'bout half way."

"They are very close to Khabnur anyway, Grandfather," Maddox said. "That city is a fortified stronghold and an easy spot to run to in case of invasion. I just cannot see what worries you about all of this."

Tammas ground his teeth, trying to still his chattering. "It is quite claustrophobic, though. The streets are narrow and the houses so close together. Where is everyone?"

They rode through the village and Gorias gestured at each house as they went. The small, brick homes remained silent. A few oozed smoke, but not many. Several had doors that looked crudely rent from their greased hinges. Aside from this, the residences were in fine repair. Their fences and even their wells were painted bright colors to reflect a sun that hadn't showed so far that day.

A few small shops in the middle of the town remained shuttered. Their striped awnings flapped and resisted the rain, but no merchants, rude or otherwise, came out to greet them.

"Something came through here," Gorias said. "Can you deduce how I figured it out?"

Tammas chuckled then appeared embarrassed when they all looked at him "Well, if there was a raiding party, wouldn't there be bodies all over?"

"Indeed," Gorias murmured. "Give the virgin a star."

"Then where is everyone?" Maddox said, frowning. "If they were raiders or barbarians, wouldn't they have burned the damn place down?"

"It's raining," Kayla retorted.

Stare full of venom, Maddox went on. "Surely, if they were afraid they would have ran to Khabnur."

"You're asking all the right questions," Gorias said.

As he threw off rain, Tammas gestured at a long brick building. On the stone steps of this edifice lay many robes. "Those appear to be priestly vestments."

Gorias agreed. "Kayla said some Prelates lived here. Looks like all of their prayers couldn't stop them from being taken by whatever it was that vacated the community."

"What tottering, flap-mouthed assheads," Maddox said. "Why didn't their prayers work, Grandfather?"

"Maybe their gods, or God himself, gets sick of hearing it,"

Gorias said to astonished faces. "Don't be so surprised, kids. Ever heard spoiled rotten brats keep asking for more? I'd get sick of that, too, omnipotence or no."

"That is hardly fair," Tammas said.

Gorias looked to the sky. "He doesn't have to be fair. He's God."

Kayla pointed her bow's tip at the end of the muddy street. "Is that the answer, Lord La Gaul?"

A shadowy shape broke the dim light in the road. While they couldn't see clearly what stretched out before them, they could all smell something dank and alien to their senses. They heard a thump and felt the ground tremble. Numerous figured melded in from the wings of the village and joined the immense shadow.

When the images grew clearer, Maddox said, "I guess that's where the people went."

Gorias shook his head, spattering rain away. "No, son, somehow I doubt it. This place is dead, but they aren't the makers of this bloodless destruction."

The creature in the middle of the street wore the silhouette of an elephant, but stood much larger than a common pacaderm. Brown hair covered the beast and its tusks curled around at savage angles, swathing his massive trunk. Atop this great brute rode an enormous, hirsute man in crude buckskins, who pointed a spear at them. This weapon held a stone head.

In front of the mammoth strode several dozen barbarian warriors. They swiftly closed in around the riders as a few more hairy elephants stepped into the street, flanking their kindred.

A clap of thunder echoed as if God himself slapped the earth.

CHAPTER XV

BROCK AND THE BARBARIANS

"Whom do you serve?" Gorias called out with dire force to the huge man on the mammoth.

The barbarian snapped back, "Serve? I serve no one." The voice, deep and brutal, matched the man. "I'm Brock Lloydson, chief of the Bellgades, tribe of southern most Vynlain. I never send lackeys to ask questions. I do it myself."

"A man who knows what he wants. I respect that," Gorias said, uncaring if the man Brock heard him or not.

"You are indeed the one they call Gorias La Gaul. Still alive. So the pickets watching you in the city aren't drunk or lying."

"I am he, Brock."

Tammas whispered, "They have spies in Khabnur?"

Gorias frowned at the bard. "Shut your mouth, kid, or the next song you sing will be out your ass." He cleared his throat and felt a cold coming on in his lungs. "I think I knew your father a hundred years ago when I killed the Nephilum collecting girls at the Zenghaus keep."

Brock snotted up a glob of phlegm and tried to spit past the tusks of his mount. He failed. "Probably." His tone wasn't of a man impressed, or angry, or really caring. "We of the Bellgades have all heard that story. They take children to the spot where your twin swords gutted the Son of God himself. Often did I wonder if the sword scars on the aged altar were just a fake indentation, if such a man as you ever really existed."

"I see."

"I thought you would be taller."

"I am. It's this damn horse."

The barbarians laughed, looking the old one over. Brock said, "I never thought I'd see one such as ya here in this armpit of the world. I heard ya were here. Good health be unto ya, warrior.

I'm lucky to see ya before I die."

Gorias wondered why such a man would contemplate death at a young age. *Probably,* he thought, *because for such savages death could be any day.*

"What are you doing in such a godforsaken place? You are awfully far from Zenghaus. Are you racing Tolin for the weapons at the Foundry of Syn?"

"Come back to our camp and we'll talk about it." Brock said and snorted. "What are these little ones here to ya? She has plenty a'meat on her."

The barbarians practically smelled the air as Kayla jutted out her bottom jaw.

"They are with me and leave it at that."

"Even the runt?" Brock joked, pointing at the bard.

"He plays for his supper and treats. No risk killing a man like that, is there?"

"I suppose not."

Gorias relied on them knowing the old barbarian proverb: that if there was no risk, there was no glory in anything. "Is the entire town empty?"

The barbarian leader gave a nod. "Yeah. It wasn't us that clear 'er out, though. Oh, we planned on scavenging Oliverian for supplies and women, but we found it as such."

Kayla spoke up, "There are no whores in Oliverian."

Brock never looked at her, but addressed Gorias with confidence. "You let your bitches speak? Ya got balls, hero."

Gorias shrugged. "It's a crazy age. She's no bitch to me. You respect women who can fight."

Brock laughed then eyed Kayla. "So ya say, eh? They're all whores to us, eventually."

They went with the barbarians out of the small town. Soon they saw a great multitude of them awaiting outside Oliverian. Maddox leaned in to his grandfather and asked, "Why do they need us if they are so many?"

"Who said they needed anything of us? They may plan to kill our asses quite badly, real soon here. It's been fun getting to know you better, by the way."

"Thanks," Maddox said, glancing back at the others. He held out his hands as the rains let up a great deal.

Gorias stared ahead at the growing mob of savage humanity spreading out before them. "Tammas, don't wet yourself. Riding with Gorias La Gaul will get you killed."

"The moment we met I thought I would die. Every extra second I live is a benefit." Tammas sounded hurt.

The rain stopped as they rode on. Several huge fires appeared as the camp grew visible. He wagered them partially covered and kept dry from the deluge. The fires peppered the expansive barbarian encampment. Gorias followed Brock to the one in the center of the pickets.

Many unrefined men and women held rabbits on long rods into the flames before consuming the flesh half-raw. Gorias took a canteen from his saddle and drank of it then dismounted. Many of the savages swilled stale wine in skins.

Brock gave out a guttural laugh and waved at his party. "Perhaps not the royalty that has contracted ya for service in the past, huh, La Gaul? Ya were never one picky fer money, or so the legends say."

"That's true enough. How do you know an old man like me is still looking for money?"

Brock took a drink, sat down on a fur mat near the fire. "Whores cost money. We all have our fatal habits. Ya are weak for loose women at a cost."

Gorias walked over near Brock and warmed his hands by the fire. "We all have our hobbies, even in our advancing stages."

Brock watched him remove his rain slicker and motioned for him to sit down. "Ya've seen better days, old one."

"No one lives forever." Gorias hesitated. "I better just stand if it is all right with you. Can't believe you brought such a force this far south of your homelands. Must be ten thousand or more of you all."

"Heh, or more indeed. If I were a slave to numbers, I'd be chained up in a school of learning, unable to breathe the air of freedom. We go as we must, like on this venture for goods and to gain the power of the foundry's weapons. Life must be adventure, not sitting on yer ass talking about it all. No use leaving the women or children behind, either."

"No argument from me on that one."

"So why in the Hell are ya around here 'zactly?" Brock spoke with forwardness. "We heard the perfumed chief in Khabnur tried to contract ya to lead the guards and mercenaries."

"The story I tell them all is that I'm here for my grandson. And I was going to visit him before I moved on. Then, I got caught up in all of this nonsense."

Brock smirked. "Yes, ever the family man."

"You're hot dung yourself, barbarian."

"Ya call me that like it's supposed to insult me." Both men laughed and Brock said, "I know yer words are educated about the ways of life. Only a man with stones would talk crap with me in such a way. Tell me why ya are really here."

Gorias' gaze wandered beyond the village, to the north. Brock looked too, as if he would see what Gorias focused on. The air echoed with hot thunder, yet hidden in the eldritch sound dwelt another tone. It ran low, monotone, almost like a man laughing under water.

"A great malevolence has come out of the desert, again. Just when you think a job is over, some ogre with afterlife envy goes and screws up things."

Brock nodded. "We've heard the bellow of the dragon. A few of the patrols claim to have seen it in the distance. If ya listen long enough one can hear the rhythm of its nonsense. I think it's singing."

"It isn't exactly a dragon. What's left of one, with the soul of a human in its chest."

Brock's hearty laughter rolled as did chuckles from the camp. "How's that possible? Perhaps a demon or dragon could squeeze into the body of a man, for a season, but how could a man do likewise? It'd be like trying to swim the ocean. I think any human carting around a dragon would explode in time."

"You'd think." Gorias took a drink of the stale beer offered to him and nodded. "Damn this is freakin' terrible." He drank some more. "Yes, I wager that would be a bitch. If the human soul were that of a real maniac, my, wouldn't that be a bad thing?"

Brock gestured at Oliverian. "Ya know what happened, of course?"

Gorias nodded. "I knew you would as well."

"Even my hardest warriors flinched at such a reality."

Kayla looked from face to face, but said nothing. Maddox, however, wasn't fettered to their rules and spoke up. "What is it? Are you saying the dragon, the Draco-lich, ate everyone in the village?"

Gorias sighed. "We never said that, did we?"

"Not I!" the barbarian chief said slyly, glancing at Kayla.

Frustrated, Maddox put out, "What are you two playing at?"

The old warrior said to his grandson, "You know how I say there are worse things than dying? Gird up your necromancer guts and listen to me. If indeed a body is raided from the dead, any body, be it Carlato Wyss or a dragon, what's needed?"

"Blood and flesh, if there's no body to be bestowed into," Maddox said. "Like Wyss in the bog. He absorbed his own worshipers. There was a skeleton but no warm flesh for it."

Brock drank heavily as children at play ran past. "That grandson, he's a brilliant one."

As Maddox frowned at Brock, Gorias said, "The Cult of the Dragon isn't as stupid as the Cult of Wyss. In theory they aren't anyway. They would have plenty of flesh for their arisen dragon or a great deal nearby."

Tammas put his hand on his stomach and he almost wretched. "You mean they sacrificed the entire village?"

"Not as so many grisly bits, virgin, but yes, in a way," Brock said. "They never trussed up hundreds of bodies for the dragon to suck into dry husks. But I'd guess that once the Draco-lich was up and about, it went to Oliverian and indulged."

"That's terrible," Tammas said.

The nicest jeer he received was from one of the children that said to him, "That's life."

"Husks," Kayla said. "If the dragon would consume the flesh

to re-create itself, then why did you say it like that? Do they indeed leave the skin of the people behind?"

Brock shrugged, but Gorias said, "Yes. I've seen this before, believe it or not. They turn a body inside out like a man eating a lobster and leaving the shell. It's not as tidy, however."

"Why don't they consume the skin?" Kayla wondered, looking to the sky as the clouds lightened.

"By Wodan, why do ya talk so much?"

"Human skin has other uses," Gorias pointed out. "Plus, that's the advantage I…we…will have here. This Draco-Lich will not be in a full body of a dragon. It has been dead for over a century, thus there'll be little but bones or a few scales left over. The body it re-constitutes itself with will be made of human flesh, thus more vulnerable than any dragon I faced in the past." Gorias gripped Maddox's shoulders.

"What?" Maddox said to the old man, whose face practically glowed. "You plan to slay it, don't you?"

"You cannot make a dragon your pet. An idea…a plan has came unto me."

"How could I believe in any god who would allow such a thing to happen to good people?" Kayla said.

"Stop it, dammit!" Gorias snapped. "I got an answer for you how you can believe in such a God — Don't if you are so inclined. I'm sure it'll break his fucking heart. He has bigger problems than you. Besides, it isn't God you should be angry with for what happened to Oliverian. It's quite the opposite."

Brock persisted, "Why do ya care about the dragon, La Gaul? Ride off into the sunset, take the little gal with ya and let us all kill ourselves. What's it that makes ya care about a dragon?"

"The Draco-Lich isn't about sucking up villages. That isn't his job or intent. He has a worse mission--one that will cost more lives than a few armies clashing together. You know of what evil Stillwell may be plotting in his private dealings?"

The barbarian chief shrugged. "Who cares? He's a damned ogre. Who can trust him? He must die."

"He's a half bugbear mutt, but you cannot trust those

bastards, either."

Tammas said, "Yet you planned on getting weapons from him before Tolin did!"

"Ya don't lie," Brock agreed. "Yet yer wrong in yer assumption that we planned on dealing with a damn ogre, or whatever ya say he is."

"What's that supposed to mean?"

Brock grinned a smile of jagged, dim teeth. "Oh, we sent our emissaries and showed Mitre much gold, but do ya think we're gonna step up and do competing cash deals with the likes of those serving Nosmada? We plan to take Mitre's supply of weapons, all right, virgin child."

"But the Foundry is a fortress!" Tammas said. "There is no way to invade it from above with an army such as yours."

Brock looked at Gorias. "Yer virgin bard is bright as well. Tell him to sing me the one about the *Way Worn Traveler*. Damn, that one makes my blood rush on."

"You savage," Tammas said bitterly. "You take me for a fool!"

"Because ya insist on actin' the role, ya pussy. Indeed, we'll send a force to the foundry, but not up to the front gate. Ya take *me* for a fool, puppy with an untouched wanker? Stillwell doesn't care who in this world wins in this fight between Nosmada's men and us, or if all of his workers die. But do ya think his fat ass will die in the Foundry? What do ya think that bastard will do if there's an attack?"

"Escape?" Kayla said.

Brock winked at Gorias. "How much for the sassy little bitch? She would be an excellent breeder. She isn't pretty in the conventional sense, but after a few children, her hips will widen enough to really be a fine woman."

Kayla tried not to make a face, but Gorias said, "The price is too high, fella. I would guess Stillwell has an escape route somewhere and there has gotta be a vent for the air not connected to the bellows or sanitation."

Brock nodded, a sinister grin on his ugly face. "We know where it is. Oh, it's full of excrement, but what treasure isn't worth treading in manure for?"

"What's your plan?"

"We know where the smaller vents are, but not Stillwell's escape route. We'll send in the children and they'll clear the place out."

They looked off at the kids in the muddy plains. Hundreds of barbarian youths wrestled in the mud, enjoying themselves.

"You will send your children off to such a horrid place?" Tammas said.

Brock shrugged. "It'll help in their man-making and, Hell, they're the only ones small enough to fit in the vents. They're curious by nature and will love the job."

Maddox stepped away from them and whispered to his grandfather, "They came all this way with a plan like that? They have balls, you have to grant them this much."

"As far as brains go…" Kayla muttered.

Gorias said to Brock, "How is it you are so certain of the plans of the army of Nosmada?"

Brock gestured for them to follow him to the edge of their encampment. There were a few trees and shrubs thereabouts. He said to Gorias, "You know of the practice of augury?"

"The reading of guts?" The old man laughed. "Yes, seen it done with many an animal."

"It works."

Gorias blinked, trying to comprehend what he saw. Maddox and Tammas caught on quicker and the bard vomited. The barbarians thought this greatly humorous. Kayla had no reaction other than a frown. The same reaction Gorias sent Brock.

At the end of a series of four trees lay two bodies clothed in leather jerkins from the army of Nosmada. One body was somewhat bloated. Gorias guessed his death occurred a while ago. However, his fellow soldier remained alive. Through the tree line was strung a gray and pink, fleshy rope. One end was tied to the first tree, and the other ends terminated in the bellies of the soldiers. The man alive screamed out many words, pleading for death, confessing everything he knew about his army and their positions. By the looks of things, he had been confessing for some time. Now, keeping him alive was simply cruel amusement.

"I told you for true." Brock chuckled. "One can learn a great deal from the reading of guts!"

They turned away and Maddox patted Tammas on the back.

Gorias murmured, "Haven't seen augury that effective in years."

"How can they…" Tammas stammered.

"They are barbarians," Kayla said hotly, as if that explained it all.

"Don't show weakness," Gorias said. "They don't bother feeding off the weak. They crush them and walk on."

"Is it weak to be human?"

Gorias paused, thinking. "No, I guess not, but it's a luxury we cannot have out here today." He slapped Tammas on the shoulder and moved closer to the edge of the encampment. Squinting, he thought he saw a dull ripple in the emerging day's glow. Was it a trick of his eyes? What did he see?

A grubby barbarian child approached his horse. "I don't believe in dragons."

Gorias glanced at him, but kept his eye on the raw desert ahead. The sun slammed into the back of the dissipating clouds. "Good for you. You can't fear something you don't believe exists."

"I don't believe you slew them all or any of such a thing."

"A boy has to have his convictions."

"Did you really do it?"

Gorias' turned his withered face to the boy. "When you go into battle you call on Wodan, your god. Ever seen one of them there gods of yours?"

"No."

"And yet you believe in them, huh?"

The boy glowed as he said with malice, "I think it's all a big story. All of it."

"What? The creation of the world and all of the spirits?"

"No." The boy smiled, showing a mouth full of bad teeth. "All of the stories about you."

Gorias threw back his mane of hair and roared with laughter.

"Really, it's silly to think a single man could kill a dragon."

"I suppose it is."

The reddish locks of the boy blew in the wind. "Then how did you do it?"

Gorias opened his cloak. The boy gasped at what he saw inside and the other barbarians gaped as well. "Satisfied?"

Pulling his rough covering tighter about himself, Gorias shuddered from the chilly wind.

Brock segued back toward Gorias and said, "Any other man would have been skinned alive by now, La Gaul."

The dim daylight gave life to the distant ruins of Larak as Gorias said, "They would have tried."

"Ya see, they think if one legend is so, then the rest must be true."

Gorias exhaled as if to show the hairy man just how bored he was with his words. "I'm lucky more than blessed. That's what you can build a fetish to—luck and chance. The older one gets, the wiser one becomes, as a rule."

"I'm not one for gods, even though we invoke some," Brock said. "I've more faith in the strength of my arms than in any deity hurling lightning overhead."

Gorias never replied.

The clear blue eyes of Brock looked at Gorias' backpack where the twin sword casings were and said, "They say yer blades are made from the wings of angels."

"That's just preposterous," Gorias dead panned, never looking away from the ruins toward the desert.

"They say that ya talk to angels."

"Who are *they* anyway? Some people talk too much. You ask more stupid questions than that kid."

Angered, Brock pressed on. "And they say that's why you make the bold pronouncement about deliverance every time ya face certain death. They say ya are counting on angelic intervention at the moment of yer death."

"A great many of these folks who talk need to listen to songs about someone else," Gorias said. "All of that is a load of hokum. I'm a tired old soldier nearing the end of his term on this filthy planet. We all want to die fighting, no? It just doesn't matter to me where I happen to fall fighting. I just want it to be worth it."

"Ya don't fear a violent death?"

"Fear it?" Gorias said as he saw a pale, glowing ripple on the edge of the town. "I'm counting on it."

Brock laughed then his voice went grim. "War is a man's means to an end. War is child's play to even the toy soldiers taking orders from Tolin. But I know something those orderly men don't know. I understand war is good. They see it as a terrible circumstance that will ensure domination for their Lord. Bah. War isn't a dirty business. War means death, but that's a part of life. War is life. War is good, so very good, and I have never felt so alive as I do now."

CHAPTER XVI

COMING TO A HEAD

An hour before noon, the rain stopped over the troops of Nosmada. Soldiers roused Tolin from sleep, per his orders. His austere face studied the sky and breathed in deep. He turned to his attendant sergeant then ordered the hulking Tubal, "Assemble the captains."

Tubal wiped moisture from his bald head, stood at attention, and saluted. "They await ya in the main tent, General. They're thirsty fer action."

Tolin imparted a wry smile. "That is good. Action is what they will be drunk on soon enough." He went into his private tent and stripped off his casual uniform and lighter armor. Tolin donned undergarments then a light leather covering. Over this he put on his chain mail armor. Once this mesh fit in place, Tolin pulled on various plates for better protection—greaves for his shins, poleyns for his knees, a couters at his elbows, light pauldrons on his shoulders, and a fauld over his groin. Placing metallic sabatons over his feet, he pulled light tassets up over his thighs then vambraces across his forearms. Securing the goret about his neck, the general grabbed his gauntlets. Once adorned as such, he exited the booth.

When he entered the long tent, his men saluted. They knew if Tolin dressed as such, he meant bloody business.

"We march as soon as you can assemble your units. We go unto the foundry to arm ourselves and press on. There is enough daylight left to make it by dusk. If we must pitch tents at the edge of Khabnur, then we will spend the night there. I believe we will overcome that goal long before afternoon dies. The wagons cannot travel on the roads, nor will we. Have your men march in columns in the roughs, armed with what they have. They will get plenty of chance to use the new weapons soon enough."

"You don't think we will pitch tents, do you?" Karter said.

"From the reports of our rangers, the barbarian force is preparing to move," Tolin said. "If that occurs, then our slower moving force will run into them sooner or later. I will take the fight to them. If they attack us in transit, I will swing the entire army into a curl and pinch them off. The moving will be slow, but not nearly as much so as if we were followed by a ponderous baggage train of wagons."

The men saluted, and Captain Karter asked, "Sir, what of the gold and jade for Mitre Stillwell? There's a great deal of it in the carts."

Tolin pulled his heavy gauntlets tighter. "What of it?"

The captains remained at attention, yet they looked back and forth at one another. Each man knew what was being asked and what the answer would be.

"If we cannot use the wagons on the roads, then we cannot load them with the weapons. Granted, we can carry out twice what we need per trooper."

"Yes?"

"Then how can we carry Mitre's payment of gold and jade to him?"

"How indeed?" Tolin mocked surprise. His long face drew into a ruthless scowl. "Piss on that ogre. He dies." He approached a map of the region, laid out on the oblong table. It detailed the city of Khabnur and the surrounding towns. Chalked in were the movements of Brock's barbarian horde. He turned to his officers unified behind him and proclaimed, "Tomorrow, all of them die. Every last mother's son and then some. One could almost start a kingdom in this place, if one was of a mind to do it."

"If we encounter La Gaul?" Tubal said.

Anger bubbled free over his face. "Do not kill the old fighter. If he is seen on the field, and I am not there, bring him unto me."

Hands behind his back, Karter said, "What of his entourage?"

"Shear off their damned heads. I care not for their souls, only for that of La Gaul. He must not die before I get to him, do you understand me?"

A few of the troopers fidgeted at these words, curious what

he had in mind for the legend.

Tolin walked outside where his horse awaited him, regaled and ready for battle. Like the rest of the mounts being readied for the coarse trip, chanfons and crinets covered their heads and necks. Light peytrals shielded the horse's chest against attack.

On the back of the saddle, next to the bedroll, sat the tiny wooden box from Tolin's private materials. He wiped a hand over it. "And they say I can only kill you once, La Gaul."

＊＊＊＊＊

Lannon gripped the handle of his sword. He stared down, not wanting to elevate his gaze toward the Chamber of Redemption.

Nosmada sat in the center of his funnel shaped hollow and stared at the gloomy sky. The sun wasn't visible. The marked man sat in a meditative pose.

Lannon faced Zillian, who peered through the single door into the chamber.

She rubbed her chest and whispered, "What is on your mind, young man?"

After a few steps back from the doorway, he went to a knee to face the elderly woman sitting on an outcropping in the stone wall. "Will it ever be enough for him?"

"Dear boy, you are a man of few years. You do not fathom all there is to know. Nonetheless, you have served your master well. You see the depths of his pain and woe."

Lannon released the handle of his short sword. He stared at Nosmada then at the walls of the great chamber. Each spot withered and quivered. Not one inch of rock could be seen. Leeches, bodies bloated with blood, covered every inch of stone. His own blood ran cold, for he could hear what Nosmada was doing. He sang.

Chilled by the words and attitude his lord displayed, gooseflesh appeared on his muscular forearms. Forcing this eerie feeling from his mind, he heard the song stop and Nosmada begin to speak.

"You find this all so hard to take in?" Nosmada said in a rather kind voice. "Do you not comprehend what's in the blood everything needs and desires? You see how the rain falls and spreads out to give life unto the earth? Not one part of humanity realizes the water returns to the sky, reloads in the clouds, and is wrung free from them to replenish the earth again. It's a wonderful image, no? Has not God in his infinite wisdom blessed us all with such a system?"

Lannon's mouth grew dry and he looked at Zillian. She stared down.

Nosmada continued. "Water changes its forms and alters itself, yet it still is a part of the world, one with the Creator's plan of redemption. Feeding, strength, and rebirth--it is all the cycle of life. It's the same with blood. You're given blood through your mother and you live on. You impart blood to your kindred and they continue on in life for you, an image of you, an extension of you. But in time, your own blood fails and you must return to the dust where all men were spawned from. And yet, you left blood, you let the flow carry on, thus, completed a part of the ultimate program of God."

Lannon noted Nosmada never used the word "gods" as most men did. He referred to but one deity above.

"Why else would God require blood in sacrifices, for blood to touch the very ground, the Earth itself, to purify? In this pious act of bloodletting, there is great power. It purifies, renews, and shows obedience to a paternal force; no matter how much some want to desire to worship something else. Animals by the score can be sacrificed and bled as homage to God above. The most persuasive form of magnificence unto God is the surrender of human blood."

Again, Lannon felt cold in a warm environment. He couldn't hide his disquiet, yet kept listening to his dark lord.

"Giving of human blood and the lives therein obligates the God of all gods to return the glory unto the man who makes such a sacrifice. This is the most exalted form of intercourse between God and man, the moment of human sacrifice. The reason? Not only does the blood cleanse the sin away, the badness of the one releasing the blood, but the spirits go free as well. You see, as with rain that never ceased to survive, the spirits of those bled return unto God who prepared them. A spirit cannot be destroyed, Lannon. Returning lives for a life, showing respect for your Creator, surely, he will offer forgiveness for the taking of a life…a single damned life…"

✵ ✵ ✵ ✵

Lira Rhan stood at the apex of the temple where Gorias and his group previously watched the armies move. Her keen observation took in all as the day brightened around the noon hour.

One of her guards approached, saluted. "The army of Nosmada is starting to stir, Magistrate."

Her words rang methodical. "Yes, I can see that from here. Most of them are starting to take advantage of the break in the rain. Any word from Gorias La Gaul?"

"The men are seeking him, ma'am. They disappeared into Oliverian and there is no sign of life there. The rangers think they are amongst the barbarians."

"Was my daughter left in Oliverian, per Gorias' request?"

"Not that we can see, ma'am."

"Thank you. You may go now."

Listening to the footsteps fade away, Lira looked at the small dagger in her hand and wondered if her courage would be enough. She would never be prisoner to Tolin, nor on his master's plate.

✵ ✵ ✵ ✵ ✵

Mitre Stillwell slept deeply and without dreams. A gallon of whiskey will do that, even to a cross-breed bugbear. His lunchtime naps were famed in the Foundry, for even the Beholders and Minorc security force took their breaks then.

In the Foundry of Syn, the afternoon shift was about to begin. The Minorc overlords prepared their whips and the gossip started to roll. The Beholders passed on their current fantasies into the minds of the workers. This sparked jealousy and resentment at each other, not where it should go.

All throughout the rigors of arduous work, the sweat rolled and the weapons were born.

Mitre Stillwell, hugging an enormous pillow as if it were his own very soul, slept with what passed for a smile on his face. His peace was as unremitting as the labor of those in the vicinity of him.

❈ ❈ ❈ ❈ ❈

Over the edge of the barren desert, a hideous laugh echoed out for all in the barbarian camp to hear. This rolling voice came from the ruins of Larak. This voice was singing as well.

The shimmering gray light at the edge of the encampment warbled and many rubbed their eyes. Surely, that wasn't just a man who walked out of thin air? Many thought it was a trick of the light. No matter to the savage group, they sent men forward to confront this stranger.

Gorias held up a gnarled hand. "Hold! I know him. He's not with Nosmada by a long shot."

"What's this man to appear from the air?" Brock said. "Some kinda accursed wizard?"

As the figure moved closer to them, heading directly for Gorias La Gaul, the old combatant said, "No, far from that. His name is Ezran Gavreel. I see him every so often."

The serene man in white smiled at him.

"I'm getting almost weary of his face, though."

Ezran didn't flinch at the bellows of the dragon behind him. The herd of mastodons nearby trumpeted and snorted, showing their unrest.

"I'd say good afternoon," Gorias said. "But something tells me it's going to be anything but a fine day, eh?"

"Days are what we make them," Ezran said.

Not acknowledging the rest of the men around him, Gavreel folded his arms under his pale white cloak. Gorias stood next to him as he looked in the direction of the singing echoes. They stepped away from the others and Brock didn't pursue them. The other barbarians let them be as well. The youths with Gorias stepped up near, but gave them some space.

With a small laugh, Ezran said, "Give the barbarian horde time and they will start to mock the song."

"Probably."

"Still, it would be an improvement over their uncouth war songs. Do you recall that tune?"

Tilting his head and concentrating, Gorias confessed, "No."

"I bet your bard would know it."

Gorias adjusted the plates of his armor. "I wager he would, but get to the point."

Tammas joined them and listened. "It is the Litany of Love by Carlato Wyss."

Gorias asked, "How does it go?"

Tammas cleared his throat and sang,

"Say that you love me, never resist.
Tell me you adore me, never to desist.
Come unto me, for as long as you exist.

I love all my children, come hear my song.
O adore all my boys and girls, all the day long.
Be one of my kind, I'll never treat you wrong.

There is no resistance, give it to your lover.
We are all one family, give it to your brother.
Bring all your kindred, give it to one another."

Gorias snorted. "I never did like songs about that. All that love stuff makes me want to puke."

"I wonder why a dragon would be singing the tunes of a dead cult leader?" Ezran said.

"You know or you wouldn't be hanging around here."

Tammas gaped at Ezran then Gorias. "Who is this man?"

"A wayfaring stranger." His nostrils flared as he snapped at the boy. "Leave us alone."

After the boy sulked away, Ezran said, "You have plans to make a man of him, do you now?"

Gorias gaze focused on the pallid face of Ezran. "You're peeping into my thoughts."

Ezran sighed. "It's late in the day for such particulars, no?"

"I reckon. I'll give him a chance to be a man really fast here."

"What do you think of Brock's plan for infiltrating the Foundry of Syn?"

Gorias smirked and suppressed his laughter. "It's downright insane and foolhardy, but full of balls. I love it."

"And all in the hands of children. Barbarians, truly, but still children."

"Brock thinks such a bloody venture will make men out of them."

"Indeed," Ezran said, looking at the sulking Tammas, then Kayla, and at last the ruins afar off. "It would. The girl loves you, by the way."

Gorias' expression remained unchanged as he compared the song the dragon sang in the distance to the words Tammas just sang. "Yeah, I reckon so." The damp air from the rain was fading and the wind of the desert felt warm in his lungs.

"Is that old hat to you, being admired by young girls? She is a sturdy woman for certain, but..."

"Why talk of love or sex so much and harp on it? It's just life. You need to make a big case out of every such event that happens? So what?"

"Some say it's overrated, love. The brethren of mine that took unto themselves wives and fell...many regret it, but they cannot restore themselves unto their appointed place."

"Life's a bitch, huh? Always easy to be sorry after the act is over."

"I am glad to see you still here, Gorias La Gaul."

"Kinda pleased to see you, in a peculiar way."

"We keep our promises."

"I never doubted that."

"Such is your faith."

"Yeah. But these idiots, they'd die if I was here or not. They are out to get even with Nosmada's troops for the hand mortification thing and just because they are also desirous of weapons."

"Also very true." Ezran wrinkled his nose. "They are not my concern this day. You are."

"Good. That sounds anomalous coming from one of your ilk--that a bunch of humans killing each other isn't your concern."

Ezran looked back at Brock as the barbarian howled orders to his troops. "Humans kill each other every day. It is a bad trend started by a really bad man. Their petty wars aren't under my scope of want."

"All of these forces clashing together, what if it really aids Nosmada's cause? Have you thought of that? You have tunnel vision over the dragon. You care not if Nosmada's plans will be fulfilled by this massacre?"

With no emotion, Ezran said, "But it won't, don't you see? Nosmada is delusional in his dreams. His desires are based on fallacies. This entire grand dance of death, all of his collection of blood and incantations that brought the leeches into this realm, it is pointless. The lives of a few thousands sinners cannot compare to what will happen if that Draco-Lich is allowed to fulfill his program."

Gorias sighed. "That's what I feared. If he can truly translate the Daemonolateria and leave it in the hands of humans…"

"There'll be no stopping the demonic horde from invading Earth from the Abyss," Ezran finished. "And do not say *he*, say Carlato Wyss. It is him arisen from the dead yet clothed in the flesh of a dragon, such as it is. Once his agenda is complete, the incalculable losses will be beyond my power to save."

"That thing will do worse than all of the curious hands of elders across time."

"They will exterminate all human life, the homunculi of the Creator."

"You could slay them all," Gorias said. "It's well within your strength. You could rise up and destroy the Draco-Lich, all of his followers, and then smite both armies for good measure."

Ezran regarded the barbarians. "Not that the world wouldn't seem more pleasant afterwards, but you know that is not how things work."

"It's within your ability."

"But not my appointed function, is it? This episode, this world, is a proving ground. That is what you all were given your miserable lives for. Prove you are worth his time and effort. Prove that he was right by loving you enough to give you life. Prove that you have the courage to save humanity. Show him you are not just trash and worth the right of existence."

Ezran turned his back to Gorias, walking into the desert. Then he simply vanished.

Tammas and Maddox joined him swiftly.

"What was he?" Tammas' voice nearly broke.

Gorias frowned. "If you think he was a winner, you should speak to demons. Come along. We have plans to make."

CHAPTER XVII

GOING TO WAR

"I think you are making a gigantic blunder," Maddox said, staring at his grandfather, who stood in front a multitude of Brock's barbarian children. Tammas was amongst the children, appearing taller than usual.

"You think badly at times," Gorias muttered and fixed the strap on Tammas' helmet under his chin.

"Sending Tammas off with those kids to infiltrate the foundry is sending him to death."

Gorias eyed Brock, who was drinking again, and then looked at the army of children, clothed in skins. "Any of you plan on dying?"

A roar flittered out from the young army, showing their confidence and bravado.

"See? They aren't afraid of this."

Maddox frowned. "I think you're missing the forest for the trees."

The aged man glared at his grandson. "And I think you are as well." He stepped away from the savage brood as Brock repeated instructions to the young warriors. "There are greater things at play here than just these tiny lives."

Maddox swallowed and gave a fast nod. "I understand that, sir."

"Do you? Of all of them, I hoped you would have learned what really is at play here. Why do you think the demons beyond our eyes desire to destroy this earth and all of its souls so much?"

"To get even with God?" Maddox hands ran down the armor.

Gorias raised both eyebrows. "Basically. When God imparts life or souls, each are a piece of him. If the demonic horde can cast them into Hell, they see it as destroying a little bit of him. They cannot corrupt him, but this is a scant victory for them."

"You would think God would have better children than us to worry on."

Gorias laughed and slapped both sides of Maddox' face as if to wake him up. "He is determined to give his children every chance. I fear that one day he'll grow weary of us and wipe the earth clean of this rabble called humanity. He'll probably start over."

Tammas suited up in a looser outfit than he usually wore. It was light armor and leather for the most part, scavenged by Brock's men in Oliverian. He also wore a small helm from the gutted men in Nosmada's army. The bard winked, secure in his undertaking.

"You must follow through on your element, son," Gorias said to Maddox gravely. "It is very crucial that you do exactly as I have instructed you."

"I hope that I can, Grandfather…"

Gorias grabbed him by the jaw, thrust his head up. "No, boy, there's no such thing as *hope*. You cannot hope for anything. Action requires courage. Men filled with hope are mooning for other men to take action. There are no more sidelines. No more playing at being Gorias La Gaul in a sand box full of kids. This is war for the entire earth and you are going to play a key role. You must allow me time to do as I must."

"No pressure?"

Gorias glanced at Kayla, who appeared dejected and apart from the proceedings. Again, he faced Maddox. "Pressure? The utmost. I have to go kill that bastard at Larak. I promised Ezran I would fight evil and I aim to keep that pledge. All of the silliness, all of the jokes, all of the acting out war games stops this time around. You have played off my name for years, ever walking in my thrall. You will soon discover exactly what it is like to be Gorias La Gaul."

The young man gripped the old man wrists and they locked eyes. "I'll not let you down."

"You had better not," Gorias said, his blue eyes glimmering. "Or I'll kill you."

✿ ✿ ✿ ✿ ✿

Brock shouted at his substantial barbarian horde, sometimes in different dialects. As Gorias, Maddox, and Kayla approached, Brock said, "There are other tribes mixed in with ours, by Wodan. I need to make sure they understand what a pinchers movement is. They know clear enough how to kill those of the offending army, though."

Gorias laughed. "They all have to die sometime." He then disappeared into Brock's main tent.

Maddox, still by the main flap of the tent, gaped at the assembled force from Zenghaus then at the sun overhead. "We have plenty of daylight left."

"Good," Gorias said.

"All of them came in hopes of destroying Nosmada's army?"

"Mostly they came for the opportunity to fight and rape the countryside. Some came to get revenge for the atrocities of Tolin north of here in the past. Others, well, they are what they are, right? They have agreed, in principle, to spare Khabnur, for now."

Maddox nodded as Brock walked near to him. He faced the barbarian chief. "Grandfather says if this comes out right, Lira Rhan's chief will be more than generous to buy you off."

Brock gave a sardonic laugh. "Yes, would we then be considered civilized if we imitated whores and accepted their cash? We should just be the rude barbarians they think us to be and take it all."

Maddox echoed his grandfather. "You fill me with confidence."

Brock pointed at Maddox. "I'm a warrior, boy, and have killed men since I was a boy. I live by a code and respect your grandfather. He has the smell of death and blood all over him. An ocean of soap water cannot remove the blood from the ghosts he has sent into Heaven or Hell. That's the only reason you breathe and that little bitch isn't riding my manhood as we speak." Bawdy cheers rose from the crowd of fighters as Brock swelled up. "But I see truth in your grandfather's words. He's right to do as he does and we will follow his plan. If it breaks, piss on it, we'll just go into the jaws of death as we planned."

"You have great courage."

"Bah!" Brock dismissed Maddox. "You talk of things babies have in my realm. I don't need to be told of anything. Too much talk, boy. You think it takes courage to die? It takes courage to live! Go forth in your grandfather's stead and take their courage from them!" He then paused and said, "Or die."

Maddox followed his grandfather into the tent and undid his cloak.

Gorias grunted as he pulled loose one of the armlets. "It'll be heavy at first, but you'll get used to it."

His hand running over the dragon skin until he touched the dew nail, Maddox opened his mouth to speak, but no words came out.

❖ ❖ ❖ ❖ ❖

Tammas jogged far from the barbarian's camp when the clear sunlight washed over their position. The army of children he marched with kept a fast pace. He looked back and saw a great, proud warrior emerge from the tent of Brock. The scales of the wyrmling armor glistened in the sunlight and even the barbarians cooed. Many invoked the name of their pagan god, Wodan. This time, the warrior of renown placed a helmet on his head and put the visor down. This helm of dragon flesh blended in with the rest of the armor. Walking across the camp, everyone gave him a wide berth. He climbed onto Gorias' white mount and rode toward Khabnur. He road alone.

A second figure emerged from the tent. This shape was cloaked in tan and walked almost with a feeble gait. He used a spear as a walking stick and made it to Maddox's horse. With great difficulty, he climbed into the saddle, and rode off in the direction of the singing Draco-Lich. He also rode alone, until a stout female archer climbed on a horse and followed him.

Tammas heart beat fast in his chest as the words of Gorias La Gaul rang in his ears:

"Free Noel."

THRALL

✻ ✻ ✻ ✻ ✻

Brock Lloydson sat atop his mammoth and held the heavy reins in his hands. His cavalry of hairy men mounted on hairier pacaderms rowed up into ranks. The barbarian was somewhat disappointed that his massive force would attack separately, on two fronts as La Gaul planned it out. He tried to deal with it in his mind, tried to fight down what he felt in his breast--the savage vehemence that all men like him knew as their guiding vigor in life. He tried to accept that Gorias was correct. He would try it the way of the legend on two legs. For now…

He roared for their attention then spoke to them in a calm but loud voice. "Know your guts and know the hearts of those you hate. They think us stupid folk. We shall be the kings of knowledge, for after this day only we shall carry the tale of what happens. This day, we will become truth." His voice raised in power as he commanded, "Seek your enemy. Hate your enemy. I exhort you unto battle, to attack and fight not for peace, but for victory!"

The cheers of the barbarians from Zenghaus assured him of their passion and determination to follow his words unto death.

A full half of his armed forces split away from the bearing he faced. On foot, what some would call the main infantry (what he called berserkers, foot soldiers and a ground attack force) moved to his right and around the city of Khabnur. This force would hit Tolin in the rear, or be waiting for Tolin's men if they retreated. It would also be in a dangerous spot—in-between Tolin's main force and the reserves he left behind at their encampment.

These ground forces carried a variety of weapons. Many carried crude swords or heavy bludgeons. Others carried maces and morning stars to go with the knives in their girdles. Toward the back, many older men and women brandished sickles, scythes, and pitchforks. Though these folk adhered to no units, they didn't meander in a haphazard fashion. They stayed true to their cause and moved forward.

He gave the battle cry indicating it was time to move the herd of mammoths forward. His forces would curl to the left and attack the main bulk of Tolin's army. In front of his cavalry a thousand berserkers would run, backed by more footmen and women. Tolin would think this was the barbarian army. He would never think that such a large forced lurked behind the mammoths.

✦✦✦✦✦

Mitre Stillwell sat in his offices at the Foundry of Syn. Sober enough after his waking necessities were preformed, he got down to business. In the bowels of the earth, he was safe. When the Minorc guards of the outer perimeter returned from Khabnur with news an enormous force approached them from the south, he was not worried, for they carried the banner of Nosmada's mark.

"It's about bloody time Tolin showed up for his weapons," Stillwell brooded, drinking his mead for the afternoon. "Are their arms assembled in the carrier carts on the main floor?"

"Yes, sire," the Beholder near his desk said.

"Good." Slamming his enormous hands down, he then reached under his desk. "This calls for a drink."

"Dear! This early after noon, sire?" the Beholder asked, a stunned look in its central eye.

"Why the hell not?" Mitre chuckled and poured from a huge wine skin into his mead cup. There was no wine, only whiskey in this container. He drank deeply. As he imbibed, his eye opened wider. "Tell me, you, did it rain all night?"

"Um, I would speculate to say so, sire."

"You'd guess so? Well, sew my ass to my bitches then! Think, you damned floating whelp, or I will rip off your stalks and let the children in the streets of Khabnur play with your self."

The Beholder called in more of its kind for advice. After a great deal of talk, they concluded that it rained most of the night and on into the day.

Stillwell finished his whiskey and sat forward, his chin on his fist. "I expected another day before they could roll in here then. Huh. How does Tolin brave the wet roads with wagons in such a way?"

"Though the sun is out now, there are more storms coming, sir."

Stillwell arose with haste and grabbed for the ceiling. He pulled down a long pipe near his large chair. He looked into a slot on this pipe and peered out on the surface of the earth. "You are smoking the herbs again, ignorant whelps. There is not a cloud in the sky this day."

The Beholders again had a conference and one said, "We hear thunder from the north."

Mitre poured himself another whiskey and laughed. "Do you, now?"

❖ ❖ ❖ ❖ ❖

Tolin's army moved slowly off the road and into the open roughs. The army, though in a strange area, kept the proficient ranks of a force in attack mode. Though marching, everyone kept to their units. Several divisions of infantry led the forces, followed by pike-men and the regulars who would normally man artillery pieces. The archers marched together, but would move to the sides of the force in a moment of battle.

The cavalry rode in back and Tolin rode with them. Most all of his men wore armored breast-plates and light chain-mail on their arms. Above their leather boots, greaves of metal protected the lower portions of their legs. All of the army wore head-gear of a fashion. Several of them wore no face plate, as they were used to open confrontation. Others carried on their laps full nasal helms.

Never was the word happy used to describe the oft melancholy General, but on this day, his Captains would recall, Tolin looked content.

❖ ❖ ❖ ❖ ❖

As the great army abandoned its camp, leaving nothing in reserve, Kayla Rhan stood beside her horse. She wept, recalling the last conversation she had with Gorias before they all departed.

"So where do I go in all of this?" she had asked him. "You have never told me where I fit in?"

"You want my advice?" Gorias said as he prepared the mounts for himself and his grandson. "My advice isn't worth that much, but don't tell Brock and the barbarians. Hell, they are staking their lives on me being bright."

"Quite a burden you carry, being you."

Gorias shrugged, as he often did. "I got used to that years ago. If one concentrates on it, that's when it gets heavy. I'm too far gone to care any more. I'd advise you to go in after the wake of crippled among the barbarian army. You can get into Khabnur through a murder hole. I'm sure you know of one."

Kayla nodded, comprehending him, but not desiring to obey his words.

"If you can slip in, get inside the main keep and be safe there. If anything, you'll avoid the bloodbath outside."

"They are all going to die, aren't they? Brock, his people, the children, even Tammas! You sent him to his death…"

Gorias never looked up from his adjustments on the saddles. "I sent Tammas to his life. It's was time someone did."

"You're going to send Maddox to his demise as well."

"I send Maddox to his destiny. On the south side of Khabnur, on the plains of Shynar, he will find himself. It will be the first day of the rest of his life."

"What if he dies?"

"Then he does. Cowards aren't worth a chamber pot or the window they are thrown out of, dear. Better a dead lion than a live chicken. No one can live forever."

"No one?" she said, a slight sob in her tone. "Not even a fable?"

Gorias stopped in his motions, took a breath., "Even fables fade to black. I will be forgotten in time. Heroes often fail. No child will be bored by the tales of Gorias La Gaul ever again."

She moved close to him. "No, you will live forever. Ones like you never die."

Gorias kissed her right hand at the knuckles and they parted.

It occurred to her then she was the only one he sent away from the war.

＊＊＊＊＊

Even in the afternoon light, Lira Rhan and her guards could see the armies on the move. Both the forces of Nosmada crowding in to the south and the force of Brock Lloydson split in half at the northern sector.

"Probably the only one who sees what's going on," she said in the zenith of the tower.

She could see the plan unfolding and could tell the barbarian horde now separated completely. The massive force of men on foot curled around Khabnur. Indeed, they meant to assail the army of Nosmada's rear. By the way the writhing snakes of human lines moved, they would do just that. These men were not running, but pacing themselves. They conserved energy for battle. The forces of Tolin marched with more vigor, a goal in mind. The main body of Brock's army would run directly into Tolin's on the other side of Khabnur.

Far beyond this force, she thought she saw the dust of a third force curling around. Lira could not comprehend their purpose, for they looked positioned to miss the army of Nosmada all together.

Down by the first wall of the city, hundreds of her armed mercenaries waited and held the lines. Would they break and run? Would they flee unto their doom? She knew not, and didn't like waiting to find out.

"All of my training, all of my negotiating and compromise to appease so many, gone through my fingertips like so much sand. I have become a slave to chance. If… ahh, there are too many ifs… It is almost enough to make a woman pray. Almost."

However, her heart lifted when word came she should direct her spyglass at a lone figure approaching the city. Lira Rhan trained her viewer and gasped.

Over the hill came the mighty stallion, carrying a fable toward her. The sun glittered off the dragon-plated armor the warrior so often hid from view. His name was whispered all over the city. Her deliverance, Gorias La Gaul, rode forward.

❀ ❀ ❀ ❀ ❀

Amid the dusty, stone ruins on the edge of the desert of Dundayin, the singing Draco-Lich paused in its labors. Flexing its claws, the red eyes of the undead dragon stared down at it servant.

The high priest of the cult bowed. "Master, a rider approaches us."

"Ah, excellent." The thunderous tones of the Draco-Lich rolled. Sand flew from the ancient stones as the mottled reptilian wings extended. "Is it my own true love?"

"It is Gorias La Gaul, Master."

Rows of fangs parted and laughter echoed from a mouth filled with fetid breath. "Let him come forward, then. I would have this done with him." The dragon tested his wings while watching the small figure on its way to the ancient ruins. Its scarlet eyes sparkled with intellect. "Gorias La Gaul, his own damned self." The Draco-Lich looked to the sky and giggled. "God is great!"

CHAPTER XVIII

FOOTSTEP OF AN ASSASSIN

Of all of the factions moving on that afternoon, Gorias La Gaul had the briefest ride to his intended target. Though all the armies prepared to converge around Khabnur, just as Lira Rhan feared, Gorias' ride away from the coming action was a short margin. However, after an hour, he let his horse rest. Then he walked through the first set of ruins on the edge of the shifting desert.

"Larak," Gorias said. Awe flooded his brain as he took in the locale destroyed not by human hands. He pulled the long cloak about himself and expanded his chest inside the armor he wore. "City by the sea, relaxation place for the mighty and aged, so long ago destroyed by a game of behemoths. I salute you." He laughed in spite of himself, alone with the grim rubble produced in a battle of angry gods.

Before he rode through the first set of gigantic stone pillars, ravaged by the weather and now mostly obscured by the sand, Gorias looked at the wreckage to the left and right of the entrance. Rectangular blocks, once arranged in perfect symmetry with the stars, now lay collapsed. This path of destruction punched out so clear Gorias could see the path whatever it was followed. Gorias reflected on the great power it took to construct such objects into a perfect circle. He then thought of the great fury it took to destroy them like so many children's toys.

The overall area of Larak lay abnormal and disorganized to the eye. A labyrinth of paths presented themselves, seeming to stretch for infinity. He saw many a narrow track in the malignant decay and felt his heart leap, so apprehensive was he of the trap that obviously lurked for him.

On the crumbled blocks near him, several engraved mosaics depicted bizarre creatures he had never seen before. Some were half men and part fish, others were tentacled creatures crossed with jellyfish. The artist or carver was mad, he thought, for the dichotomy of size concerning the creatures was erroneous. Inside were piles of crumbled walls, once well masoned, now lying in disintegrated mortar and beams pulverized to dust.

The clear sky was rent by a ripple most men would take for approaching thunder. His ears popped as a voice drifted into his head at a great, baritone volume, vibrating through him, reaching to his toes.

"Stories are spun about Asmodeous destroying the city of Larak out of spite," the voice intoned. "The fallen Cherubim became disgusted when many refused to make him the center of their sexual rites in the circles of the sun. In his wrath, Asmodeous smashed the city by the sea and took the sea with him. Behold the corroding of the ages, La Gaul."

Gorias gazed across the endless desert, then at the image shifting behind many rows of broken obelisks and shattered temple walls. Finely crafted marble columns in rows looked to have been slapped down by a gigantic hand. The desert had swallowed inner segments of the city completely as the lumpy outer edges of the city contested.

"Must have been before I was born. Larak has been rubble since I first saw her as a boy."

The voice dropped in from everywhere. "You saw this place at the beginning of your life? Excellent. Now in your twilight years, you return to witness it again. This is an unhealthy place for you."

"Are you going to impress me with a better vista now?"

Silken robes fluttered through the series of phallic stones in the ruins.

"Of course," it said and laughed a little, sounding like an echo in a cavern. "How is this?"

From out of the tall series of obelisks the Draco-Lich glided into view. Suspended on two large, bat-like wings, the undead dragon set down on bony, clawed feet. All around him in a semi-circle stood the Cult of the Dragon dressed in greenish robes.

A rush went through Gorias' chest, for it had been a long time since he beheld anything like a dragon. Truly, in his heart of hearts, he hoped all his fears were for naught concerning the resurrected beast. Yet the little priests in emerald robes, practically masturbating at the sight of their living god, confirmed his dread.

Spectacular, even in its undead state, the dragon appeared as grand and as imposing as any he had slain in the past. Even with its flesh reconstituted and not gleaming, save for where the sun struck the platelets, the dragon made him pause. Poised on two legs, not unlike those of a vulture, the Draco-Lich had uncanny grace. The long front legs were like those of a man's arms, save for they terminated in hideous claws. The striped underbelly of the Draco-Lich was akin to that of a snake or lizard, but it bore an upper torso that ran almost humanoid. Down its limbs trekked raised scales that would prove deadly if dashed against flesh.

As with any dragon, the wings and face made the creature. The wings appeared constructed out of puzzle pieces. These colossal flaps came together at the Draco-Lich's back, while its long legs sprouted from the torso. The head was more quizzical than he would have thought for a blue dragon. Bizarre was its humanoid facial expression, yet the elongated skull showed more kinship with a lizard than a man. However, the orbits of the eyes and structure of the nose proved much more human than reptilian, and this aided its humanlike facade. Fins and spikes were packed in tight rows up the nose, then back down the head like slicked hair. In the middle of its scalp a grand series of razory spikes perched like a rooster's comb

It is not a wonder lesser men worship such a thing, he ruminated, still taking in the creature. However, when he focused and the dragon pranced a few steps, actuality set in. The sun reflected off a few scales--original pieces of the brute still left. There wasn't much of the authentic dragon remaining. The patchy lattice of its flesh attested to this verity. Time and the elements had taken its buried tissue as it did with any animal.

The beast wasn't unlike the corpse of Carlato Wyss resurrected by his pathetic followers. The Cult of the Dragon, however, knew their craft better. There were no bits of sand or dirt on this beast. This network of scales held a uniform surface, pretending to be scales, but what shaped the armored platelets was

not dragon. Upon closer inspection Gorias saw it was parallel to human muscle, but not on a magnificent degree. No, it was as if several biceps and calf muscles were melted together to construct this breathing monster from the primeval epoch.

He recalled the missing villagers of Oliverian and realized where this tissue had come from.

"You've seen healthier days."

The Draco-Lich roared with laughter that came to an abrupt stop. "You as well. But you are mistaken, aged foe. I am not a dragon. I am your executioner. I am your devil and god. I am Carlato Wyss."

Gorias rode his grandson's mount and the horse faltered, ill used to the old warrior's movements. The Draco-Lich made no move to attack him. If anything, the creature appeared bemused by him. Squinting in between the pillars, he beheld a section of the city hardly touched by the all encompassing devastation, or maybe reset by large hands. This zone stood with complex symmetry. Some perplexity spread on his face, as he did not comprehend what blew in the wind amongst these columns. The materials seemed to wave at him.

Unsheathing his two swords caused the cult members to back up a step. Their Lord never moved as Gorias said, "You know me, then, and what I have done."

"Yes. The tales of yore spread far when you slew the dragon that was this one."

Gorias watched the Draco-Lich run its claws carefully over its muscled chest before he said, "I'll kill myself to see you die."

"You are no fool, that is true, and you break your code, for you speak to me too much before the action begins. You expect to break me? That is a fine jest, La Gaul. You killed me already, do you hear? You killed me years ago."

"You are just a crazy murderer, Wyss. Directing the law to your activities caused you to be dumped in that bog. I never cut off your head. Now you have a body to match your ego."

"Murderer? Me? If I started on a binge of murder, little man, believe me, there would be none of you left."

"That's what you have in mind, no? Destruction for all

empires of the earth, so ripe for your taking." Gorias recalled the mind games of Wyss, played on the youths of Shynar. "You're all about death and pages from the Daemonolateria. You will murder the earth."

The rows of fangs in the dragon's maw parted. "The earth should die and all of her kingdoms with her. Everything that walks or crawls should cease to be. In a blaze of fire, it should go the way of the dragons. Let its utter corpse belong to the flies. Then I shall be its Lord."

❖ ❖ ❖ ❖ ❖

Never had so much terror been in Tammas' breast. Running miles with the barbarian children proved an exhausting exercise. Though no great thewed warrior, Tammas was quite fit and didn't falter in the long run. Even the primal children knew to pace themselves for the coming enterprise, jogging as if a trained troop.

Luckily, there was an open prairie and not a clotted landscape for them to overcome. If anything, the tall, dead grasses of winter hid their advance. Tammas felt the thrill of subterfuge as they jogged.

He lost his sense of direction a few times, but the barbarian children slapped his head. They goaded him to follow on and he did so. As one of the collective, they understood the way.

On the eastern side of the Foundry of Syn, the land dipped low. A rotten stench filled his nose as they saw the deep valley and treacherous cracks in the earth serving as the depository for wastes.

"The ass of the foundry," Tammas named the series of pipes. The name was true, for every form of waste shot out of the metallic tunnels at regular intervals. The ejecta wasn't a flood, just minor dribbles. Tammas gritted his teeth and controlled his gag reflex while traipsing in through this route.

Just as Brock and Gorias figured, there were two Minorcs guarding this horrid spot. Both sat down, incredibly bored with their duty. Tammas absently wondered just how worthless one would have to be at their work to be assigned this duty. The youths snuck up in silence, then made signals at Tammas to support their coming attack.

The children struck. They arose in a wave of humanity that confounded the Minorcs. A rain of rocks was the first thing to fall on the guards, making them unready for the rising of hundreds of lean, wild children. A dark haired boy leapt onto the thighs of one, swiftly raising a stone axe above his head. The Minorc would have cast him off easily if half a dozen bodies weren't weighing down each arm. With a sickening splat, the skull of the Minorc broke. He fell backwards, the youths stabbing his body repeatedly, killing him more times than he needed to die. The youth shouted the name of Wodan and laughed. Tammas thought this one looked a great deal like Brock, but he never asked, nor did the boy trumpet the fact. He just fought.

The same operation happened on the other Minorc, but this one arose and threw off his oppressors. Even though dozens of them surrounded the guard, it felt as if the last two folks on earth were Tammas and the giant creature. Letting go of his sword, Tammas unslung his bow. The beast stepped toward him though biting children hugged his calves. He fixed an arrow and let it fly. The projectile hit the Minorc's chest plate and deflected. A curse word slipped, then Tammas pulled his sword. The flood of children couldn't stop the Minorc. He reached out and knocked Tammas to the ground with a balled up fist.

His head full of lights, nose gushing blood, Tammas tried to rise, but the creature loomed over him. Feet stomping echoed in his ears and a flood of bodies hit the ogre in the back. He stumbled forward. Tammas shouted in anger and utter fear, raising his weapon. As if by design, the creature fell hard, his skull directly aimed at the short blade of Tammas. On top of the bard, the Minorc wretched and breathed his last. Brains oozed from his nostrils as his skull popped partially open like the claws of a lobster.

All around the dead Minorc, the children danced.

Tammas shouted, "Roll this damn thing off me!"

The barbarian children did so and Tammas stood. The bard wiped brains and blood from his face and laughed in spite of the act. The tall barbarian youth took blood from the dead Minorc and painted marks on Tammas' face, then his own. On some primitive level, Tammas became one of them. However, he allowed the youth to lead them into the pipes. He wasn't crazy.

✿ ✿ ✿ ✿ ✿

Several hours of drinking passed before Mitre Stillwell lay down for a second nap. He oft awoke in a state of delirium, afraid he was back in time at the door of some great horror. The Minorcs or Beholders would never go to wake him at a time such as this. They knew to stay outside, safe from his accidental rage. Nevertheless, Stillwell awoke coughing, a-feared that he was a young man again, trapped in a burning house that his legion had razed.

"Out of my way, you bastards," he shouted, swinging his meaty arms at phantoms in his mind. Stillwell rolled off his large couch and landed on the floor of his office. In his ears rang the panicked shouts of the Beholders who stood vigil at the Foundry of Syn. In his nostrils snaked the stench of smoke and ash.

"Mitre," one of the Beholders howled both in his ears and inside his mind. "There is something wrong with our ventilation system."

"Sharp fellows for Beholders, you are." he said as he climbed to his feet. Wiping his mouth, he recoiled again from the stench in the air. The door opened and the floating Beholder gaped at him. "What's going on at the filters? What do the guards report?"

"They have never returned, my Lord!" the Beholders said. "It stinks worse than bodily functions across the entire foundry."

Mitre's huge nose wrinkled as he swore. He grabbed the overhead scope and raised it to observe the surface. Dropping the scope fast, he reached for the twin headed axe on his wall. Spinning this weapon no human could handle, he then grabbed up a triangular shaped shield off his other wall. Many thought these items a display to show the foundry could create any sort of weapon. However, these were minted just for the hands of Mitre Stillwell.

"What is it, Lord?" Fright crept into the Beholders' eerie voices.

Mitre returned to the wall and strapped on a long sword also made for his size. He said nothing.

The Beholder persisted, "What did you see?"

With one fluid motion, he snatched the Beholder's eyestalks in his right hand, bringing the creature to his face. "I saw a barbarian child passing water on the lense of my scope, that's what I saw."

Stillwell threw the Beholder against the wall with an incredible backhand swipe. The floating being couldn't stop itself and the momentum of the blow made it bounce off the wall. As it wobbled in the air, the Beholder returned near to Mitre, who swiped with his axe, dividing the creature in half as if it were a melon. The pieces flew and stayed afloat for a brief moment before plummeting to the floor.

The two Minorcs and other Beholders receded from the office as Stillwell stepped out, stomping the lower half of the severed head as he went..

Two Minorcs ran up, holding a smoking blanket between them. A single Beholder cautiously floated behind them, saying to Mitre, "Here it is, my Lord. A series of these things were clotted into the vents. The passageways are open now and the air will soon clear."

Visibility was dim on the main production line behind them, but he put down the axe, reached out, and snatched the covering. He cursed and threw it down. "It is mammoth hide, damn their eyes. We are under attack."

The Minorcs looked at him, dumbfounded, and the Beholder said, "Surely not, my Lord. It is a simple jape by children."

Like the suddenness of lightning, the cheers of hundreds of voices flooded the outer office. Mitre shoved his way past the Minorc and looked over the terrace onto the main floor of the foundry. Confused, he shook the railing violently as if he could banish what he saw.

Countless barbarian youths, some clad in animal hides, others running naked, stabbed and slew the guards of the Foundry of Syn. One of the Minorc overseers beheaded one of the boys. The head rolled across a series of women's hands cooling blades in water. It plopped in the liquid and vanished, but the barbarian's slayer soon felt the wrath of this child's brethren. A spear perforated the Minorc's colon. Barbarian children used knives made of bones to stab bellies, while nail boots kept them steady on the meshed cat-walks. Many guards flailed, mouths agape in screams.

The Minorcs swung fast at the savage children, but the barbarians wriggled between their legs like puppies at play. Often, they stabbed the thighs of the Minorcs. Just as Brock taught them, even a Minorc would fall if his hamstrings were cut. Though the Beholders faired better at eluding the children, some of these overseers were stabbed and used as playthings in a brutal game of death, not unlike dodge ball.

The Beholder's panicked, trying to use their mental power on the children. It was like trying to tame a herd of rats, and oft their power bounced off the Minorc's minds. These guards fell and went into convulsions, the power of the Beholders fracturing their brains.

Mitre howled a cry louder than the insane war songs of the children. All was still for a moment as he shouted over the production floor.

Putting his axe down he pointed and screamed, "You are all dogs and have no will of your own! These barbarians are here for the weapons. Shut up and let them take what they want!" He looked at the group of children in front of him and gasped, dropping his arm. A pair of figures stepped forward from the mass of barbarians and bleeding guards. "You bastard!"

The face of Tammas, painted in stripes of blood for war paint, was familiar to Stillwell. However, the man who loomed next to Tammas caused the head of the foundry the greater concern. The towering man, his back a cruel network of scars, raised muscle bound arms. All of the workers could see the reality of what caused Mitre to scream out in terror: Noel was free.

Worse yet for Management, Noel was armed. He held Stillwell's twin headed axe in his left hand and a fresh broadsword in the other. No regular man could weld such objects and fight. Noel, though, corded and sturdy, had the ability. He jumped onto the production floor away from Mitre. At the lines of workers, he broke their interlocking chains. One by one, Noel freed several workers held together by a long communal link. At times, he would swing the axe up, killing a Minorc who tried to stop him in his labors. One Minorc nearly did cut his head off. Noel dodged the savage blow, put down his sword, and gripped the heavy axe with both hands. Swinging overhand, he cleaved the Minorc's skull down to the bottom teeth.

Noel grabbed the sword again then pointed, showing the others to take up arms and kill their oppressors. In the air heavy with sweat and oils, now blood and brains intermingled, giving the laborers a new breath of what was to come. Noel never told them what freedom tasted like, but in a moment, all of them realized what swam near to their palates.

They reached out and took the nearest piece of steel, men and women alike, then shouted screams of rebellion. Quite a few were slain outright by the Minorcs. Many brains burst under the power of the Beholders, but there were too many of them to stop at once. Chaos ensued and Noel was its emperor. The workers slew and fought, some even using their chains as weapons.

The laborers of the foundry were human to the core. The seething hatred boiling for too long exploded, and they settled old scores. Anger and petty jealousy rose up inside dozens of the workers, who slew each other in the morass of bloodlust on the production floor. At one point, two men threw a Minorc into the smelting pot then fought hard until one cast his brother in as well.

Tammas trudged in the wake of Noel and concentrated on slaying the Beholders. He could feel their power in his mind, but he could also taste their panic. It hung heavy and chewed as thick as bacon in his maw.

Noel performed like a berserker unleashed, slaying and killing any Minorc who dared step close to him. Once he paused to stop a female worker as she scalped another woman. When he lifted her by the hair with one hand, Noel gave the woman a curious look. She held up her bloody trophy, the scalp of her hated enemy, and acted as if she just won the war. Noel dropped her and shook his head.

Then he went for the stairs, after Stillwell.

Several of the Minorcs scrambled in retreat, and Mitre beheaded two of them with his large sword. "Yeah, run you little pricks!" He planted his feet, staring down Noel, who faced him on the cat-walk. "You have always wanted a piece of me, you big sonofabitch! Come take on the power of—"

While the bugbear's bluster reached its crescendo, Tammas loosed an arrow. It struck Stillwell in the good eye. Mitre dropped his sword and shield, roaring to the ceiling.

"You took away my sight!" he screamed and stamped about, causing anyone nearby to scatter, save for Tammas and Noel. Mitre raged, "You will kill me like a dog, damned coward! That's the way of all you scum, eh? I'll rape you in Hell for eons, Noel!"

Tammas shouted out, "You took away Noel's mouth and all of their souls. Your state seems a fair exchange to me."

Noel reached down and picked up Mitre's sword. He placed it into the hand of the supervisor of the Foundry of Syn. Mitre gripped the weapon, holding it true. He staggered, failing to adopt a defensive stance. Then Noel buried the axe in Stillwell's right leg at the knee.

Noel didn't disappoint, for after he split Mitre's knee he pulled the axe out and buried the weapon in the chest of the creature. At first, Tammas thought Noel meant for Stillwell to suffer more, but this proved false. Mitre grabbed the blade on the curl as it sank into his abdomen and he tried to hold it close to him. Noel pulled the weighty metal weapon back, his whip flailed flesh contorting as he mutilated Stillwell's hand.

Mitre rose up on his good knee then dived at Noel. He grappled with him briefly, wrapping him in a limp bear hug. Stillwell bit at Noel's stomach. Reaching down, Noel dug his fingers into the cheeks of the creature who'd stared down at him for so long from afar--looked down at him and had grinned every day--the man who took away his voice and dignity. With strong fingers and long, sharp nails developed on the assembly floor, Noel dug into that hideous face and ripped Mitre's cheeks down off the skull.

When Mitre howled and rolled to the floor, Noel grabbed up

the sword and promptly vivisected the overlord of Syn, see-sawing the blade over and over.

The Foundry of Syn became awash in blood. From the production line to the quality control offices, those who oppressed the slaves died, badly. Their blood painted the walls, floors, and mouths of the arisen workers. Many old scores were settled as sweating slaves rose up to find those who stabbed them in the back, and stabbed them in the front.

Tammas wagered that none of them realized that Gorias also figured: After these hundreds of workers slew the Minorcs and Beholders, they ran out onto the surface of the Earth.

✴ ✴ ✴ ✴ ✴

Tolin had confidence in his men. They would stop outside the Foundry of Syn and behave as if they were there for the purchase of the weapons. Once the Foundry was unlocked and his men were inside in great numbers, they would start the assault. What were a few Minorcs against trained men? The gelded guards were accustomed to whipped masses of slavery, not real fighting men aware of their craft.

When the first reports came that there was a terrible disturbance in the distance, indicating a huge movement of the rival army of barbarians, Tolin wasn't that concerned. "Savage fools," he cursed now as he looked back over the territory they just came from. The jogging barbarians came up fast. This was the spur of the Northern army that broke off and headed around Khabnur to the west.

Captain Karter watched these barbarians stop, then assemble themselves into crude lines. As they did this, the hairy men took deep breaths and prepared.

"There are a great many of them," Karter said. "If I didn't know better, I would think the barbarians are assuming a phalanx formation."

Tolin nodded, never wavering in his confidence. "We are spread out. Those maniacs will ram into our flank and do us damage.

Curse them." He shouted and gathered the attention of the cavalry around him. "Move the cavalry to the front of the columns! Get the pike-men ready and closer to our rear! Regular troops first followed by the greener ones. "

The army of Nosmada stopped dead. Hundreds of pike-man then archers peeled off and tried to get into position to take the brunt of the rear assault. Elite troopers in heavier armor marched in to support these lines.

"Sir!" one of the troopers near the front of the force shouted, pointing to the northeast.

Tolin didn't follow his point. "Yes, we are very near the Foundry of Syn…"

"No, sir, look!"

While the city of Khabnur loomed in front of the military force, off to the right of the city stood a stationary, dark line. This long line snorted and breathed. Behind this dark, hairy line of animals came a rising shout growing louder.

"Damned barbarians," Tolin said. "Only they would make a cavalry out of mastodons."

Tubal directed most of the light infantry and green slingers to swing around to face this line. He then divided the pike-men and moved up the forces of the cavalry. "They will out number us still, General. The force in our rear is several thousand. Their force on the elephants can only be a couple hundred or a few more. Behind them, yes, perhaps over a thousand men. Rest assured, we have five hundred pike-men alone. This will be good exercise for us."

Tolin frowned. "I'd feel better with the new weapons." He watched the force of pike-men divide between the two fronts. "The men are fighting with obsidian implements not much better than the barbarians."

"But we're well trained…General!" Tubal pointed back at the foundry.

Far south of the army near the foundry figures started to pop through the ground like gophers. A few, then dozens of small barbarians ran into the open. These boys waved short swords that gleamed in the sun. They paused as more bodies trickled up from an unseen opening.

"My confidence wanes," Tolin said in a droll voice. "Now we are attacked by children? Tell the archers to fix arrows, and the core of engineers and back up green infantry to charge when these babies hit our flanks. I will not be bullied by—"

"General," Captain Karter said and pointed at the outer wall of Khabnur. "With respect, sir."

Pouring out of the city came hundreds of rough, fighting men. Many looked like bar room toughs, others like well-oiled warriors. They were all armed with steel and stood in no formal ranks. Most wore light armor. Next came a back-up force of crudely dressed and sparely armed common folks of Khabnur.

"Will they throw stones at us next?" Tolin said, causing many of his men to laugh. "They are drunken fools and have not the courage to attack us. At the first drop of warm blood on their faces, they will flee."

From the midst of the mercs emerged a great white stallion. The army of Nosmada collectively gasped and exchanged looks as the huge figure on horseback came into view.

He who held reins through the mouth slot of his helmet was a giant of a man. In his hands, he gripped two gleaming swords. On his body was blue armor skinned from the hide of baby dragons.

Down the lines of the army of Nosmada the cry went like wild fire; *"LA GAUL!"*

The rabble roared toward the armies' flank, head and center. Tolin reached back to his attendant and grabbed his helmet.

"I have had enough of this legendary bastard," he said. "This day, my revenge is completed."

Then, all hell broke loose.

CHAPTER XIX

ALL HELL BREAKING LOOSE

The right leg of the Draco-Lich extended, grabbed one of the stone obelisks, and drew back to heave it forward.

Gorias kicked the horse hard and darted for an avenue of rubble buildings. Just in time, he left the main boulevard as the granite effigy crashed down where he just stood firm.

"Damned nag," he cursed the horse of Maddox, alien to his manner of riding.

"Come now, hero of the ages," the Draco-Lich said with humor bubbling in its voice. "Approach and kill that which is already dead. What is one more dragon? Bring delight unto the kings of the earth once again. Climb on my back and ride me to your eternal reward."

"You're no dragon," Gorias called out, unsure if the creature could hear him or not. He then stopped, trying to hide behind a lone temple wall.

Abruptly, the crumpled wall split in half and the horse reared up in the rain of dust. The Draco-Lich's long neck extended and the face of the monster loomed near. The beast made no attempt to strike him as he nearly fell from the spooked horse.

The Draco-Lich said, "You eat meat and kill things that are better than you are. The breath of virgins sours in your gullet, fool."

Gorias crossed his swords and struck out at the dragon. The monster pulled away, easily avoiding the blows. For a moment, the face of the Draco looked disgruntled, or angry. This unrefined emotion faded. Gorias surmised his lack of fear didn't make the creature happy. Wyss lived for the taste of human terror on his tongue. Gorias wouldn't feed his habit.

The dragon's wings unfolded, knocking down more walls of the ruined shrine. "You exterminate all dragons, create a holocaust of death, yet you cannot understand why your son turned out to be a murderer." The Draco-Lich took to the air as it giggled. "You made your child what he is, La Gaul."

Talons of the Draco-Lich swept down rapid. Gorias dived off the horse. The dragon scooped up the animal and left him in the dust. When the Draco-Lich tried to strike at La Gaul with his other foot, Gorias slashed his swords in defense. Blades crunched into then bore through bone. Savagely he removed one of dragon's toes.

The creature threw back its head in startled pain, and Gorias said, "My son is dead."

Still in flight, the creature glowed aqua-blue and the human muscles of his frame glistened. The horse in its claws still writhed. The creature was shredded, bled, liquefied, sucked into the form of the Draco-Lich. The toe Gorias extracted returned before his eyes.

Gorias looked at the extracted toe on the sandy street. The outline of the dragon digit washed out into a green light and the shape of two skinned humanoids fell apart. The two hugging corpses rolled apart, abandoning their former union then lying still as statues.

Gorias darted away in-between stone pillars and inadvertently confronted three members of the Cult of the Dragon. Two wore green robes and one wore a more formal blue gown.

The man in the blue robe spoke with authority. "You cannot escape the…"

The priest's words stopped, for his head separated from his shoulders. The criss-crossing swords sliced clear through the meat of the cleric's throat. Gorias then impaled both of the retreating cultists in green, striking the powerful deathblow to each under the heart. The stab was fast and final. The cultists fell, hands clutching their wounds, blood flowing in-between their fingers as they hit the sand. Their cowls fell back and Gorias discovered they were both women. Never once did he look back as he passed them over.

"Too many make the mistake of listening to you idiots," he said, then shouted at the Draco, "They are helping you! You can't absorb at will. These bastards have to cast spells to assist you. If I knew where your soul crystal shelter was I'd stomp it down."

The dragon passed overhead and spoke again from

everywhere. "They are my fathers and mothers in this new flesh. I am their creation, as are your children. I am just a reflection of them, flesh and bone." Gorias slumped and hid, resting as he listened to the Draco. "They created me from what they had, what they were, and I expanded on this with those nearby." In its words lurked grotesque satisfaction at the homicidal act it performed in Oliverian.

With great velocity, the dragon fell from the sky. Gorias dived and avoided the clutches of the beast once more. The dragon grabbed up the corpses of the fallen priests and started to add them unto himself. Parts of the dragon's flesh that were spotty became clearer and thicker with the accumulation of three more bodies.

He was well aware Wyss held no real magic in this dragon state. His mind raced. He couldn't find and kill every cultist aiding the dragon. Then again, he had a plan.

"You are insane," he said, slipping down another narrow avenue of ruins, trying to work his way back to where the ordered sector remained. When he saw all that precise order, he thought of the outside of Larak and of Asmodeous thrashing around.

"Long ago, when I lived before, being insane meant something." The creature took to the air again, circled overhead. "Now, everyone is insane in this world. It should perish, a failed experiment, a bad trial of a lunatic beyond the realms of your understanding."

"But if you believe he is there…"

"Why follow him, old hero?" the dragon said and roared with immense malice. "I chose the reflection I know better, like my own. I am god, I told you once before. I see excellent possibilities in my new form for great procreation. If it is all about love, I will give them a god of love, all right!" The dragon's words stopped. "What is happening? How…oh I see!" The confusion left its pitch as it spotted the reason for its angst. "Kill my followers, will you now girl? What is your game? You are just meat for the beast, little feminine."

Gorias sprinted on as the dragon started to knock the obelisks over like blocks. From out of the shadows fell more cultists in green robes, but these folk were already dead. In their backs and in their fronts were arrows. Fleeing the path of the dragon was Kayla Rhan.

"Damned girl," he said and smiled, holstering his swords, frowning down at the meager leftovers of the horse. In the mess of gunk not taken into the Dragon lay his saddle and the broadsword. Gorias unsheathed this long blade and ran after the dragon and Kayla. He stopped and looked at the place where objects waved in the wind. The dragon didn't destroy any of these pillars.

"Kayla!" Gorias ran toward the series of pillars away from the rest of the ruins.

Exhausted, she loped after him, turning to fire blindly at the Draco-Lich.

The flying creature took the arrow deep and Gorias saw it wince. It pulled back as its two attackers darted in-between the columns.

Gorias grabbed Kayla by the wrist, stopped running. "I'm not going to lecture you for following me, because I'm glad to see you." She smiled at this, weakly, but he went on. "You gave me the distraction I needed to discover something about that thing." He shouted up in the air, "Not as durable as your old flesh, is it? What am I saying? You were never a dragon, Wyss! You were hardly a man."

Her eyes flared. "What are you trying to do? Provoke it?"

"Did you see it as it pursued you? It was tiring. Real dragons don't tire that easy. It's probably consuming its followers for energy now."

The unfathomable tenor of the Draco-Lich drawled out, "I cannot bring myself to hate you. I admire you. You are a pioneer. You all call me a killer and a murderer, yet who here has killed more humans? It is but a matter of time before you all kill yourselves on this planet, anyway. My program will help it along, fulfill your aspirations. You say I am evil or a devil, but I am just what lives inside each and every one of you."

"Mouthy bastard," Gorias said as he waved at the hanging objects.

Kayla asked, "What's all of this stuff here?"

"Short answer or the complicated one?"

She shrugged as they changed positions again. "Both."

"In short, this is the Daemonolateria translated from the memory of Carlato Wyss. In the longer version? These are the inhabitants of Oliverian, well, their skin, anyway. These are being dried and will be pressed for future grimoires for wizards for generations to come. Ever wonder where those spell books on human flesh come from? Here you go."

She grimaced at an open mouth on one of the sheets of stygian text. Locked in a silent scream forever, the mouth was on the upper right hand corner of the page, sans teeth.

The deep voice from the sky intoned, "You are a swift thinker. That is why I love you so. I cannot detest you nor judge you, but it is time you stopped living the lie you call life."

Gorias directed Kayla stay behind a column, then spotted something out of the corner of his eye. Stepping forward with caution, he saw the Draco-Lich at the end of the series of pillars. He swung around a pillar and practically cut a cultist in half.

As this body fell, he shouted to the dragon, "So you're the one who decides who lives and dies, eh?"

The Draco-Lich stared him down. "And who else is to decide this? You? Who gave you the right, old man? I can smell an angelic being in these ruins, yet he will not lift a finger to help you. Why is he here? Why do you work so hard to appease one such as him?"

"That's my affair, ya maniac, just like making sure ya die again is," Gorias said as the Draco-Lich's neck lowered behind the pillars. "Your followers are dying off, Wyss. Soon, you'll follow them. Don't you care that the ones who love you fall dead so often for you?"

Unconcerned, the dragon replied with a strong but amiable voice, "You think I made these men believe in dragons and worship a dark force? They come after the world with sacrificial knives, but they learned how to deal death from you, not me. I just taught them to stand up better."

"So I'm a murdering prick. What's your point?"

"You would do well to respect those who bring death on wings of scorpions, La Gaul. They are all coming to Earth and nothing you can do will stop it. Hades, I will not even bring the dark forces here. You and your kind will. You humans can will your own destruction. You can call up Belial, an angel fallen so far he craves dead babies for revenge on the creator." The dragon held up a long piece of human flesh, baked, tanned, pressed into what looked like parchment. "Here is how you can call him up. I cannot quote a page number, but she was a housewife, gardener, mother of six…"

Gorias stepped into the open and reared back with both hands. With all his strength, he threw the broadsword like an axe. The long blade twirled, end over end, and flew into the lower abdomen of the dragon. Since this creature wasn't made of armored plates, the blade easily buried itself and disappeared from sight. The creature reared back its head and howled.

Kayla fired arrows at the creature, over and over, as Gorias ran forward. He disengaged his twin swords from the crude pack on his back and hopped onto the edging of a pillar. He meant to jump on the folded wing of the Draco-Lich, but Wyss was too fast for him. His left hand descended fast and clutched Gorias in a fist. Kayla screamed, fearing him dead. However, Gorias had drawn his two swords near to himself, like a soldier at attention with arms at the ready. The grip tightened and the Draco-Lich growled in hurt. With one move, Gorias expanded his arms, pushing his swords out. The blades sliced through the muscle and bones, removing the fingers of the dragon.

Gorias fell to the ground and rolled. He came up on his knees, gasping. Kayla saw blood on his stomach. "This chain mail isn't good for holding back the wind," he declared, missing his dragon-plated armor. He tried to rise up, but his left leg nearly collapsed.

"I shall be whole again," the Draco-Lich promised, reeling, wincing in pain, shaking off its left hand.

The long tail of the dragon snapped around, battering Gorias before he could attack anew, sending him into one of the obelisks. He felt ribs crack and tasted the strong tang of blood from inside his throat. Gorias spit scarlet ichor down his beard as he flopped on the ground, barely avoiding the second lash from the tail.

The Draco-Lich informed him as it picked arrows off its

belly, "I was the greatest conjurer of my time, old sinner." The voice labored some, hurting. "Yes, I fear it was true and will soon be again. I do not need more followers for my life to be restored. I talked with angels and demons, thus, that is why I knew all of the Daemonolateria."

On all fours, he thanked the dragon for reminding him that hand-to-hand combat wasn't the way to beat this creature. He forgot his purpose. Recalling it, he was up and bolted down the avenue of narrow columns. Swords out and slashing, he attacked the freshly inscribed banners of human flesh.

"No!" the dragon howled and rose up on its wings. Narrowing its eyes at Gorias, it charged the tapered avenue.

✤✤✤✤✤

Nosmada's army tried to assemble itself for the coming assaults. The problem was, since the army of nearly ten thousand was so spread out, it became difficult to form a solid unit as the barbarians attacked.

The berserker force advancing around Khabnur threw themselves into the rear of the army. Nearly two thousand screaming barbarians brandished stone axes and clubs, attacking hastily assembled units of pike-men, infantry, and archers. Usually, the artillery and projectiles from archers or longbow classes softened up a charging foe. Few arrows loosed before this barbarian force of berserk killers attacked, though. Many of the archer's bows were hampered because of the rain, thus, making the strings ineffective.

The manner of the savages ran vile and unpredictable. Solid units of trained pike-men, well skilled in fighting with stout lances, met this initial force. One force of pike-men stood, supported by a thousand regular infantry fighters with crude bronze short swords and long shields. Hundreds of archers tried again to aim, but only a few dozen managed to loose arrows as the barbarians first thrust hit.

The heavy slaughter ensued, destroying a hundred pike-men and two hundred infantry in scant time. Many of the barbarians died, but their push proved irresistible. The on-sweeping hordes attacked with communal entreaties to their god, Wodan, and the army bent. Their push caused a few hundred in the cavalry to retreat and take up a different position. With great valor, the pike-men and infantry fought. They met the attack, struggled, and died hard.

The bloody clubs and axes of the berserker force was only stopped by the armored legion, a thousand elite men in stern body armor, fighting with interlocking shields. Many of these men of Nosmada perished, but more attacks came forward as they went down. An auxiliary cavalry charge, led by Tubal himself, supported by more units of the armored knights, stopped the rear attack of the barbarians cold. The terrible fighting went on, but the barbarians ceased advancing.

Brock's mammoth cavalry trumpeted and they charged ahead from the opposite position. The ordered lines of the army of Nosmada felt the earth tremble as over a hundred of the giant beasts trampled forward. No matter what Captain Karter's forces threw at this thundering advance--arrows, spears, axes--nothing could stop the irrepressible stampede of flat feet. Through lines of scattering infantry and cavalry, these monsters thundered. Men on back of these beasts shot and stabbed as they went. They used arrows mostly, but they carried extra men on the back who dismounted. These men swung stone axes. Axes then did what axes do--they crushed bones and killed people. Quite a few were struck down from their mammoth mounts by the infantry, but the great beasts still crashed on, stumbling through the army of Nosmada. Tusks flaring, feet crushing, the barely tame creatures went wild once their riders were gone.

From behind this force of mammoths came thousands of warriors from Zenghaus. More berserkers plus regular fighters with any number of weapons poured into the devastated ranks. The bloodlust flooded forward, crashing into the gaps left by the monstrous beasts. With the lines scattered and in tatters, hand to hand combat quickly became the order of the day. Unable to fight as units, many of the infantry in this forward section fell back or fell dead.

Even the one-handed and the women came up and fought

in the wave of heated battle lust. They attacked the horses of the scattered cavalry. Once the men were down from their horses, pitchforks and knives fell onto their breasts. Several of these cripples died as the units of pike-men and green light infantry units hurriedly reinforced the bleeding nose of the army.

With both ends of the army assailed and dented in, re-organization proved slow. Tolin led a force of cavalry, infantry, and pike-men against the forces exiting Khabnur. These fighters, led by Gorias La Gaul high in the saddle, were truly a division of rabble. A hundred police constables and their deputies; several dozen of the palace guards of Rhan; hundreds of poorly armed citizens that made up a militia; and a few hundred mercenaries, also ill-trained but armed and angry, came out to fight. These men saw a fable on horseback, the great Gorias La Gaul in his dragon armor, leading them onward. So caught up were they in his majestic wake and grandiose fame, they clung hard to be a part of it. They would follow him into Hell itself, but for now they followed him into the only section of the army of Nosmada that counter attacked.

Tolin led a few hundred of the cavalrymen right at these forces. His hope was to break them fast with a show of power. Indeed, fear showed on the faces in the militia and many others, but the mercs, drunk on La Gaul's thrall, went on into the killing maw. Even those far behind on the castle walls cheered and shouted their encouragement as the fight was joined.

With flashing swords, La Gaul cut two riders down. He stabbed, slashed and fought like a man possessed, not stopping as gouting blood painted his armor. Spears broke on his famous armor, unable to penetrate the dragon skin. Almost elegant in his acts of murder, La Gaul wasn't denied. Both blades dropped on either side of him, both finding homes in the shoulders of pike men. They had rushed to La Gaul and hesitated, truly afraid of the man they knew as larger than life. Gorias ended their fears forever. A loud chunk echoed as the blades found flesh. Armor rent, collar-bones collapsed, and the blades crunched down into the ribs of the men.

Archers drilled him with arrows, but they glanced off his armor. Even the long bowman's offerings were rejected.

Never once did the fabled killer hesitate. He rode deeper into the lines, making his horse rear up and spin. Even La Gaul's mount fought for him. Harden veteran infantry-men drew back, hesitating for that crucial moment. When they found their courage at last, when they decided they indeed wanted to be the man to kill Gorias La Gaul, a swipe sheared off their sword arms.

Blind in his odium of Gorias, Tolin charged forward, ravenous for the ultimate kill. All of his senses flared at the sight of the warring man, killing everyone around him, dropping the blades so often one would think he chopped logs.

Several of those in the cavalry fled rather than attack Gorias. Quickly warriors and mercs aided La Gaul, buoyed by his undaunted bravery. It was the wedge they needed and they drove it deep into the side of the dispersing army.

Tolin's skin crawled as he reached La Gaul. The armored legend never flinched. He reached out with a blade and blocked Tolin's first sword thrust. Gorias even kicked the general in the hip as he passed. La Gaul played with him. Tolin heard him laughing as he kicked a pike man, caving in his ribs, then hooked a passing cavalry fighter with the dew nail of his armor, ripping loose a string of guts and a loud scream.

And yet…there was something about the combatant that made Tolin's senses shriek. What was wrong?

The fighters from Khabnur threw their lives into a meat grinder, but many prevailed. They fought like men possessed, men who were part of a parable in a drunken song. They waded into Tolin's troopers and used them as meat to dull their swords. These were not men accustomed to discipline or long fights. They didn't have to be, Tolin mused, as he swung around for another shot at Gorias.

Again, he charged the marvel on the horse. Again, La Gaul repelled him. Tolin reined back, flummoxed. He witnessed his great second in command, Karter, charge in with an extended lance. For an instant, Tolin believed Karter would impale La Gaul. No shock overcame him when Gorias pivoted in the saddle, causing the lance to miss his side. La Gaul then swung his left sword down,

246

snapping the lance. Karter's momentum carried him close to Gorias and an overhand smash from a gloved fist. The brain buster caused Karter to falter in the saddle and tumble backwards from his mount. Twirling, he landed on his back then rolled on to all fours. Shaking the cobwebs free, Karter tried to rise, but his head hung. He never knew La Gaul sliced at him and missed his head. La Gaul then shouted a single word at him. Karter raised his head up to look. The blade of La Gaul fell.

Tolin howled when he heard the brittle crunch as the sword bit to bone depth. Captain Karter fell flat on his chest, arms out, and his soul departed.

The general bellowed and charged La Gaul. Again, he crossed swords with Gorias and the scream of blades whined. The warrior moved fluidly, repelling the attacks with ease. With a circular twist, Gorias motioned his right sword and Tolin's weapon flew from his grasp.

Tolin caught himself drawing back in fear, for he inadvertently left a killing avenue open. Yet, Gorias never took it. *Strange, an aged fighter would do such a thing...*

With rage in his mind, Tolin realized what was happening. He had been deceived. His horse shuffled back as he reached down for the spike headed mace hanging from his high-pommel saddle.

✵ ✵ ✵ ✵ ✵

The mammoth cavalry had shoved a great force of the Nosmada's infantry back towards the Foundry of Syn. Pouring out of the Earth came four hundred well-armed workers, crazed in a primal blood desire. Into the back of the retreating infantry these workers plunged with vigor.

Tammas saw the children who he came into the foundry with charge into a skull splintering frenzy as they took on the reforming pike-men units. Embodying their savage nature to the fullest, they flooded into the battle lines. The trained pike-men impaled a few of the children, but were unready for the chaos of so many shorter attackers. These children cut low and the lines of men bowed.

Tammas joined them in their quest for a lower assault, stabbing and slicing, pinning the feet of the troopers into the ground with knives or bone-honed daggers.

When the children squirted into the next lines, they encountered armored swordsmen. One of these men stepped up, slew a youth and easily disarmed another. However, his mirth at the ease of his moves allowed the unarmed youth to tackle his shin. Finding a gap in the greave, the barbarian youth sank his gnarled teeth into the tendons in the swordsman's lower leg. With a shout, the swordsman sliced the boy through the back, and then stabbed him through the heart once he rolled off his leg. Staggering, the swordsman faced Tammas.

The bard charged, swinging his weapon hard. Though the blow was blocked, the swordsman couldn't plant his leg and it gave out from under him. He fell to his knee awkwardly and Tammas stepped forward. Making sure the boy never died in vain for his act, Tammas sliced into the belly of the swordsman and then removed his head. It took his a few chops, but he got it done.

The multitude of youths charged into the blinding war with Nosmada's men and vanished. Tammas fought well, impaling a cavalry officer with a broadsword from the Foundry and then ascended to his horse. This cavalryman stumbled and fell, forcing a third of the blade back out of his body as he impacted on the Earth. The wash of blood on the thin grass was so prevalent the horse nearly slipped.

Almost as if his mind screamed it, Tammas bolted the field and headed back toward Khabnur. Once near that raging battle, he thought of the ruins of Larak where Kayla and Gorias disappeared. On his lips was a tune. On his lips was a song of death. On his lips was a smile.

❖ ❖ ❖ ❖ ❖

Brock Lloydson rode his mammoth across the bodies of many warriors who tried very hard to kill him. The tusks of the great animal ripped and disposed of men far more intelligent than

Brock. He sent arrows into the faceplates of soldiers of great breeding. Truly Brock killed, trampled, and ground into the earth many mother's sons. He thought it funny and exciting. The blood rushed in his veins and spattered across his beard. The scents of brains, intestines, raw horsemeat, and elephant dung drifted on the evening breeze. He felt unashamed over the erection he sported because of it.

His long bludgeon swung from the mount and Brock kept on his path. To crush through the lines of infantry wasn't enough. Dispersing the cavalry and crushing the spines of horses didn't do it for him either. Brock directed his troops to keep running up and down the length of the army.

When he witnessed the flood of bodies exiting out of the steaming Foundry, both in the form of armed children and the workers, it made him smile. At last, he dropped off his mount and waded into the scattered pike men attacking as reinforcements for their comrades. Brock picked up a sword dropped by a dead foundry worker and put it to better use.

A cavalry rider attacked him and Brock attacked the soldier's horse. Predictably, the animal went down and the rider fell to the earth. This man's helmet fell off, exposing a huge soldier, bald and bruised. He drew a great sword and swung at Brock. The barbarian took to a knee and slashed backwards. Brock cut through the back of the rider's sword arm, slicing off much of the tricep. Standing tall again, Brock fully removed the bald fighter's limb with a grunt.

The bald mad staggered, drawing out a dagger from his girdle. "I'm Tubal, son of Norasha, kindred of the line' of Seth himself."

Brock replied, "I don't care," as he ran him through with his sword, blade just below his sternum, like his father taught him. Face near enough to kiss the bald warrior, Brock felt his warm breath as he exhaled, then heard him up close as he gagged--a natural reflex to the turning of the sword. Brock pushed him away. Tubal fell, dying and convulsing on the bloody grass. Dark fluid bubbled from Tubal's maw like a crimson spring. Brock spit on him and moved on.

While he sliced another warrior of Nosmada open, Brock

saw La Gaul get off his white mount to fight a tall man in well made armor. The twin swords flashed and the fable took the big man down. Another leapt in to fight Gorias, to defend the fallen man. La Gaul slashed the soldiers' neck quick. The head teetered and fell off backward, sending jets of blood into the sky. Gorias stepped over the fallen man, a General probably. La Gaul put his twin swords side by side and raised them above his head. When they fell, the general blocked the move with a broadsword. The twin swords exploded into glittering shards. Brock heard the general laugh.

CHAPTER XX

DELIVERANCE HAS COME

Gorias loped as best he could on his injured leg. His broken ribs screamed at him as he raised weary arms and slashed. He dodged between pillars, renting and shredding the human flesh that constituted the pages of the Daemonolateria. He noticed one sheet of skin sported the tattoo of a scarlet spider on it. Behind him, the howl of the Draco-Lich mingled with what he anticipated: The fall of many of the perfect obelisks.

In its abiding fury, Carlato Wyss charged. It aimed to discontinue Gorias from destroying the pages of the grimoire just translated. In his haste, Wyss thought too much like a man and not like a dragon, just as Gorias anticipated. The long wings and bulky body of the Draco-Lich slammed into the pillars and obelisks. These objects teetered and fell, smashing into others on their way over, and they into others. Such stood the symmetrical alignment of the stones made to perfection by the fallen angels, whispering to man to be obsessed with the stars. This perfection led to a swifter destruction.

What fleshy pages he failed to slash the dragon buried in the sand, grinding them together amidst the stones, ruining the words etched by the creature. In time, the monster tripped over rolling stone columns and lurched forward. It smashed into the remaining pillars, snapping many more off. It injured itself as it knocked more structures down.

The debris ejected during its fall threw him to the ground. Certain a few of his fingers snapped in the process, he tried to ignore the agony of his broken body and rise up to his feet. He failed, making it only to his knees. Blood poured from his stomach through his busted chain mail cover. He held his fists, still clenching his blades, to his belly. Fingers steadily weaker, his temper correspondingly thinner, he trudged on. His aged eyes saw the chest and abdomen of the undead dragon were broken, bleeding out muscled humanity. A few errand arms and legs fell away from the collective body of the Draco-Lich.

"Gorias!" Kayla called out from a great distance away.

The world twisted and tilted in the eyes of La Gaul. A rush went threw him and he felt his heart thud in his chest. His blurring vision focused on the Draco-Lich, still not finished, stumbling amongst the broken pieces of the pillars, stepping on sheets of human flesh. The dragon stumbled greatly and its leg went deep into the earth. It was caught, unable to pull its limb from a hollow place below.

Up at last, he advanced, though staggering. Kayla ran to him, full of fear at his appalling condition. He waved this off and pointed down at the fresh gap in the earth. "The sunlight shows it well. Look! It's the reservoir for the soul crystals. That's where Wyss will retreat to if I kill this sonofabitch. He'll go back to a jewel and await another return."

Holding a sword under his armpit, he drew out a dagger, and looked to his left. In the open stone street stood Ezran Gavreel, arms folded. This time he wore an immaculate white cloak and a hood. Ignoring him for a moment, Gorias spoke to Kayla as he gave her the blade, "Get down there and destroy the jewels. This will cut them. It will cut anything."

Her eyes streamed rivers of tears. "Lord La Gaul, you are dying."

He gripped her by the shoulders, steadying himself. "Sister... Kayla, we're all dying. Get down there and destroy the damned jewels. I can't."

"How can I break a jewel?"

Gorias squeezed his sword in her hand. "It's made out of stern stuff, girl. You have to be as well, so be strong for me. It can do it. You can do it. Now go." He then looked to Ezran Gavreel, as did Kayla, He saw her stunned expression when another persona just like Ezran stepped out from behind him—no, she gaped over the fact that *he'd divided into two beings!*

"Go!" He shoved her and disengaged his swords again. "Deliverance shall come."

After those words, he ran with great energy and leapt onto the back of the Draco-Lich. Kayla slithered down the hole past the shifting leg of the monster. Gorias took a few halting steps on the creature and found the joint in the spine where the wings connected. His legs slid down, straddling the shifting monster. Thighs tight, head pounding, he dug in where no plates lay, the serrated edges of his leggings digging ruts in the soft flesh of the Draco. Like a drummer pounding a huge skin, Gorias went to work. Repetitively, the swords fell. Over and over again, like a man trying to swim the ocean, he slashed and stabbed at the dragon's back. Not every blow fell on the wings--some were insertions to probe for guts.

The earsplitting cry of the dragon sounded. The Draco-Lich tried to dislodge him with its tail but failed. One leg trapped in the underground chamber, the monster floundered.

Gorias rode the creature like a wild horse, still striking down. Alas, the wings fell free and onto the ancient stone pavilion. The Draco then threw back its head enough to slap him. He tumbled off, rolling to the side, falling just beside the injured creature.

On all fours in the pool of muck spewing from the wounded, he looked up at his enemy, and then over at the two men in white. They stood, watching placidly. Was it a trick of the sun or his addled, wounded head that made them appear to glow? Gorias looked to his left and saw the handle of the broadsword he lost earlier in the gut of the beast. Too weary to put his twin swords back, he left them on the ground and grabbed the broadsword handle with both hands. With great effort, he yanked it free.

He stood, stumbled, looked from the struggling creature to the two glowing beings. Gorias saw the tattered remains of the translated book on demonology torn asunder in the clutter of fallen pillars. He raised the broadsword high.

"Stop it now, La Gaul," the Draco-Lich gurgled, trying to use its wounded hand for support but only worsening its position. "Can't you see that you are dead already?"

"I have just one life," Gorias said as blood spurted heavy from his nose. With each breath, he blew out streams of crimson. "No regrets, no remorse...No mercy."

253

With shaking steps, the ancient warrior charged and leapt. He landed badly on the down-turned snout of the dragon, feeling bones in his left shin give way. The force was enough to drive the broadsword through the top of the dragon's skull, impaling its brain. This wasn't enough to stop the creature, for its tail curled around and swatted him. The swipe knocked him off, but his fall was halted by the right fore-claw of the Draco-Lich. It grasped Gorias tight, but with a sudden jerk it released him. He dropped only a few feet to the ground and staggered, remaining on his feet. The Draco-Lich convulsed then plummeted, limp. It went down with a wet groan and never rose up again.

Coming up from the hole, climbing on the dragon's still caught leg, Kayla displayed a handful of glassy shards with pride. "I did it!"

Gorias took a breath, saying, "Just in time…" His eyes fixed on the two glowing beings, muttering faintly, "…Ezran and Gavreel, glad you could arrive just in time for the climax."

Then, Gorias La Gaul fell.

On his knees, he faced the two lustrous beings, hands on a piece of rubble. He turned his back to the last dragon ever to walk the earth, staring fate in the face. The world spun, and he rested on his right side.

Kayla scrambled, screaming wild. She grabbed the huge shoulders of the old man and turned him over to his back. The dragon had done more damage than she'd expected with its final squeeze. Gorias' chest heaved and blood painted his thick beard in full.

"You cannot die!" she said, shaking him as if the action of it would call him back to health.

"Come on now, girl, you never disappointed me," he said as her black hair matted over him. "Don't start now."

Tears almost blinding her, she raised her head and shouted at the two personas of white light, "Help me! Please, I beg you both. Help him!"

Ezran said, "Gavreel and I intend to do just that." Yet, they made no move forward.

She climbed on top of Gorias, trying not to put any pressure on his crushed body. She sobbed and held his head in her hands. "I love you. I always have! Can you realize how much I love you? You are everything to me. You always have been. Every dream, every hope, every moment of my life, I love you more than I can say."

His blue eyes flickered open, the whites colored red. He smiled a little through crimson tainted teeth. "I know, Kayla." He coughed and his body shuddered. "You made me happy for a little while." His hand touched her hair and felt the tears on her cheek. "For that, you're a princess without compare…mine, always and forever." His eyes twinkled. "My little princess, for all time."

With the last bit of strength in his mighty arms, Gorias pulled her closer to him. Her mouth went to his and she kissed his bloody lips.

Kayla felt him leave. His last breath exited into her, but he wasn't in it.

She held him for a long time, wailing, before Ezran spoke behind her. "The time of reckoning has come."

She twisted about and held out the heavy dagger he gave her. "Stay away from him."

Both men looked at the blade. "No, thank you, we have our own." From the backs of the men in white unfolded two sets of wings. At first, they weren't unlike those of eagles, save for they had longer feathers and shined like steel platelets.

Gavreel said in a voice identical to that of Ezran, "Protecting his body is admirable, but you forget what happens to the dead on this world." The men raised their hands in unison and Gorias La Gaul's corpse levitated into the air. "This is what he wanted and this is the deal he struck. We always keep our promises."

"Angels." Kayla wiped her face. "You really are angels. Damn you both. You let him die!"

Never acknowledging her statement, the two figures of light made Gorias float to a spot outside the rubble of the pillars. On a flat granite slab, his long body came to rest.

Ezran gazed at Gorias and touched the top of his head with his fingertips. He then bowed down and kissed the dead man's forehead gently. "Blessed are you, good and faithful servant. You have done well." The two angels stood at either end of the fable of the world. They then reached to their belts. Though they held handgrips, no blades existed for their weapons. A burgundy colored flame sprang out. Gorias La Gaul was afire.

Kayla fell to her knees. She couldn't make more tears come.

Gavreel's eyes reflected the flames. "Leave this place, girl-- you and your friends. There are those who will not treat you kindly if they ascertain what dwells inside you for Gorias."

Confused by his words, Kayla returned to the side of the dragon and retrieved Gorias' swords. She then walked back to his body on the pyre. Gorias' profile, though afire, seemed to wear his characteristic smirk.

The body of the Draco-Lich began to break down. At first, the creature started to spew corpses from its stomach. In time, all that was left of the dragon amounted to several bones, a few scales, and the skinless populace of Oliverian.

Ezran said to the weeping girl, "Gorias La Gaul sits at a place where the real heroes go. He is at rest. I shall sit and talk with him this very day. Please, you must leave him now."

But as the young are want to do, she didn't listen. Kayla saw Tammas ride up on his horse outside Larak. He dismounted and she tearfully explained what happened.

They retreated out of the area and watched as the two angels bathed the ruins in flame via their swords, scattering the ashes of La Gaul, burning the pages of the Daemonolateria to cinders. The two beings then walked in circles around each other and became one again. Ezran Gavreel vanished.

Tammas held Kayla and they both cried. They then sat down and talked for hours. This was a mistake.

Several horses rode up. This never disturbed Kayla or Tammas, for the lead rider wore the dragon-plated armor of Gorias La Gaul and rode the white stallion of the fable. They knew it as part of the ruse that Maddox La Gaul wore the protective covering to trick the mercs into fighting for him.

When this rider dismounted he pulled off his helmet and

Kayla screamed. Tammas tried to arise and fight, but it was futile.

Tolin La Gaul threw down the helmet and raised both hands. He chopped at Tammas on each shoulder, breaking each collarbone and sending the bard to the ground. He grabbed Kayla's face, her mouth still red with Gorias' dried blood.

"Where is he?" Tolin raged as her hands gripped the dragon plates on his forearms. "Where is Gorias La Gaul?"

She said nothing and he threw her down in the dust.

He grabbed the two gleaming swords and his glare blazed as he looked at them. "Yes! These are the real thing! Not the imitations the whelp played with on the battlefield."

A trooper dismounted. "General, we really must meet up with the remnants of our forces. This debacle cannot be righted by traveling farther north. The barbarians will regroup and head out this way."

He gazed back toward Khabnur and the general grinned. "I would still make that city my wash pot, soldier. Damn them all." Tolin then turned back and ran amongst the confounding ruins, screaming, "Where are you Gorias? Where are you? Damn it all!" He returned to face Kayla and, behind him, a small line of smoke ascended to the heavens. "Where is Gorias? He cannot escape me."

Tammas sobbed but stood up.

Tolin glared at him and crossed the swords. "Get down, fool. If you are lucky, we will take you as a slave like that other young idiot in Gorias' armor. I have a special execution awaiting him. Where is La Gaul? I sense the Draco-Lich is no more, for my flesh screams this unto my ears."

Tammas sang,

> "While gazing on that city, just over the narrow flood
> A band of Holy Angels came from the throne of God.
> They bore him on their wings, they bore him all the way home
> And joined him in his triumph.
> Deliverance has come."

With an inhuman roar, Tolin crossed the two blades again,

this time removing Tammas head from his shoulders. The bard fell straight backwards, stiff legged as his heart beat its last in Larak.

Kayla bolted and tried to make it onto the general's horse-- Gorias' regular mount. Tolin dropped the swords and grabbed her backside. Her hands gripped the saddle and bedroll, dislodging the tiny wooden box tied on the back.

The wooden box tumbled to the gravel, smashed and broke open. The contents spilled there for all to see.

What looked like a puppet, near to a wooden child save for a jewel setting in its chest, rolled out. On closer inspection, the creation contained little wood, but was mostly constructed of bones.

Tolin held Kayla's scalp and whispered in her ear, "That is where La Gaul should be. My prisoner in this humiliating shell forever. He deprived me of my body, my dragon's life, and caused me to live here in the flesh of a rat bastard human for all time. My reward to him would have been slavery, to be my little thrall in a box for my amusement. Now I must find another to live on in Nosmada's fetish to his kindred."

She gawked at the hideous doll as Tolin started to mumble an incantation. Suddenly, the soul jewel glowed emerald and the eyes of the doll flickered open.

Tolin laughed. "Though not Gorias, any soul just freed will suffice for now. Your headless friend will sing for me again in his new home. Soon, my master down south will realize his fetish is gone, used for my own purposes, thus, I can never return to him. Gorias..."

"He beat you, for he escaped," Kayla said, expecting her own death to arrive shortly. "Gorias La Gaul died as he lived--a hero. No force, no demon, no dragon, no man could stop him. Kill me if you like, but he still won."

Tolin raged, one hand about her neck and the other clutching her stomach. As he prepared to push her neck backwards, he paused. His nostrils flared. "Damn, I almost missed it if not for my magic. I doubt you know yourself, little bitch." A cold smile spread over his ruthless features. "I was going to kill you and place your soul in the homunculus, instead of what I snared from the ether world a bit ago. Now, I smell a better punishment." He held her throat but patted her belly. "I will take what Gorias has planted in your flesh and make it mine. Oh, this is even better than killing him."

She glowered at him as he released her. "Are you a lunatic? What do you mean?"

Smile gone, lips peeled back, Tolin declared, "My senses and magic tell me things mortals do not know. You have conceived, girl. You carry the child of La Gaul in your self, damned little pig." His hand slid to her chin. "And when your piglet is born, I shall have a great day of sacrifice indeed, no?"

He cast her down. Her head hit the ground and her feet flew up. Tolin howled at the sky, cursing Gorias La Gaul. He then turned and saw the ashes flittering overhead. Tolin looked down and saw Kayla crying.

"Put her in chains," he ordered as he retrieved the swords. "But do not make her walk with the other slaves. No, this thrall will be on a cart and be a gilded flower indeed."

When the soldiers took hold of her, she stabbed the one on her left in the belly. He screamed a shrill that punctuated the coming night. She twisted away and went at Tolin with the dagger of Gorias, lashing at his exposed face. He stood his ground and sliced the swords through the air. Her right hand came off and she fell, clutching her wrist.

Tolin told the soldiers, "Seal the wound." He knelt by Kayla. "You do not need both hands to have a baby, slave."

General Tolin placed the helm of dragon skin on his head again, then climbed onto Gorias' horse. He put down the visor and laughed.

€PILO6U€

In the fortress of Kanoch, Nosmada watched as events north of him unfolded. Distraught, he stared into the caldron of Zillian. His disfigured brow furrowed and he turned away from the sight of Tolin at the Larak ruins.

Zillian almost fell, yet held herself up at the edge of the caldron. When she did this, her cloak fell open, revealing her naked chest. Though Nosmada looked, he never glared at what grew there between her diminished breasts. Lannon did. The guard couldn't help but stare at the bulging object which moved.

"Don't be so surprised," Nosmada said with calmness in his voice. "You thought the old one could not sport something so common to wizards as a supernumerary teat, whereby she can suckle a familiar devil?"

"I…" Lannon stammered. "Forgive me."

Nosmada smiled. "Such an easy request to forgive, no?"

Followed closely by his servant, Nosmada exited Zillian's chamber. He walked far to the Redemption chamber, Zillian and Lannon accompanying him.

In the center of the chamber, he removed a circular stone disk and stared down. His corded limbs dipped into the well and confirmed what he suspected.

"Gone," Nosmada said. "He has stolen the last bone fragments of my brother for his peculiar purpose. Damn Tolin to Hell, and damn me for respecting my kindred's bones until the moment of redemption drew near. It was the last bit of respect I had for him, such as he was."

From this well of despair, he roared a cry to Heaven. The sound rang ghastly and echoed out forever.

Because of this cry, he never heard Zillian whimper or fall. He also never heard Lannon move forward and dash into the chamber.

All the same, Nosmada's senses weren't so dull that he didn't hear a weapon cutting the air. With reflexes like lightning, Nosmada sidestepped the deathblow, and gripped the wrist of Lannon. Though Lannon was a tall, thickly built guard, Nosmada controlled him as if a child attacked him. He yanked Lannon around with his arm behind his back. Nosmada disarmed him by crushing the bones in the servant's wrist.

"You come to kill me with a knife made of bones?" Nosmada said. "More than enough, surely, for a regular man. You come not fearing the curse of the one who kills Nosmada, I see. Great must be your faith in God." The dark lord's brows lowered, the disfiguring mark on his forehead rippling to reveal its full nature--a deep, black X. He whispered, "Go to your God then."

He rose up and smashed his forehead into the brow of Lannon. The cracking of the skull echoed, and the leeches on the walls chattered in mock-approval or glee.

Zillian climbed to her feet, held onto the frame of the doorway as her chest heaved. "Nosmada!"

As he dropped the body by the open disk at his feet, the dark lord glanced back at her. "Sometimes I tire of my false name, a play on backwards phrases, and the quest which I have cursed myself with." He touched the mark on his forehead. "Ironic, no? A curse to obscure a curse? But will he really be appeased with all of this blood? That's what he wants, correct? The first time was never enough, for I offered from the earth, so I must make it right. I must appease the Father."

Zillian faced Lannon, a tear dropping through the cracks in her withered face. "I fall prey to sentiment, as Lannon was my nephew and a friend."

Nosmada shrugged. "You are forgiven. He plotted against me and would take unto himself fame for killing me. That would follow him and be his curse. Hmm. Perhaps I should have let him slay me."

"Did you have to kill him?" she snapped, showing real anger in her voice. "That was just murder..."

The tall man bubbled with vehemence. "Speak to me of murder?" His growl was like that of a wounded bear, but if one listened long enough, one could tell it masked laughter. "Speak to me not of murder, elderly woman, for I created murder." He then looked up to the clear sky of the late afternoon and to the leeches writhing on the walls. "Speak unto the Lord of Heaven a name forbidden, all of you. Tell the God of all gods the name of me, his bastard grandson, who wants to come home!"

"Nosmada," Zillian pleaded. "Just stop…"

Unabated, the big man shouted out to the leeches, "Venerate the name accursed of all the earth and stars forevermore!"

From the maws of the undead hissed a single word that couldn't be misunderstood:

"Cain!"

THE END?

ABOUT THE AUTHOR

Steven L. Shrewsbury, from Central Illinois, enjoys football, books about history, guns, politics, mystery shows and good fiction. 365 of his short stories have been published in print or digital media. His novels *STRONGER THAN DEATH, HAWG, TORMENTOR,* and *GODFORSAKEN* run from horror to historical fantasy. His collaboration with Nate Southard *BAD MAGICK* was his first hardback release from Bloodletting Press. His collab novel with Peter Welmerink, *BEDLAM UNLEASHED*, was recently accepted by Belfire Press for an early 2011 release. The novel *HELL BILLY* is also on the horizon, to be published by Bad Moon Books in 2012. When not writing new tales or working on collaborations with Maurice Broaddus and Brian Keene, he searches for brightness wherever it may hide.

Connect with Steven online at:

www.stevenshrewsbury.com
or add him on his Facebook page at:
www.facebook.com/stevenlshrewsbury

Check out the following pages to see more from

All Seventh Star Press titles available in print and an array of specially priced eBook formats.

Visit www.seventhstarpress.com for further information.

Connect with Seventh Star Press at:
www.seventhstarpress.com
seventhstarpress.blogspot.com
www.facebook.com/seventhstarpress

Immerse into epic fantasy and let your imagination soar with two incredible series from the mind of Stephen Zimmer.

Epic Fantasy-Fires in Eden Series

Explore the lands, seas, and skies of Ave in this epic fantasy adventure, as eleven individuals from the modern world find themselves in lands both wondrous and dangerous. The enigmatic figure known as The Unifier has unleashed a war to end all wars, but the nature of it is far more insidious than any of the kings and rulers supporting it can possibly imagine. The fate of Ave hangs in the balance, as the eleven exiles discover the reasons for their presence, and the choices that they will have to make in response.

Book One: Crown of Vengeance
ISBN: 978-0982565612

"This is definitely a book for people who like character driven stories with gorgeous and detailed descriptions of a fantasy world and their inhabitants mixed with beings who follow devious plans who will face more resistance than expected....."

-Only the Best SciFi/Fantasy

"For me to say so many great things about a fantasy book is an accomplishment as these types of books used to be towards the bottom on my list that I was willing to read. This book with the help of Mr. Zimmer has restored my faith that fantasy makes for some thrilling reading."

-Cheryl's Book Nook

Book Two: Dream of Legends
ISBN: 978-0983108627

Available December 2010

Epic Urban Fantasy-The Rising Dawn Saga

A shadow falls across the world, and realms beyond, as a war that has raged since the dawn of time itself draws closer to a decisive clash. As groups aligned with a movement called The Convergence speed up their efforts to bring about a global economic and legal order, resistance mounts after the host of a syndicated radio show, Benedict Darwin, discovers the true nature of a virtual reality device that has come into his possession. The Rising Dawn Saga will take you into mythical, supernatural realms as it unfolds, as the most unlikely of individuals rise to confront powers that have existed since before the world began.

Book One: The Exodus Gate
ISBN: 978-0615267470

"With The Exodus Gate author Stephen Zimmer sets the stage for an adventurous new science fiction fantasy series that is sure to entertain the reader from beginning to end. Zimmer has weaved a tale of fantastic realms populated with exotic creatures. Keep a sharp eye out for this new series."
-Mark Randell, Yellow30 Sci-Fi

"…a book that Fantasy Book Review recommends for lovers of thoughtful-fantasy. It is also a book with an ending that is near-prophetic, written as it was before the world's economic meltdown."
-Fantasy Book Review

Book Two: The Storm Guardians
ISBN: 978-0982565636

"This novel transports me from my bedroom to the edge of an upcoming storm — a battle to be fought by incredible villains and noble heroes of all forms. I love Zimmer's imagination, as each of his creatures play a pivotal role in the bigger picture. Unfortunately, for every auspicious being there is an ominous beast lurking in the shadows. Zimmer's weave of fantasy and religious fables leaves the reader sated"
-Bitten By Books

"The scope of The Storm Guardians is massive, opening up and expanding on the conflict only hinted at in The Exodus Gate. The intrigue and action promised in the first book is fully developed and mercilessly exhibited. The Storm Guardians is a non-stop thriller that lives up to the promise of The Exodus Gate and points at an even more amazing denouement in the final book of the series. Once again, Zimmer has used his command of cinematic imagery to give us a spectacular vision of war both heavenly and hellish. Two thumbs up on this one."
-Pure Reason Book Review

Coming Soon

 **SEVENTH STAR PRESS**

brings you an amazing YA fantasy series
from award-winning author Jackie Gamber.

The Leland Dragon Series arrives in 2011,
with Book One, <u>REDHEART</u>, in early 2011,
and Book Two, <u>SELA</u>, in the summer of 2011.

www.ingramcontent.com/pod-product-compliance
Lightning Source LLC
Chambersburg PA
CBHW052019020726
47501CB00004B/1132